AT FIRST SIGHT

AT FIRST SIGHT

Patrice Wilton

The characters and events portrayed in this book are fictitious. Any similarity to real persons, living or dead, is coincidental and not intended by the author.

Text copyright © 2013 Patrice Wilton
All rights reserved.
Printed in the United States of America.

No part of this book may be reproduced, or stored in a retrieval system, or transmitted in any form or by any means, electronic, mechanical, photocopying, recording, or otherwise, without express written permission of the publisher.

Published by Montlake Romance, Seattle
www.apub.com

ISBN-13: 9781477817476
ISBN-10: 1477817476

Dedication

I would like to thank my editors from Amazon, Maria Gomez and Hai-Yen Mura, for their continued support, and to Charlotte Herscher who diligently worked her magic to make this book the very best it could be. A big thank you also goes out to the amazing author team that works so hard to promote and ensure that are books are highly visible, so that we as authors can concentrate on our job to write.

A special mention to Doctor Craig Skolnick, an eye specialist in Jupiter, Florida, for his kind assistance and information regarding injuries and surgeries for my sightless hero.

On a personal note, I'd like to thank my darling Ralph for his patience when I'm working so hard, and love to my extended family, and all our beloved grandchildren.

EPISODE ONE

CHAPTER ONE

Natalie Connors stood in the doorway watching the recently blinded vet and his best friend as they discussed her possible employment. Their argument was heated, peppered with profanity, and she wondered if it was in her best interest to quietly retreat. Shane, after a breakfast meeting near her hotel this morning, had offered her a job as a live-in aide to help his buddy, Brent, settle in and readjust to civilian life. Not an easy chore, but she could handle anything for a month or two and then be on her way to a new life—a life filled with hope and promise, and the absence of fear.

This temp job might not be ideal but it seemed doable, or would be if Brent Harrington wasn't so vehemently opposed.

She took two steps forward and froze.

"Forget it, Shane. I don't need a nursemaid," Brent snapped. "Since you hired her, you can damn well fire her."

The anger in his voice, his physical size and stance made Natalie rethink her decision. After her recent escape from a volatile man, she preferred calm, courteous, soft-spoken.

This wounded war veteran was none of those things.

He continued shouting, as if she wasn't there. She might be low on funds with no place to live, but this was not going to work. It was too similar to the situation she'd just left.

She'd been wiping her damp palms on a tissue, and now she stuck the shredded piece back in her handbag and lifted her chin. She opened her mouth to let the two men know that they didn't need to argue. She would not take the job after all.

Her mouth slammed shut as Brent took a step in her direction. Did he know that she was standing inside the door, cowering from a safe distance?

"Is she here?" he whispered in a low, angry voice.

"Yes," Shane answered, "although she's probably frightened to death. Come in, Natalie."

Natalie hesitated, then took one step farther into the room. She'd tell Shane she couldn't be an aide for his friend, and then be on her way. To what, she didn't know. But one thing for sure, she couldn't stand this amount of friction, or his shouting. Not for one second. Already her nerves were frayed, her anxiety peaking, and she'd worked so hard in the past few months to relieve that stress.

Brent swung around, his hand out as if searching for her.

"Why the hell did you hire someone without asking me?" he spat out the words, turning back toward his friend. "I'm fine. Learned a few things in rehab, like how to take care of myself."

"Don't be an ass," Shane replied. "I'm not worried about you so much as everyone else who lives in the building." He turned his back to Brent and waved her forward. "I'm sorry, Natalie. Don't be afraid. He's as stubborn as a mule, but he doesn't bite."

She kept a wary eye on Brent. One wrong move and she'd be out of there so fast, both their heads would spin. She might need the position, but safety came first. Damn, if she hadn't learned that the hard way.

Brent turned sightless eyes in her direction as she drew near. Sunlight streamed through the windows and she blinked twice to see him more clearly. He looked to be in his early thirties, tall, with really broad shoulders, but was painfully thin, his skin pale. His face was lean but strong, with a well-shaped nose and a rigid jaw now pointed at her. His dark hair was shorn, and she could see the faint scars still evident from his head injury. If he wasn't wearing that angry scowl on his face, she might think him a handsome man.

Taking a deep breath she walked toward the two men, determined to squash her fears and behave like a professional. She reached out a hand.

Shane made the introduction. "Brent, this is Natalie Connors. She's willing to stay here 24/7." When Brent didn't offer his hand, she put hers down, realizing he wasn't being rude. He hadn't seen the hand she'd offered.

She couldn't imagine how difficult it would be to live in a world of darkness when you'd had vision all your life. Shane had called him "Eagle Eyes," saying Brent had an uncanny sixth sense, was an excellent helicopter pilot, and flew by sheer instinct. He'd flown for CAL FIRE before going off to war, putting out dangerous forest fires in smoke so thick you couldn't catch your breath. He'd been a warrant officer in the Army, flying Black Hawks in Afghanistan, and had miraculously survived flying into a mountaintop during the dark of night.

She understood this man was a hero, but she had an agenda, and taking care of a man filled with rage was definitely not on her list. She'd spent the last few years in a tormented relationship, pacifying a control freak, dodging his cruel comments and equally cruel fists.

"I'm having second thoughts about that," Natalie said, warring inside. "This might not work out for me, after all."

Shane swore softly. "Look what you've done," he told Brent. "You've frightened her off."

Brent ran a hand over his shaven head and dropped his eyes to the floor. "I'm sorry," he said, glancing in her direction. His fingers fisted at his side. "But I've already gotten rid of two aides, and I told Shane I wouldn't have another. How did he find you?"

"My friend owns a home health care business and she's given me some temp work. Said I might be interested in this." She licked her lips. "You see, I just arrived in the Long Beach area a few months ago and won't be staying long." Natalie forced her gaze away from his clenched hand. "Look, I can ease the transition from group living to living alone, Mr. Harrington, if you'll have me. I did a little research this morning and learned about the rehabilitation center you were in. Operation Freedom Bell has an excellent reputation for their work with wounded warriors and—"

His full mouth lifted in a sneer of contempt. "I'm not a warrior, just a pilot who'll never fly again. And as far as that program, I've learned enough. Don't intend to be blind forever, so why waste my time?"

Shane shook his head. "Denial is part of your problem. What if you don't get your sight back? What then, smartass?"

"Then I'll be fucked, won't I?" he snapped back.

Natalie knew from her quick research that Operation Freedom Bell was a six- to nine-month residential program for blind and visually impaired wounded warriors. The Department of Defense offered this to their veterans, and yet Brent had left. He must be pretty darn sure he would get his sight back, or he was a damn fool.

"I can help you learn to be independent," Natalie spoke up, looking at the two men. "I mean until your sight comes back. But until it does, your life can be greatly improved. Blind people, or those with limited sight, manage to live very productive lives." She sucked in a deep breath. Why didn't she just walk away? This job, low pay and all, was certainly not worth fighting for. And she didn't have the heart to fight even if it were. "But that's up to you. You can stumble along on your own, or accept help," she told him. "Your call."

"Who the hell do you think you are?" Brent hissed.

Her shoulders went back, and her chin jerked up. "Nobody. Just a school teacher in need of a temp job. And I don't like to be yelled at." She took two steps toward the door.

Shane ran a hand through his shaggy blonde hair, looking clearly frustrated. "Wait. I'm sure we can work this out."

Natalie stopped walking. She turned, folded her arms, and looked at Brent. His face was flushed with anger, his mouth grim, but there was something behind his defiance, a weakness, perhaps? His shoulders were too big for his body, which didn't even begin to fill out his clothes. His cheeks were sunken, making hollows in his face and emphasizing his strong bone structure. Obviously once he'd been a big, strong man, but now he seemed both terrified and frail.

"She's right," Shane said. "Blind people lead productive lives. They don't sit around and mope all the time, like someone I know."

"Cut me some slack. I don't need to explain myself to you. Or anybody." Brent reached to his left, his hand finding the top of the sofa. Natalie noticed his fingertips never left the fabric as he felt his way around the side and sank down to the couch. It must totally suck to have to feel your way around your own apartment, after being sighted all your life. Hell, she'd be angry too.

"I'm just trying to help," Shane said and grimaced.

"I don't want help," Brent shot back, and then glanced in her direction. "I'm sorry, lady, but you'll have to find another pathetic soul to look after. I don't need you here, or you, Shane. You hang around and make me feel as helpless as a baby."

"You're acting like one right now, and you need to man up and stop feeling sorry for yourself." Shane sent her an apologetic look. "He's normally not such a prick, but if you don't want this job, I understand."

She needed a job for the next month or so—until the work permit came through. Then she'd be off to Europe to tutor three young children and live in some wealthy family's country estate in the Loire Valley. A dream come true—especially sweet after the years of hardship she'd faced. She didn't want to waste money on cheap hotel rooms, and live-in positions were few. "I can try it for a few days." Natalie spoke quietly and took another hesitant step forward. So far, she didn't like this man who would be her charge, but he'd gone to war and paid a heavy personal price too. Guess he'd earned the right to be surly.

Decision made, she moved toward Brent and reached for his hand, giving it a firm shake. "Let's start over." He tried to pull back, but she held on. "Brent, I'm Natalie Connors from Kelowna, Washington. I've been working at the agency for the past couple of months. My last charge was an Alzheimer patient who is now in a home." When he didn't answer, she continued in a low voice, "I'm fluent in three languages but can get by in two others. Back home I taught both French and Spanish in middle school. I'm not familiar with working with the blind, but I'm a teacher, Brent, and will help you all that I can. You be honest with me regarding your needs, and I'll give you space. Will that be all right with you?"

Brent snatched his hand away and stood up quickly. He wobbled, regained his composure, and took a couple of steps forward, only to smack into the coffee table. He cursed, his strong face pale and etched with pain. "I just want to be left alone." He counted the steps and found the corridor to his bedroom. They heard him bang into a wall, and then the sound of the door slamming shut.

Natalie understood that sentiment completely. Alone. She'd learned there was safety in solitude.

"Guess that's settled then," Shane replied, giving her a weak smile.

"It doesn't look promising, but it's obvious he needs someone." She lifted her head and met Shane's gaze. "I'm not sure why you hired me instead of someone who works with the blind."

"Not sure either. Call it a hunch, but I'm a pretty good judge of character. Besides that, you seemed anxious for the job. The pay sucks, so you must really need it." He gave her a serious look. "He didn't like the guy I hired, or the old lady with grandkids. You're the same age as us, so I'm hoping he'll be able to relate to you."

She swallowed her nerves. "I can try, if he'll have me."

"Good. That's settled then." Shane rubbed his jaw. "He's my best friend, and I love him like a brother. Trust me, the guy has a good heart. He's just scared to death right now. Probably a helluva lot more than he ever was flying choppers in enemy territory and being held captive for days."

"I understand. And as I said, I'll give it a try. That's all I can promise." If he threatened her in any way, she was out of there.

"When do you want to start?"

"I'm staying at a hotel and I'm anxious to leave." The cheap room was gobbling up her very limited funds. "I can start today."

Shane nodded. "I'll let Brent know what's up."

"Let me tell him," Natalie spoke quickly, not allowing herself a chance to change her mind. "He's going to have to accept me, and it might as well be now."

"I'll wait here." Shane took a seat on the couch.

Natalie walked down the hall and stopped before the bedroom door. Knocking softly, she ignored the nervous butterflies in her stomach and the fact her palms were wet. She tapped again. "Brent. Can I come in?"

He didn't answer, so she carefully opened the door a crack and peeked in. Brent lay on his side, facing the wall, his back to her. He didn't shift his position or look her way.

It was obvious he didn't want her here, but that was too bad. In a month or two she'd move on—but for now? She needed a place to hide out. Where better than with a man who couldn't see?

Keeping a safe distance from the bed, she cleared her throat. "Brent. I'm going to the hotel to get my bag. I'll be back in an hour. Is there anything you need before I leave?"

"Yeah. To be left the hell alone."

"I can't do that," she said, keeping her tone light. "Sorry." She took a step back, studying him. His wide shoulders turned inward, creating a frail impression. Empathy welled as she allowed herself to feel his pain. She hardened her voice, knowing better than to show weakness. "I'm not a bad cook. What would you like for dinner?"

"For you to fuck off."

His harsh words didn't evoke the fear her ex-boyfriend's had, but she still took an instinctive step backward. "Here's the deal. I understand wanting independence. I'll help the best I can without interrupting your pity party." She drew in a breath, and rushed on. "It's no big thing. I'll cook so you don't have to burn the house down."

"I can cook."

"I saw all the old frozen dinner containers on the counter." She edged closer to the door. "I'm not going to babysit you. You want something, you can damn well get it. But if I can help, you ask. Laundry, cleaning, whatever. Okay? Does that work for you?"

His shoulders stiffened, but he refused to turn in her direction. "Get out of my room. Can't you leave me alone?"

"I can but I won't." Her voice cracked, her heart heavy at the desolation in his voice, in his body. He looked as hopeless as she'd recently been herself. She'd been at the bottom of the dark, dank well of despair and was even now climbing out by her fingernails. "I can help you. But I won't take any shit from you. You hear?"

"Get lost."

The order lacked oomph. "I'll see you in an hour. Why don't you take a shower while I'm gone? You're starting to stink." It wasn't exactly true, but she hoped to prod him from his lethargy, which was more deadly than self-pity. She marched out of the room and closed the door not so gently behind her.

Shane jumped to his feet, his brow arched. "Well?"

Natalie blew out a breath. "I think we'll get along fine."

Shane chuckled. "I had a feeling you two might hit it off."

"Like a house on fire."

She followed him down to the street, and he stopped by her car. In her old life, she'd driven a year-old VW bug. Now she was grateful for the ancient silver Toyota Corolla she'd paid cash for. Funny how a new house and nice things used to matter, but for now her wants were simple. To have a roof over her head, food on the table, and to know she was safe.

"I'll come back later to see if you're settled," Shane told her.

"Great. I'll pick up some groceries. Anything your friend calls a favorite meal?"

"Pasta." He opened the door to his Honda SUV and she noted the infant seat and booster in the back.

"You've got a baby?"

He gave an embarrassed grin. "Not yet. We just found out a month ago, but hey, I wanted to be prepared. His older brother, Josh, is seven and uses the booster seat. He's small for his age, and his mom's a little overprotective."

"That's nice. You're a lucky man." Children, a family. Pushing those dreams to the past where they belonged, she slid into her car and fastened the seatbelt, glancing around. The present required being "present," and Natalie remained alert... watching, waiting. Vigilant.

"Thanks. I think so too. Lauren, my wife," he said proudly, "is an ER doctor. I'm in my second year of medical school. Not as gifted as my wife, but eventually I'd like to work with other vets like me."

"Is that how you lost your hand?" She glanced down at his I-limb, a high-tech mechanical hand. "In Afghanistan?"

"No. Iraq." He darted a quick glance at her. "So what's your story?"

"No story. Nothing to tell." Natalie looked straight ahead. "Just a relationship gone bad. Decided I needed a change of scene." She shrugged. "Figured Alaska was too cold."

"So you ended up in California. You like it here?"

Wherever her son-of-a-bitch ex-boyfriend couldn't find her was good to her. If it turned out to be Alaska, she'd buy a parka. "I like sunshine and the warmth."

He slipped a hand into his pocket, pulling out a silver keychain. "I almost forgot to give you the keys. The big one is for the outside door and the small one for the apartment. You need anything, call my cell."

The words were barely out of his mouth when his phone rang. He turned away and answered.

She heard the words "Yes, she's pretty, but not as gorgeous as you," and realized he must be talking to his wife.

He waved to her and slid behind his wheel, still talking as he backed out of the parking spot.

She jumped in her car and followed him down the road, then turned at the light, heading toward the cheaper side of town. She had ended up in Belmont Shore in southern California for two reasons. Her best friend from college who ran the home health care business with her husband had invited her many times. They'd welcomed Natalie into their home and given her work. More importantly, it was sufficiently off the radar, and probably the last place Carl would look.

CHAPTER TWO

Brent got out of bed the moment his supposed best friend left, along with the pushy hired help. She had a silky voice when it became her, but he'd heard the iron will behind it. She also had an attitude, one he didn't appreciate. He sniffed at his clothing and realized he did smell a little off. So what? It was his own place, wasn't it? Besides, getting in and out of the shower wasn't frickin' easy when you couldn't see a damn thing. He'd show her she wasn't needed—damn well show everybody. After all, his place was organized so that he could function as normally as possible.

His bathroom was only a few feet from his bed and the shower was on the left of the commode, easily accessible. Automatically, his hand went to the light switch, and then he remembered he no longer needed it. He smacked his knee on the toilet seat and felt around the shower stall until his hand reached the tap. He tossed off his clothes and waited for the water to warm.

It had been a couple of days since he'd showered, and the moment he stepped under the warm stream of water it felt good. From memory, he guided his hand to the bar of soap and used it to wash himself down. He might be a useless prick, but at least he could be a clean one.

The hot pounding of the water relaxed some of the tension and strain in his shoulders and neck. He tilted his head back and found a little half empty bottle of shampoo on the ledge next to the soap. He squeezed some in his hand and massaged his scalp, careful to avoid the sensitive scars on his head. He didn't have much to shampoo now that he wore a buzz-cut.

He turned the water off and climbed out of the shower. He felt for the towel and when it didn't slide off the rack, he gave it a good yank. He heard the clink as the rack separated from the wall, then cursed as the sharp metal edge caught his chin. Feeling around for the dropped towel, he found it and held it to his face. How long to apply pressure? He touched his chin, and his fingers came away sticky and damp. He dabbed at it with the towel, frowning. Hoping for the best, he finished drying himself off.

Wrapping the towel around his hips, he went into the bedroom for some clean clothes. He heard the outside door open, and paused, expecting to hear Shane's voice call out a greeting. Man, did he have some choice words for his friend.

Halfway down the hall, he stopped when he heard the woman call out, "Hey, Brent. I'm back, and Shane's just arrived too. He'll be up in a sec. Wait until you see what he's bringing you." She used the nice company voice, not the sharp one she'd directed at him when they'd been alone in the bedroom.

"I'm not interested." He turned, eager to get dressed, but the sound of a dog barking stopped him. "What's going on?" Unable to see, he relied on his hearing and sense of smell, his intuition. He'd always paid attention to his gut instincts, and now they were sharper than before.

Something that smelled like a freshly shampooed dog snuffled over his bare feet, a sandpaper tongue licked his toes. "What the fuck? I didn't say you could bring a dog into my home. Is this yours, Natalie?"

Shane answered. "Meet Sam. He's a retired service dog. I pulled some strings to get him and it's on a temporary basis only. If you get your eyesight back the dog can be returned for adoption."

"When I get my sight back, you mean." He turned to Natalie. "A CSH, Combat Support Hospital unit had to do an emergency procedure in the field. After a CAT scan they burred a hole in my head over the site of the hematoma. Flew me to Landstuhl once I was stabilized. Never did get my sight back even after they drained a blood clot. Few months later, back here at home, none of the doctors could figure out why I still couldn't see. Eventually I had another scan, and they discovered cerebral edema and an obstruction of fluid affecting the occipital lobe. Bottom line is even after that final medical procedure I'm still visually impaired. Seems there's no permanent damage. Doctors say it's a conversion disorder or psychosomatic, they use a few terms, meaning it's all in my head."

"I see." Natalie added, "That's good then, isn't it?"

Brent nodded. "Yeah. I keep telling Shane that, but he doesn't want to believe it."

"It's not that I don't want to believe it, I just want you to be prepared for the worst," Shane answered. "Your helo crashed nearly a year ago and it hasn't come back yet. Didn't doctors say that it should return within six to eight months?"

"Not always," Brent replied. "Hell, after flying into a mountain you can expect your vision to be screwy. It'll come back, you just wait and see." He kicked his foot and attempted to nudge the dog away. "Get him off of me!" Brent hated feeling so vulnerable. "You can give him back right now. I don't need a frickin' dog. Just another mouth to feed."

"Sit, Sam," Shane said in a firm voice. "Sam's a golden retriever, and he's getting on in age. He'll be a good companion and knows all the commands."

"There's gotta be a lot of people who need or want him more than me," Brent muttered. "He'll just get in my way."

"True—you're not exactly appreciative, and this is an exceptional dog. Figured you could train with him too. Get out of the house a bit." Shane bent down to pet Sam. "He's sitting here, tail wagging, eyes bright, as though waiting for another command. Got intelligence, haven't you boy, which is more than I can say right now about your new master."

"I don't need to take shit from you," Brent snarled. "And I won't be doing any training either. Told you, it's a waste of my time."

"Shane's trying to help you. Why can't you accept that?" Natalie spoke up.

"What did you just say?" Brent glanced her way.

"I said Shane is knocking himself out to help you. Most people would be grateful to have a friend like that."

"Well, lady, I don't need him or you."

"Come on. Give the tough guy image a rest." Natalie moved forward and touched Brent on the face. "What happened? Your chin's bleeding. Let me get a bandage."

He pulled away from her. "I'm fine. Why don't you both take the dog for a nice long walk, preferably off a short pier?"

"I didn't expect thanks, but you don't have to be an ass." Shane sighed. "I told Natalie how to care for Sam, so it won't be any extra work for you until you're ready. I know how much you used to like the great outdoors. Sam will make it possible for you to go anywhere, to walk, run, hell, damn near everything."

Real terror sucked at his gut. How could he face the world with a mutt as a guide? "Stop trying to fix me. Why don't you go back to work, or hit the books? You think you're going to get any studying done once that baby arrives? Forget it, man. You'll be up all night."

"Yeah, I know. I'm leaving. I have to pick Josh up from school." Brent heard Shane walking toward the door. He opened it and said, "Take care of Sam and he'll take care of you."

"I don't need another fucking companion." Sour, angry, frustrated, Brent added with a jut of his chin, "Now I've got two bitches instead of just one."

Natalie erupted from his left, coming out of the bathroom in the hall. Her voice quivered when she spoke, "I won't stay if you call me names."

"You know where the door is."

Obviously hoping to defuse the situation, Shane said, "A couple of days, okay Natalie? Please?"

Brent waited, hoping he'd pushed her enough to quit. Hell, he had a dog now, he sure didn't need both.

"A few days." Natalie brushed past Brent and he heard her opening the cabinet in his bathroom. "Nothing but a cotton ball in the other bathroom," she muttered.

"Good luck, everyone. I'm out of here." Brent heard the click of the door as Shane left. No doubt glad to be gone. Just like his pal to drop a bomb—two of them—and leave.

The dog's heavy pants sent puffs of hot breath against his calves. Shane had told Sam to stay, and the dog listened.

Natalie came back a second later. He heard her quick breathing and the sound as she ripped open the bandage. "Stand still, so I can put this on." Her voice was no longer soft and gentle, but bristled with anger.

Well, he'd certainly hit on a few sensitive buttons.

He lifted his head and felt her fingers brush his chin as she fitted the band-aid in place. He could smell some scent, a fruity perfume, and noticed how her fingers trembled. He sensed her fear, and wondered if that's where her anger stemmed from. Had he frightened her? Was she afraid of the crazy blind guy with the piss-poor attitude? His conscience lifted its head. He didn't want to bully the poor girl. He just didn't want her around.

"I'm not going to hurt you," he grumbled. "No need to be afraid of me."

"I'm not afraid," she said, but he sensed she wasn't telling the truth.

"It's nothing personal, but I'd rather figure things out on my own. You know ... it's frustrating enough without having a witness."

"I know. I get that." She sighed. "I don't want to make things worse for you, but I have no place else to go. Money's tight."

"We're a sorry lot then, aren't we?"

"I suppose so." She stepped away from him, and he felt like she sucked some of the air back with her. "You need to get dressed. Can I help with your clothes?"

"No, I've got it." His clothes were sorted out in the dresser, underwear and socks in the first drawer, T-shirts in the second, and jeans and shorts down at the bottom. He grabbed one of each. "You going to stand there while I dress?"

"No." He imagined she was probably blushing from the way she explained in a rush, "I'll unload the groceries. Come with me, Sam."

He heard her leave, and a small smile tugged at his lips before he remembered he had nothing to smile about. Once he was dressed, he walked back into the living room without bumping into anything.

"So what does a conversion disorder mean? It's not neurological, so that's good, right?" Natalie asked. "Shane said it was like a temporary memory loss and might or might not come back."

"He doesn't know shit. Turns out, I don't either. The doctors aren't sure if or when I might see again. They say it could be psychosomatic, which is a conversion disorder. Means it's not physical, just a head thing. But I don't know about that."

"Did you fracture your skull? I know you flew into a mountain."

"Yeah, I remember my head being jolted around so hard, I thought I'd have a broken neck for sure. Dead or paralyzed, that's what I figured."

"You were lucky to survive. Were you hit by a missile?" When he didn't answer right away, she asked, "Do you mind talking about it?"

"Not my favorite topic, but I'll give you the basics. We were brought down by small arms fire. Insurgents were hiding all over the mountain range—we were on a rescue mission, trying to bring back a high-ranking officer being held in one of their camps. They knew we were coming, but we couldn't spot them until they fired."

"It's amazing any of you survived at all."

"Guess it was. Didn't seem like a miracle at the time though." He ran a hand over his head, feeling the scars. A constant reminder, not that he was likely to forget. Sweat trickled down his back as he remembered the fear. "We were surrounded immediately and couldn't be rescued. Myself and the other half dozen guys on board, plus Captain James, none of us could get treated for days." They could hear the gunfight around them. The QRF, Quick Reaction Force team had arrived to save their hides and were held off by the insurgents. No one knew from one second to the next if they'd be eating the next bullet. "But I'm here, which is more than I can say for a few of the poor bastards."

"It must have been awful being trapped like that. I can't imagine. I'm also surprised they let any of you live."

"Rules of warfare. But then, I was in and out of consciousness, so missed most of the action." The terror never left him, it was his bedside companion. How could a man sleep after that?

"That was probably a blessing in a way," she answered. "How many men did you lose?"

"Three." He felt his way to the couch and plopped down. The dog padded over and rested his head on his feet. He needed to change the subject—talking about this only made the pain in his head worse. "So enough about me. What are you doing here?"

He heard her rattling around the kitchen, opening cupboards and the fridge door. "Needed a change of scene," she answered.

"Why's that?" he asked. "Didn't like your teaching job? Boyfriend trouble?" He imagined the things that forced a seemingly intelligent woman to duck for cover. Most likely a man, he figured. "You running away from something?"

"Just the usual. A bad break-up. We used to work together and I didn't want to stick around after he broke my heart. I needed to get away."

Right on the money, he thought. "From Washington? That's a long way to ditch a broken heart. Hell, I used to be able to drive across town to get over a chick."

She gave a short laugh. "Yeah, well. I can see you're real deep."

"Nobody ever accused me of that." He turned toward her, shifting his body on the couch in what he hoped was her direction. "Did you happen to pick up any beers?"

"Shane bought you a case. Told me to only give you one a night since you're on medication."

"How about I skip the meds and drink instead?"

"Very funny. I might not be a certified nurse, but I'm no pushover."

"You could learn. We'd get along a lot better."

"I expect we'll get along fine as long as you don't yell at me. I don't like to be yelled at." She didn't say anything for a minute, then added, "And I don't like being called names. You want that beer now, or after dinner?"

Yeah, he felt bad about that. These days his temper rode the edge of acceptability. "Now's as good a time as any."

She opened it, the scent of barley easing into the air. She plopped it on the coffee table. "Here you go."

"Thanks." He sensed her studying him and cleared his throat. "What time's dinner? I might watch some TV."

"TV? You can't... Oh, you're joking. Unless you want to listen to the news? That's a good idea." The awkward silence deepened and he bet she wondered how he occupied his hours and hours of free time. "What do you do when you aren't...?"

"Sleeping? Eating? Cutting my chin on the bathroom rack?"

"Ouch. I didn't mean it like that. That was my lack of experience talking. But my other home care patients were mostly just old. Forgetful of meds, or that they had something on the stove." Her tone brightened. "You're different—younger, more physically and mentally abled. We could do lots of things together, like go for walks or swims. And I can read to you. I love books. Do you?"

"Never read much. Didn't have time for it. But I used to run a five-minute mile. Ski, surf, you name it—I did it." He crossed his arms, doubting he'd ever do any of those things again. His life would be reduced to armchair activities, something where he couldn't hurt himself. "Now I use my treadmill and my stationary bike. I like to swim. There's a community pool where I sometimes do laps."

"That's great. I'm glad you're getting exercise." She was silent for a second, then suggested, "Maybe the three of us can take long walks together for starters. Since I'm unfamiliar with the area, it'll take me a couple of days to get the lay of the land. Belmont has a boardwalk, right?"

"I'm not going to a boardwalk. Not like this."

"Why not? It would be nice." She added, "Don't worry, everything will work out. Soon I'll know my way around, and then I can do the shopping, banking, and anything else you need."

"Shane does that."

"He won't have to anymore," Natalie responded. "And I love to be out. The weather here is so perfect. Is there a park nearby? I could take Sam for runs and swim laps with you too." She laughed. "You see, I also like exercise."

"Why? Are you fat?"

"No, I'm not fat, but I will be if I stay cooped up all day with you."

"Yeah, well, that's bad luck, because I'm not interested in doing the blind-man walk."

"Come on. Get over yourself." Her voice was all sparkly when she added, "We could enjoy the fresh air and get used to Sam. It'll be fun."

"Fun for you. Me, I'd rather stay inside."

"And do what? Oh, I have an idea. I could teach you to knit."

"Very funny. Didn't know you had such a sense of humor." He drained the beer, and because she was being so damned chipper and eager to help him, he crushed the can like an angry teenager and then tossed it to the floor. Frustration and rage boiled inside as he listened to the skid of aluminum on tile. His life wasn't worth living anymore. Every minute of every day was an agony—punctuating how useless he'd become. He couldn't laugh anymore. He had no hope, no future, no joy. Why hadn't he died with his men and his captain on that damned mountain?

Her voice lowered. "Don't expect me to pick that up."

"Suit yourself."

He got up and stumbled over the dog. "Fucking hell. I don't need a mutt!" The days of running free with a dog at his side were long gone. His career as a helicopter pilot both here at home and during his deployment had essentially made it impossible for him to have a beloved animal that needed him. Better this way—the less responsibility the better. No one to disappoint.

The families of the soldiers who'd died had all sent condolences to the hospital after he'd been rescued. He knew they'd been wondering why he'd survived and how. He didn't know himself. He'd heard the gunfire around him, and had no idea why he'd been spared. The surviving crew members had been exceptionally lucky, he supposed. No one had come back unscathed, but they weren't in the ground. And blind was better than dead, he tried to tell himself. But was it really? Blind kept him trapped in the darkness, helpless against memories, vulnerable to those last terrifying moments as the chopper crashed.

Brent's gut knotted, and as if sensing his pain, Sam stuck his nose in his hand. He found himself scratching the dog's ears, dropping to his knees to bury his head in the thick fur. His throat ached, his shoulders stiffened. Why him? Self-pity sped through his veins like a poison, making him physically sick. He knew he should be grateful, but couldn't find the courage to face life as a blind man. As a victim of Fate, of war. Crippled, that's what he was. Tears burned his eyelids.

A sob tore from his chest, a painful rip of emotion. His shoulders heaved and he heard Sam give a low, commiserating growl. Tears he'd been unable to shed earlier broke past the barrier he'd hastily thrown up against hope. He wanted to die. He should have died.

The gentle weight of Natalie's hand settled on his shoulder, but he shook it off. His humiliations kept piling up. But what did it matter, anyway? "Get away from me. I don't want you here. Can't you see?"

"I can see a whole lot better than you." She paused as if afraid she'd said too much. "As an outsider, looking in, let me tell you what I see." Her voice softened. "A man, brought down by circumstance. You used to be a lot of things, but that life is over now." Natalie brushed a scrap of hair back from his forehead, and just that bit of human compassion stirred a glimmer of hope. "I can help you with the little things, Brent, but only you can dig deep down and find the will to not only survive, but thrive."

The dog licked his face. "You don't know anything about survival."

"I know more than you think."

He hated that determined tone in her voice—it meant she wasn't leaving, damn her. "Which is why you're hiding in my house?"

She sucked in a breath, her tones now turning frigid. "This has been a long day. Since you're such a whiz with the microwave, I'll leave you to it. I'll walk Sam for tonight, but starting tomorrow, it's your responsibility too."

"No!" Brent shouted. "No," he said again, with less heat. "I don't go outside except down to the pool."

"That's rather limiting, don't you think? You're a man in the prime of your life, and that's it? You want to give up?" She walked away, and he heard the roll of her suitcase as it went down the hall.

Brent's breath hitched and he could feel himself sinking into that bottomless hole. He threw his arms around Sam's neck, and couldn't stop the dam of tears once they started. He cursed himself, he cursed Shane for bringing Natalie into his home. The last thing he needed was a woman here to witness how vulnerable he'd become, how pathetic and weak. God, he hated living this way. He wasn't even man enough to take a bullet and end it all.

CHAPTER THREE

Natalie shut the door firmly behind her, angry with him for lashing out at her, but more angry with herself for not shutting up and letting the man have his breakdown. Oh no, she just had to stick her two cents in when it was obvious he'd needed a good cry. Sobs like that didn't come naturally to anyone, and a strong man, a man who had shown the courage to leave his home, his country, and go off to fight the Taliban in Afghanistan? Well, like it or not, the guy was a hero.

She needed to work on her compassion, but Carl had stripped it right out of her. To survive, she'd had to toughen up. Perhaps she'd need that toughness because it was preferable to feeling too much, especially for someone as needy as Brent. He was broken right now, without strength or a determined backbone, a spindly marionette, but she wasn't a puppeteer and had no idea how to pull his strings to make him upright again. Someday, no doubt, he'd be the man he was, but she wouldn't be around to see it. Her time here was brief, and all she could do was offer him comfort and hope.

It wouldn't do to become too friendly, as it would only leave him more desolate than before. Two months tops and she'd be on her way. A new life. The one she'd always dreamed of building for herself.

Unpacking only took a few minutes. She'd escaped so quickly that all her personal items, including old photographs and childhood tokens, had been left behind. There had only been enough time to grab the basics. Like his keys and her purse.

For weeks, months, the better part of a year, she'd dreamed of escape, and then one night it happened. Detective Carl Warner came home after a hard day, and she'd known the instant he entered the kitchen that it wasn't gonna be a good night. He hadn't said a word, just poured himself a double scotch and drank it straight up, then poured another, watching her.

He liked dinner precisely at six thirty—not a minute before, and five minutes late would cause a stink.

Natalie remembered how pretty the set table looked, with candles and a small bouquet of lilies in the center. Dinner, his favorite beef stew, was warming in the oven. After teaching all day, she'd stopped for a loaf of sourdough on her way home. All she needed was to toss the green salad and warm up the bread.

She'd uncorked the bottle of fine red wine, wishing for the courage to ask how his day had gone.

"What are we having?" he'd asked, sniffing the air.

"Beef bourguignon. I bought the tenderloin beef at the butcher's you like, and the vegetables from the green market," she'd told him, fighting back nerves.

Even now, Natalie remembered how carefully she'd planned the meal, making sure everything was right, every detail answered, so he'd have nothing to complain about. But she'd also known from experience that it didn't take a logical reason for his anger to flare.

"Dammit. Thought we were having lamb." He'd slammed his drink down. "Didn't I say that I'd like a rack of lamb to you this morning? I'm sure I did."

In hindsight, she should have been more agreeable. But that night, she'd said, "No, I would have remembered that if you did."

"Are you calling me a liar?" Carl's face paled, his lips a furious red stitch in the center of his face.

"No. I'm telling you that I'd have remembered it. That's all." Seeing the look in his eyes, she'd taken a step backward.

He had advanced forward. "So all I'm getting for my troubles is a stinking stew?"

"You've always loved it," she'd stammered, watching his face, knowing what might come next. If only her feet would move and take her someplace safe... but she was frozen with fear.

"Can't you ever be original? Do you always have to cook the same things day after day?" He smirked. "Think outside the box. How would I ever catch a criminal if I didn't use my imagination?"

"I know you're bright." She'd smiled. "That's why they made you Detective, and you're not even forty." Flattery sometimes worked, but she'd known deep down this time it wouldn't.

"Don't get sarcastic with me." He'd slugged back his double scotch and wiped the back of his mouth, his eyes never leaving hers.

"I'm not. I just said that your hard work has been rewarded," she'd answered, trying to keep her voice steady. Giving in to fear would be a mistake. Fear excited him.

"Some reward." His eyes had glittered. "That asshole partner of mine is going to get his head blown off some day. He's not a team player, if you know what I mean. And he's mouthing off to the wrong people. Hell, I don't want the guys to think I'm a whistle-blower either."

"I'm sure they won't. Especially when you make your dislike for your partner so well known."

He'd stepped forward and was within inches of her. "You've got an awfully smart mouth on you this evening. What's got your gander up?"

"Nothing. I just want us to have a nice dinner together. Why don't you sit and I'll serve it up? Everything's ready," she'd whispered, watching him warily.

"I'm not. I want to know what you've been doing all day. You look all hot and bothered. Did you have someone over this afternoon? That new hockey coach maybe?" His eyes had cut right thought her. "I saw you talking to him in the parking lot the other day."

"How could you?" she'd stuttered. The accidental meeting with the coach had been nothing, nothing at all, but of course Carl, with his twisted mind, wouldn't see it that way. He liked to think she was doing it with everybody, any man who looked sideways at her. "Weren't you working?"

"Yeah, but I took a drive around the neighborhood. Wanted to see what my fiancée was up to. You should be happy that I'm always looking out for you."

The memories of that evening were so vivid that Natalie hugged her middle as Carl's jeering face loomed in her mind. She'd said, "Checking up on me is more like it." A mistake, but one she couldn't take back. Nor would she if she had the chance. After all, it had gained her her freedom.

"What did you just say?"

"Nothing," she'd said, coaxing him to sit. "It's six twenty-five."

"That gives me five minutes, doesn't it?"

She'd forced a smile, her body tensing. "For what?"

"For this." And then he slammed his fist into her face.

When she'd come to, sprawled on the kitchen floor, she'd tasted blood and smelled the burned stew. Her blood was everywhere—on the tiled floor, splattering the counter, the back of a chair. Her clothes had dried blood on them too. She touched her face trying to estimate the damage. She was prone to nose bleeds, but it didn't feel broken. Her lip was cut too.

The sound of the shower running upstairs warned her he was still in the house. She lay there, terrified, until some small part of her brain prodded her into action. The beatings were becoming more vicious and frequent lately, and she knew she had to end it once and for all. Staying was no longer an option.

Although she ached all over and could barely move, she'd pulled herself up, grabbed her purse and phone and ran out the door. His car, parked behind hers, had stalled her for a minute. She'd almost quit, but she knew if she stayed she'd be dead within the year.

With that thought in mind, she ran back inside and grabbed his keys from the hook, deciding to take his car, a black, 2012 high-performance Mustang coupe. She'd been unable to pack, and it hurt her to think about all that she'd left behind. Her childhood photographs, pictures of her mom and dad in their happier days, her sister and her, both grinning—wearing ridiculous costumes for trick or treating—birthdays, first proms, and graduation pictures—a lifetime of memories. She'd left a nice-sized saving account in the local bank, a small inheritance when her grandma had died, and hadn't touched any of her accounts since.

Carl had taught her to be prudent. He'd taught her many things, most of them lessons she'd prefer to forget.

Sitting on the edge of the sofa bed, Natalie put her fingers to her temples and rubbed a dull ache. She'd never be free of the memories, not until she knew that she was truly safe. Europe was her safety zone. Carl would never think to look for her there.

She glanced around at her little room. It was painted a soft egg-blue and contained a sofa bed, a nightstand, and an armoire with a small TV. A computer desk sat next to the side wall. Nothing menacing here. For a short time she could hide without fear.

She'd been lucky to escape that night, and luckier still when she'd sold Carl's car to some sleazy car lot on the outskirts of Portland. The guy had taken one look at her thick lip and bruised face and had given her $7500 cash. She'd pocketed the money, walked a few blocks until she came across a silver dented Corolla in someone's driveway with a For Sale sign in the window.

No title, no insurance, no credit cards—nothing that could give Carl a way to find her. Brent had zeroed in on the secret that she was hiding. She'd have to do a better job convincing him she was outrunning a broken heart.

Leaving the safety of her bedroom, she returned to the living room and found it empty. She noticed the door to the patio open, and there was Brent in a lawn chair, with Sam next to him, standing guard.

Imagining his fears, his demons, helped put hers to rest. She could only guess what he was going through, the fears plaguing his mind, the day-to-day horror of waking up and discovering his world remained completely black.

She could hear the faint sound of waves breaking, and glanced over the railing, catching a partial glimpse of the shoreline. She breathed in the ocean air, wondering how someone could ever leave a place as lovely as this to go off to war.

"Brent," she spoke softly. "Can I get you anything before I start dinner? I'm sorry about what happened earlier. I can be a little defensive sometimes."

"I'm fine," he grumbled, his jaw set. "No need for dinner. I'm not hungry."

"I'll just toss something together. Eat, or don't." She went to the kitchen, calling for Sam, who seemed torn between following her or staying with Brent. She put out the dog bowl that Shane had brought and filled it with half a can of dog meat and some kibbles, winning him over. She also filled his water bowl and watched as he chowed down.

Brent might not think he was hungry, but she darn well was not going to let her charge starve. She decided a simple meal would be her best option until she had more time to get used to the kitchen and be better prepared.

She'd bought some angel hair pasta and a pound of shrimp, so all she needed to do was make the scampi sauce and toss a salad together. Nothing fancy, but it would do.

When the dinner was ready she went outside to coax him in.

"Dinner's on the table. I made a shrimp scampi and a green salad. Come, I'll help you to the table."

"Told you I was fine."

"I know you are, but even if you're not hungry, you need to eat." She hesitated. "I would really like the company. I told you my last patient was an Alzheimer patient? Sweet man, but every day he thought I was a stranger coming to steal his silver. I would love to have a real conversation."

"I don't have anything to talk about. Don't have any silver to steal either." His self-pity pushed all of her buttons.

She bit her tongue to hold back the sharp retort. As Carl used to say, she had a smart mouth and didn't know when to keep it shut.

"When was the last time you had something besides frozen dinners or canned soup? Surely you can smell the garlic from the scampi?" He lifted his nose and inhaled. She continued, "I might let you have another beer, or half a glass of wine."

"You know that's bribery."

"I won't tell if you don't."

"I'll take the beer." Clumsily, he pushed himself out of the cheap lawn chair and followed her inside.

She glanced at his flimsy patio set and wished he had something more sturdy and comfortable as he whiled away his days. He was a big man, and the woven weave in the chairs was already frayed and looked ready to give. She might mention it to Shane, who obviously had Brent's best interests at heart. She wouldn't be here long, but she'd like to leave him better off than he was before she came. The poor guy was more of a prisoner than she'd ever been.

He shook off her arm and counted the steps, feeling the back of the sofa as he passed, then touching the edge of the table, before settling into the dining chair. Having read some of the literature from Shane, she said, "Salad bowl is on your right, at one o'clock, and I cut the pasta in half so it'll be easier to eat. I prefer it that way," she told him. "Would you like extra Parmesan cheese?"

"Give me a second to taste it, and I'll let you know."

"You also have a water glass next to you, left at eleven. I'll go get your beer."

A moment later, she returned with his beer and a glass of wine for herself.

"Thank you." He slurped down some angel hair pasta and swiped at his mouth. "Good. You must like to cook."

"Not so much anymore." Carl had taken that joy, and every other, away from her. "I hope you don't mind if I keep it simple."

"It works for me." He stabbed his fork around until he found a shrimp and plopped it in his mouth. Like a man starved, he devoured his plate of pasta without tasting his beer. "Excellent," he said. "Is there more?"

She laughed, pleased. "No, but you haven't touched your salad, or your garlic bread. Here, let me help you." She slid his plate away and moved his salad and bread in its place. "I'm glad you're enjoying it."

She picked at her own dinner and watched him eat.

He was a very handsome man, even with his shorn hair and visible scars. Must have been a real heartbreaker. She couldn't help but wonder why he'd left his life here to go off to war. He'd had a good job, and possibly a woman too.

"Shane said you both worked for CAL FIRE. Didn't you like the job very much?"

He hesitated, as if ready to blow her off again. Instead, he answered. "We both loved it. I was a Forestry Fire pilot and he was a medic."

"Then what made you quit a job you loved to go fight the Taliban?"

"Multiple reasons, but one of them was because of Shane. He went to Iraq a year before me. Could never understand why. He had a nice gal here, we both were living the good life, but he was on some kind of mission and left. Anyway, to make a short story long, he was captured and tortured. Bastards cut off his hand."

"So that's how it happened." She grimaced, imagining the horror and pain that Shane had gone through. That being the case, why would Brent enlist? It made even less sense. "But still, that doesn't justify you signing up. Matter of fact, I'd say that was even more reason to stay put."

"You'd think that, but that wasn't the way it was between us. When this happened to my best buddy, the war became personal. You see, we grew up together and hitchhiked here from Florida right after high school graduation. He was closer to me than my two brothers. I couldn't wait to get my hands on the people that did that to him."

"But once he got back he probably needed you here."

"True, but I'd already committed. Due to my helicopter experience and the couple of years I'd spent as an Army cadet, I was being fast-tracked. Besides, by then I wanted to go. The war was never supposed to last this long, and I just wanted it to end. I figured I needed to do my part to see that it did."

"Again, why?"

"My father's a general. I come from a military background. I spent a couple of summers at a military academy when I was eleven and twelve." He laughed. "Before Shane came along. After that, I wouldn't go and Dad was furious. You see, in my family it's what we do. We don't start fights, but we damn well end them."

"Did your father expect you to become a career officer?"

"Might have when I was younger, but not once I started with CAL FIRE. He didn't even know right away that I'd signed up."

He took a long sip from his beer and seemed to enjoy it. Shane had bought him a dozen O'Douls, the non-alcohol beer, figuring Brent wouldn't notice the difference. He said he didn't want his friend using the bottle as a companion, as he had once done.

"I see." She mulled that over. "Well, you must have had a girlfriend." She gazed at his strong jawline, the straight nose, his beautiful hazel eyes that could no longer see, his full sensual mouth, and her heart ached for him. If his sight didn't return, his life would never be the same.

"I had a long-time girlfriend but she got tired of waiting for a commitment. We broke up and she hooked up with someone else right away. She was pregnant by the time I left. Must have a toddler by now."

"I'm sorry."

"You shouldn't be. She's a helluva lot better off without me."

Natalie didn't have anything to say to that. The way Brent felt about himself right now, he wasn't good for anybody. He needed to accept the new reality and learn skills that would help enrich his life.

"Tell me more about your family," she said. "Is your dad still a general? Do they live here in California?"

"No. Dad's retired. Mom died a few years back and he remarried a woman thirty years younger."

"Oh. How do you feel about that?"

"Well, good for Dad, I suppose. But Tiffany's an airhead, and I don't know how he can stand talking to her."

She grinned. "I doubt if he married her for her communication skills."

He laughed, and her heart skipped. She wanted to make him laugh. And often. It was the only nice thing she could do for him.

"You're probably right." He tilted the beer can in her direction. "So what about you? What's your story?"

Prickles of fear slid over her. She needed to hide for a time until she could figure her next move out. The police were like a brotherhood, banding together, protecting their own—she knew from experience. She'd been hospitalized once, and the police officer who took her statement made it clear that he didn't believe her. Carl had told them that she'd fallen down some stairs. Said she had too much to drink, that it wasn't the first time. When she attempted to tell him the truth, he'd said that perhaps she didn't remember the incident clearly because of the alcohol in her system.

Had she defied the cop and been firm with her story, Carl would have exacted his revenge on her the moment she got home. If he didn't do it, he'd send someone who would. So she stayed quiet and made excuses every time he lost his temper. The police hadn't protected her before, and she didn't expect them to now.

She was the only person who could do that. She had to disappear, and in order to keep the trail cold she had to keep on moving. "I already told you. A broken heart."

"Before the broken heart," Brent insisted.

Natalie thought that over. It had been a while since anything but escape and survival crossed her mind. "I have an older sister, and she's married with three kids. We don't have much in common but that's no excuse, I suppose, for staying out of touch." Natalie gnawed on her bottom lip. "Actually it's really bad when you think of it. I haven't seen her or her family since the youngest girl was born three years ago."

She couldn't tell him that had been her choice, not wanting her sister to see how Carl mistreated her. She'd never told anyone. Except her friend Lori.

Lori had repeatedly asked her to leave him and come to California, but she'd been afraid to go, knowing if he ever caught her he might possibly kill her. But the longer she stayed, the more she realized he might one day snap and kill her anyway.

"Where do they live?" he asked.

"My sister? Seattle. She's amazing, a real brainiac. She started a business on the Internet, called 'Name Your Price.' Whatever the buyer wants, she acquires, as close to the stated price as possible. And David, her husband, is a pharmacist. Their three girls are all beautiful and bright, and even the three-year-old goes to school. Half days so Melanie can work."

"They sound nice enough."

"They are. It's probably my fault we never got along. She's an A-type personality and a real go-getter. Not the warm, fuzzy type. She knew what she wanted even as a young girl and went after it."

"And you didn't?" He toyed with his cutlery, brushing his thumb along the edge of the fork.

"I did, but life didn't work out the way I'd hoped."

"Why not?" he asked.

"I wanted to travel, and so I studied languages, hoping to either work with the United Nations in some capacity, or with the Peace Corps. Something amazing, where I could live around the world." She gave a short laugh. "My sister was already married and having her first baby when Mom got sick. She had cancer and Dad didn't stick around. He left her after twenty-three years of marriage, just six months before she was diagnosed with a brain tumor." Her father leaving like that had been incredibly painful—she'd worshipped her dad, and this seemed like an unbelievable betrayal, not only to her mom, but also to herself. She'd struggled with that for years, and their relationship was still strained. "I finished my studies, got my masters in education, and became a local teacher so I could help out with my mom. She had surgery and chemo and did all right for a while, but then it came back. Within two years she was gone, and by then I was teaching and had met someone." She shrugged. "My dreams were gone, and I had responsibilities."

"And now?" He tapped at the table, his energy palpable. Obviously a man used to being on the move. He had the heart of an adventurer, even she could see that.

She didn't want to tell him about her tutoring position in the Loire Valley. Europe was her freedom from Carl, and the fewer people who knew about it, the safer she'd remain. She had always enjoyed music, so she would share that instead. "Now I know what I want, but it's not realistic. I could never make money at it."

"Ah—you always wanted to be a home care professional," he joked.

"Yeah. Right." She shrugged, forgetting for a second he couldn't see her. "No, this is a means to an end, but I'm hoping this move to California might be a positive one."

"So what is this secret passion? You want to be an actress." He snapped his fingers. "That must be it! Hell, doesn't everybody who comes to California?"

"No, I don't want to be an actress." She swallowed and confessed, "A songwriter, which is just as ridiculous."

"Yeah? Why don't you give me some of your lyrics and I'll see what I think."

"I'm not going to do that. No way." She pushed back from the table, wishing she'd never brought it up. It was her own private thing, more a comfort for her than any overwhelming desire.

"Come on. I can't see anything. It would be nice to hear something."

"You mean you want me to sing?" She gave a harsh laugh. "No you don't."

"Why not? You can sing, can't you?"

"I'm not very good at it. That why I write music, so others can bring it to life." She added softly, "Besides, I'm rather shy."

"You sure don't need to be shy with me. I can't even see you." He glanced around behind him. "Go look in the bedroom closet. I have an old guitar lying around somewhere. You can use it if you like."

"No, it's all right." Her chin lifted stubbornly. Carl had laughed at her attempts at songwriting and ridiculed her every chance he could get.

"Why not?"

"It's just a hobby." Writing music had given her an outlet when caring for her mother, and it had been an escape from the miserable existence with Carl. It was her happy place and she wished she hadn't shared it now with Brent.

"Oh, that's thinking big."

"I don't have to think big, or be like my sister. I'm just me." She studied his earnest face, glad he couldn't look back. "Not very interesting."

"You're the most interesting person I've met today."

She decided to turn the tables. "So are you any good?"

"At what?"

"The guitar. Do you like to play?"

"I used to. Haven't touched it in probably ten years."

"It might be fun for you." She jumped up. "You know I have lyrics and if you played it would give us something to do. As long as you don't laugh."

"I wouldn't laugh. I'm sure you have a very nice singing voice. Even if you didn't it wouldn't matter."

"You won't make fun of me?" She shot him a glance, hating to put herself into a situation where she could be mocked. She wasn't strong enough for that. Not yet.

"Of course not. What kind of jerk do you take me for?" He sighed. "Why don't you get me the guitar? Not even sure if I remember how, but I could try."

"Okay. I'll do that."

He got up from the table. "I'll put the dishes away. Make myself useful."

"Can you find everything okay?" She paused, uncertain.

"I'm not completely useless," he said with some heat in his voice. "I was in rehab for a couple months, they taught me to be independent. At least in the small things."

"Okay, okay, just asking." She backed away, not in fear, but because she was still tiptoeing around him, not wanting to get him riled up. "No need to get testy."

He picked up his plate, found hers, and took both into the kitchen. "I normally use plastic plates. But this is fine."

"Sorry. I didn't know." She watched him for a second to make sure he could get around without harming himself or anything around him. "I'll leave you to it, and find your guitar. Be right back."

She left and a second later she heard Brent curse and heard the sound of glass crash and splinter as it collided with the tile floor. She rushed back into the room. "What happened? Are you all right?"

"Damn dog. I tripped over him."

Sam hung his head low and slinked off to his bed in the corner. She knew it hadn't been the dog's fault but he was trained to help the blind, not to hinder.

"I'm sorry, Brent. I'll clean up. You better sit down because there's glass everywhere."

"Look. I think I'll call it a night after all." He stormed off toward his bedroom. "I knew I'd be better off alone," he muttered, shutting the door firmly behind him.

Natalie stared after him, wishing the evening had ended on a better note. They'd been nice to each other for a whole hour or more. Now they were back to square one.

She mopped up the mess on the floor, then took Sam out for a walk around the block. Although it was a much nicer neighborhood than she had inhabited lately, she still glanced warily around her, looking for danger lurking in the dark.

Against Natalie's wishes, Lori's husband had talked to a friend of his, a cop who worked in the Narcotics Division. He'd mentioned her situation to his supervisor, who'd promised to contact the police headquarters in Kelowna, Washington. When Lori told her this, Natalie had packed her bag and left their home that very night. She'd moved into a cheap motel, and that's where she'd been staying for the past few weeks. Best intentions aside, her friends had put her in jeopardy.

Carl could be anywhere.

CHAPTER FOUR

Brent couldn't sleep. His mind twisted, sensing there was more to Natalie's story than what she'd told him, but hell, everyone had secrets and whatever she was hiding made no difference now. She could even steal him blind, for all he cared.

The thought made him chuckle. Hey, was that a blind joke? What the hell was wrong with him? He'd enjoyed her company tonight, and had encouraged her to bring out the guitar. That was so not going to happen. He was needy right now, and it would be easy to mistake any act of kindness for caring.

She'd be gone in a month or so, and he had to prepare for the possibility that his sight might never return. He needed to stop wallowing in self-pity. There were a lot of things he could do without sight, and if he'd stayed in that Wounded Warrior program, Operation Freedom Bell, he'd already be fully functional, but his stubborn pride had gotten in the way. Figured he didn't need it—after all, he wasn't going to be blind forever. No way in hell. Hadn't the doctors told him it was in his head, that it wasn't neurological damage? So what was taking so long?

He wasn't a basket case. He had some stress disorder thing, but didn't darn near every soldier who came back from war?

Hell, the program was living-in with a bunch of blind vets for more than half a year—no damn wonder he'd walked out. He just needed to be patient for a little longer, that was all. If his sight didn't return soon, well he'd have nothing but time on his side to learn what he needed.

Meanwhile, the last thing he wanted was to sit around the apartment with a woman who had an enticing smell—what was it? Something natural and fruity, like a peach or mango, and she had soft hands. He also imagined, equally soft curves.

He flipped over and buried his face in the pillow. The more he tried to sleep, the more he tossed and turned. Somewhere in that twilight zone he found himself back in Afghanistan—seized by panic as he lost control of his chopper. Hit by a round of small arms fire, he frantically fought to maintain control, but the Black Hawk continued a spiral spin. An ice-packed mountain ridge loomed closer and closer. He felt the impact, heard the shouts from the crew, saw the shattered windshield as his head went through the glass. His body felt as if it had been severed in half, and then the stench of burning flesh, sounds of mortar fire, shrieks and screams of the men dying around him.

God—what had happened during those first few hours? He'd been blind. Useless to his own men.

A scream ripped from his throat, and he flailed madly about in the darkness, springing forward, groping walls.

"Brent?" Hands were on his shoulders, shaking him. "Brent, it's me. Natalie. You're having a bad dream. You're here, at home. You're safe."

His face was soaked with nervous sweat. "Where am I?" he stammered, his hands searching around him.

She brought his hands to her cheeks. "I'm right here. And this is your home."

He pushed her hands away and didn't answer. Several minutes passed as he sucked in air, coming to grips.

"Brent. Can I get you anything? Did you take your medication?"

"I'm fine. Yes. I'm sure I did."

"I'm so sorry. I should have paid more attention."

"I don't need you to hand me my pills. I'm blind, not stupid."

"I don't think you're stupid at all. But I'm here to assist you. I got carried away with our conversation and didn't do my job." She touched his arm. "It's my fault."

"Forget about it. I'll live," he snapped. "Go back to bed."

"I will, once I know that you're all right."

He sighed. "Look, I have nightmares. If you're going to stay here at night you'll have to get used to them. There's no need to come in. I'm not going to hurt myself."

"I see. Well, that's good news then, but I'm not as comfortable with your nightmares as you are. Can I just stay until you fall back asleep?"

"No. I don't want you standing here looking at me."

"Fine. How about if I sit on the edge of the bed and sing you a lullaby?" she said with a smile in her voice.

He turned to face the wall. "Thought you didn't like to sing." When she laughed, he mumbled, "Go away, please go away." To his humiliation, he heard his voice break. "How many times do I have to tell you that I'd rather be alone?"

She didn't move for a few seconds, but then he heard her murmur something and leave the room.

He was alone again, with nothing but darkness.

EPISODE TWO

CHAPTER FIVE

"Rise and shine," Natalie called, rapping on Brent's door.

"I'm sleeping. Leave me alone."

"It's seven, and you can't spend the entire morning in bed."

"What are you? A drill sergeant?" He cursed. "I can damn well sleep in as long as I want."

She cracked the door open and saw him sitting up. His chest was bare, and he wore only plaid flannel sleep pants. Even painfully thin, he was still a mouth-watering sight. Had she not had a Carl in her life, she might have wanted to work a little longer in this new job. But her immediate future was focused on remaining safe until she could escape for good and live in a place of serenity and beauty—where Carl would never find her. Not romance—she didn't have room in her life for that.

"You're a military man. Discipline. Remember?" she teased. "Get up. I can't find the coffee, and you don't want to see me when I need a caffeine fix."

"Don't want to see you anyway," he replied, sliding down the bed, putting the pillow over his head.

Treading softly, she stepped into the room, sneaking up on him and grabbed his pillow, resisting the urge to tickle him. "Up. Now." He flailed at her with one arm, and she stepped back. "Come on, Brent. I need coffee. Where is it? Please tell me you have some?"

"In the freezer," he grumbled.

"Thank heavens." She gave an exaggerated sigh. "I'll get it started while you shower and dress."

"Were you like this with your boyfriend?" He shifted and perched on an elbow. "No wonder that relationship went bad."

She froze for a moment. She'd done everything right, tried so hard. It hadn't been her fault. Carl was cruel. It was his DNA. Not hers.

"I was nice to him and I'll be nice to you," she whispered in a soft, low voice. "If you behave. If you don't, watch out. I can be your worst nightmare without a cup of java in the morning." Something deep inside her, a playfulness that was not quite dead made her reach for his blankets and rip them off. "Now, get your skinny ass up!" she said, hiding a grin.

His head snapped up, and a few seconds later, he started to laugh. "Okay, Sarge. You sure you weren't in the army?"

She watched in surprise, mesmerized at how different he looked when he wasn't angry. Younger, nicer, and a little too handsome. But she knew from experience that physical appearance didn't mean squat. Nice on the outside didn't mean nice on the inside. Still, she was starting anew, and she couldn't let Carl's actions poison her every thought. All men didn't fit in that same barrel. She needed to remember that.

She turned away. "I'll get breakfast ready."

She made the coffee and set the table, then decided they'd both have two eggs on toast. She poured him a small glass of orange juice and remembered to use plastic plates.

Everything was ready, and she could hear him rummaging in his drawers searching for his clothes. A minute later he entered the kitchen wearing his T-shirt inside out. "Something smells good," he said and reached in the cupboard for a mug.

"I have your coffee poured," she told him, not wanting to make a big deal out of his shirt. She'd just make sure they were all packed away properly from now on. "What do you take in it?"

"Just black. But you don't have to do that. I can get my own. Breakfast too."

"Good for you. One less job for me to do." She bit back her frustration. If he didn't want her to help him, she had no idea what she'd do all day. The last thing she wanted or needed was to be a babysitter for a frustrated, six-foot-something, ex-linebacker with mood swings. "Today though, I fried us some eggs."

He took his coffee and bumped into her, splashing a little on her arm.

"Ouch." She grabbed a towel and mopped the coffee from her arm.

"What did I do?"

"Nothing," she said, not wanting him to feel bad. "I just sipped my coffee and burned my tongue."

"Thanks for the warning." He took a seat. "Is the food on the table?" He felt around and found his knife and fork.

"Here it is." She placed the plate in front of him. "Over easy? Is that all right with you?"

"I'm not picky. I survive quite well on cereal in the morning. No need to go all out."

"I didn't. This only took a moment." He used his finger to locate the egg and the toast, and it took great will power for her not to interfere. She wanted to take his knife and fork out of his hand, cut up his food, and hand feed him. Instead, she sat down with her plate and began to eat.

He carved the toast and egg into jagged pieces, and brought the fork to his lips. She focused on her own breakfast and ate quickly, hating to see him struggle. "Are you still hungry?" she asked, pleased that he'd finished his plate. "I bought fruit."

"No, that was good. Thanks."

"Would you like to go out today?" she asked cheerfully and cleared their dishes. "Sam needs a walk and I would like to see the neighborhood."

She would like his company, not that she was afraid or anything. Still, she glanced out the window, calming her nerves. Even if Carl had been interrogated by his superior, it didn't mean he knew her whereabouts. She'd be long gone by the time he did.

Lori had used her contacts to get Natalie the tutoring job in France and was working hard to get her a work permit fast. She'd been angry with her husband for telling his cop friend about Natalie, and feared for her safety.

Natalie kept in contact with Lori by phone, who knew she'd taken this job with Brent but not the address. It was safer for everyone that way.

"Naw, I'm good. You go and enjoy yourself. I have some stuff to do."

"Really? Like what?" She rinsed the plates and put them in the dishwasher, then straightened up to look at him.

"Might see if I can remember any of that Braille they were teaching me in rehab. Better than sitting on my dick all day."

She nearly laughed, but said instead, "That's a great idea." If he found something to interest him, his whole perspective might change. She needed to do a little investigation herself in helping the blind. "If you'll be all right on your own, I might go visit the library after I walk Sam."

"Sure. As I say, I'm independent. I don't need someone hovering over me all day long." He finished his coffee, staring at nothing on the wall.

"Good. I don't intend to hover." She studied him for a second, wondering what it must be like to see nothing all day. A world gone dark. She kept the sympathy out of her voice when she spoke to him. "You seem in a more positive frame of mind than you did yesterday. I'm glad."

"Well, don't get too excited. My mood swings from high to low and back again. Especially when I'm not on antidepressants." He stood up abruptly. "Don't want to be in la-la land. I'd rather just learn to deal with it."

"Did the doctors prescribe them?"

"They did. I took them for a couple of months, then stopped. Don't see any reason to tell them either." He felt his way to the couch and plopped down.

"When's your next appointment?" She followed him, and stood a few steps away, arms folded, watching him.

"None of your business. You just go about yours, and I'll go about mine."

She sighed. "Brent, I'm here to help you—get you on the right track. Seeing a doctor and doing what he tells you will get you better quicker. You must want that."

"I see him when I need to." He ran a hand over his shaved head. "I spent enough time in hospitals and rehab. Had my share of doctors and psychiatrists telling me what I can and can't do."

She tried to take it all in, but it was confusing that with all his medical treatment, he still couldn't see. No wonder he was angry. "I understand your frustration, but you still need to take your meds." She glanced at his set jaw, knowing he was going to be stubborn. "If you won't listen to me, at least listen to Shane."

"Shane needs to butt out."

"Well, I can't. I'm your caregiver. For now, anyway."

"Well, that can be short-lived." He pushed himself off the sofa and went into the kitchen for another cup of coffee. "Anytime I decide I don't want you here, I'll pack your bags and put them out on the street."

"If you don't want my help, I'll leave." She held her breath. Would he kick her out? She had no place to go and little funds to carry her through the month.

"Not sure yet." He leaned against the kitchen counter and sipped his hot coffee. She saw him wince and figured the coffee had burned his tongue. Being macho he didn't complain, but she noticed he didn't take another sip either.

"So, you're sure you don't want to come for a walk? It's a nice, sunny day."

"Told you no," he growled. "And hope I don't pack your bag while you're gone."

She shrugged. Okay, he wasn't coming. No big deal. Let him remain in a vegetable state. She was going walking. She was getting the hell out of there, and no one was making her a prisoner again. Fear was only a frame of mind, and she wasn't going to allow it to control her. She was stronger than that.

She picked up the dog's leash from the counter and clicked it to Sam's collar. "You can stay in if you like. Makes no difference to me. I'll still get paid."

"Not if I have anything to do about it."

She stuck her tongue out at him. "Oh, yeah?"

"Get lost."

She studied him for a moment, anxious to see her new environment and check out the safety aspect of it, but she felt a twinge of guilt. He needed her, but was too stubborn to admit it. "What would you do without me?" she said lightly.

"Bring the strippers in." His lips twitched into a smile. "Yeah. That's what I'd do. Throw a big party too."

She laughed. "Good luck with that." Sam was jumping around at her feet. "Come boy. Let's go for a nice long walk. How far is the beach? Do they have a boardwalk?"

"Not the local beach. Boardwalk's about five miles south of here." He glanced in her direction. "Dogs aren't allowed on the beach. Gotta stick to the sidewalk."

"Oh, too bad. Maybe we can find a park nearby."

Sam barked, then jumped up and down, biting at the leash.

Natalie turned her head. "Okay, take it easy while I'm gone. Should be back in fifteen minutes or so."

"Don't rush back on my account. Take all day if you want."

She glanced at him, shook her head, and left. She knew it was fear holding him back, just as it had her, but until he was ready to break the chains, she couldn't do anything to help him.

∼

The moment the door closed behind her, Brent wandered around the apartment wondering where in heck he'd put the material he'd brought home from the training center. He'd shoved it somewhere, but in the past month two aides had come and gone. They'd only lasted less than a week each.

He had a bad feeling about Natalie. She seemed determined and stubborn enough to hang on to this job.

Then again, if he could learn the stuff he needed to, she would have no reason to stay. How was that for motivation? He would be well adapted, completely independent and alone.

He picked up his cell and called Shane, knowing his number was first on his list.

"Hey Shane? You got any idea where I put those books on Braille and that other shit from the center?"

"How would I know? Probably tossed it in the closet or in a corner. Where do you usually keep stuff like that?"

"I don't normally have stuff like that. Not in my real life, anyway."

"Well, sorry to say, but this is your real life right now, buddy." He cleared his throat. "So you're thinking of getting back into it?"

"Yeah. Figured if I could do a little more, I could get rid of Nat the rat."

"Why? What's wrong with her?"

"She's nice and sweet when you're around, but you haven't seen the lippy side of her." Brent didn't need a woman like that around—with her sweet smells and damn sympathy. Why did Shane hire her anyway? "I don't need that kind of shit."

"That right?" Shane chuckled, which infuriated Brent. "You're probably not all that pleasant, either. Look, here's the deal. She pretends to be tough, but there's something going on that she won't talk about. I can see it in her eyes, and the way she flinches when you yell. Down on the street she's always looking around, nervous-like. I think she's hiding from something, and your place is a good place to hide."

"Why? 'Cause I'm fucking blind?"

"Well, that's one of the reasons. There's safety in that. It would certainly give her refuge until whatever she's afraid of becomes less of a threat."

He let that sink in. "So basically you're saying, I need to keep her because she's in trouble and I can help her out? She needs me more than I need her?"

"Yeah. Something like that."

"Well, that's ironic, isn't it?" Brent thought about it for a long second. Maybe he could help her out a little. The place got awfully quiet with just him around. "A month. She can stay for a month, then she'll just have to figure out her own problems. I have enough of my own."

After he hung up, Brent went out onto the balcony, feeling the warmth of a bright sunny day. Almost, but not quite, wished he'd had gone with them, except he didn't want anyone around when he did venture out. So damn awkward. How did babies and little children deal with blindness, when a grown man like him couldn't?

He returned indoors and sat waiting. It seemed like a long time before Natalie returned with Sam. He felt the dog rub up against his leg and settle near his feet.

"Good walk?" he asked pleasantly.

"Wonderful. This is a beautiful neighborhood, and we did find a park. Sam wanted to play with the other dogs, but when I gave him a command he obeyed instantly. And he's so sweet."

Brent listened as she rummaged in the panty, ripped open a bag, and tossed the dog something. Probably one of the dog treats.

"Before you go out again," he asked, "do you mind looking around for my books? Might be in a closet or a drawer somewhere."

"Sure. I'll look."

"Sorry, but I had two aides before you and I don't know what they did with them. Not much help, am I?"

She stepped toward him. "Well, aren't you being nice, all of a sudden," she said in a teasing voice, then laughed. "What did you take when I was gone? A personality pill?"

He glowered in her direction. So much for being nice. "I told Shane I'd put up with you for a month, and figured maybe we could try to be polite. If that's a problem, forget it."

She came up and put a hand on his shoulder. "I shouldn't have been snarly. I'm grateful that you're going to let me stay, and yes, I can be polite too."

He smelled her fruity scent and wondered where it came from. Shampoo? Body lotion? Whatever it was, it was both enticing and annoying. He removed her hand and felt its loss when she walked away.

"I'll be back as soon as I find your books," she said. "And nice works for me."

He heard her open the sliding doors to his closet. "Here's your guitar," she shouted. "There's a lot of junk lying around, but I can't see any books."

"Keep looking," he shouted back. "It's there somewhere." Brent rested his head on the back of the sofa, staring upward at what would be the ceiling. Time passed, and he grew impatient. Is this what the rest of his life would be like? Endless hours, endless days?

"I think this is what you're looking for, but if you need anything else, I'm going to the library and can pick something up." She'd come back into the room, and dumped some books next to him.

He felt the books. How could he tell what he was supposed to learn if he damn well couldn't see? It was a ridiculous idea. "What do I have here?"

"You have a couple of books in Braille, something for computer software, a book about activities for the blind, another one on job training, and one more on hobbies and sports." She guided his hand to the books. "All good stuff."

"Good, if I knew how to read it."

"That's what we can do together. Study Braille. Do you remember anything?"

"I remember some." He felt a moment of panic. This was going to be harder than expected. Why the fuck had he walked away from that training center when he didn't know shit? Because he'd been so sure that his sight would have returned by now, that's why. After all, the eye specialist hadn't found any neurological damage. So what was his brain waiting for? Did he need another smack on the head or traumatic event to get the gray fog away? What if his sight never did come back?

He swallowed hard, not wanting her to sense his fear. "You go, and I'll play around with this."

"Fine. But I'll make a sandwich for you first, and then I'll be off."

He heard her puttering around the kitchen. She was singing softly, and it sounded like French. He couldn't make out the words but it sounded sexy. A few minutes later she returned and told him his lunch was on the kitchen table, and he could eat it when he was ready.

"What were you singing? Was that French?"

"Oui, oui, monsieur." She laughed. "Gotta keep current. Never know when I'll get another teaching job or find a Frenchman to care for."

"I see. Being a language teacher, you need to keep your skills up." He closed his eyes and tilted his head back on the back of the sofa. "You're free to leave for the day. No need to rush back."

"Thanks for making me feel so wanted," she said in a teasing manner.

"I'm being polite," he said, careful to keep his face neutral. He hated having this woman in his house, seeing him weak and pathetic. He'd been something of a big shot once, now he was nothing but a zero.

"Fine. Have a nice afternoon." She opened the door, and called out, "Bye, Sam. Take good care of him while I'm gone."

Brent waited until she left, then fingered the books until he found the Braille. His finger tips followed the indentations, and slowly he was able to figure out letters and words. Due to his slow pace, though, the meaning was lost on him.

After what seemed like an hour, he tossed the book on the floor with disgust.

"This is no life," he muttered aloud. "Why couldn't I have died instead?" His conscience niggled at him. He could have ended his life, but he wouldn't do that, not to his family, not to his friends, not to those who'd died instead of him.

He closed his eyes and lay back on the sofa, remembering the men who were on his Black Hawk that day, and one special woman too. He'd been surprised to see his captain was a woman, but he'd seen how the men respected her, and quickly learned why. She'd graduated from Princeton and had four years on active duty. She was tough, gritty, competent, and had hoped to become Special Ops one day. Had she made it out alive, she might have been one of the first women to join the elite forces. But Linda didn't live long enough to see the Defense Secretary lift the ban on woman in combat.

His fault. He'd been flying with the aid of night-vision goggles while on a search and rescue. He'd seen tracer rounds lighting up the sky, coming right at him, and had tried to dodge the bullets, but they'd suffered a direct hit.

Brent tossed to his side on the couch and tried to find peace in sleep, but as usual Captain James's face popped into his head. He could clearly see her wide-set brown eyes flashing, her mouth twisted in a familiar tough-girl snarl.

He heard the sound of her voice and tried to muffle it with a pillow.

"Move it, Harrington," she whispered. "I don't mind going down for the USA, but I sure as hell do mind you lazing around and feeling sorry for your damn self. You have to live for all of us. Schooner, Hamilton, me. Drag your ass off the couch and learn what you need to know—hell, you learned code better than anybody! How hard could it be for a smart boy like you? Learn how to laugh and love, maybe even get yourself laid. Wouldn't that be something! But don't waste the sacrifice we willingly made for our country on self-pity. Got it, Harrington?"

Her face began to fade, and he fought to keep it with him for a minute more. He wanted to remember all of them, but she was the only one who hounded his sleep and hadn't given up on him.

As the captain, Linda James ran the show. She'd been quick with a joke, but just as quick to push back if any man crossed the line. They'd flown their first mission together in tandem—hers was the lead copter, he trailed. It was a recon over a suspicious area a few miles from base. He'd flown at night in training, but this was his first real mission, and it had him jumpy with adrenaline. He'd always lived for the thrill of danger and this was no different.

With no moon, no light, the Black Hawks were darn near invisible. The goggles cut his vision forty percent and played havoc with depth perception. He'd accepted the challenge with the same daredevil spirit that made him fight fires back home. Not a god complex like some pilots were accused of, but more of a guardian angel thing, being able to swoop down in his helicopter and save who needed saving.

Suddenly, pops and flashes of fire caused her copter to break left. He followed, as trained. The door gunners readied for return fire, though that hadn't been the mission—somehow their cover had been blown. Theirs was a search and rescue team, but they were still soldiers, through and through.

"Harrington. Watch your rear," Captain James radioed.

The first flare of light coming toward him pissed him off. Didn't those bastards know who they were dealing with? After the first rush of anger, he settled himself and followed procedure, calling in for Apache backup. Captain James had shown some mighty fine flying skills and he'd had a hard time to keep up, dodging fire coming every which way. His respect reached a paramount level that night, and he'd never had cause to change his mind. The event solidified their team. Their Black Hawk family.

His mind relaxed, and eventually Brent fell into a peaceful sleep.

CHAPTER SIX

Natalie came home around three and found Brent sprawled out on the couch, a beer can next to him, and the books tossed on the floor. Sam was sound asleep in his doggy bed.

The silence was almost eerie, she decided. It was time to put a little life in the place. Turning the TV on, she found the music stations and scrolled down until she came across Andrea Bocelli. She turned the volume on low, not wanting to startle him but to give him something pleasant to listen to.

Brent shot forward. "What the hell?"

"'The Prayer'—beautiful isn't it?"

"Turn the damn thing off." He rubbed his face. "Couldn't you see that I was sleeping?"

"Sure I could, but it's the middle of the afternoon and I came back with all kinds of toys for you. Learning devices for people with limited sight." She purposely avoided using the word blind, because she didn't want to believe that was what his future held, anymore than he did.

"I'm not in the mood." He had a hangdog expression on his face, and looked so down and dejected that her heart softened. She wished she had a magic wand to make everything right, but nothing would ever be the same for him again. Well, she couldn't fix him, but she was here to brighten his life the best she could.

"What happened to Mister Nice? Come on, Brent. Why are you snapping at me? I was hoping the music would cheer you up. And I brought stuff to help you learn." She stepped toward him, stopping only a few feet away. Sam eyed her suspiciously and made a low growling noise in the back of his throat. She ignored the dog and said to Brent, "What would you like to do today?"

"Well, I'd like to take my board down to the beach and hit the surf, or engage in a fast, grueling game of tennis, or something simpler, like fly again. But since that's not likely to happen, I think I'll just sit here and suck it up. Does that work for you?"

"The sucking up part does, but not the bitching." She busied herself picking up his books and stacking them on the coffee table. "Want to see what I got at the library?"

"No." He rubbed at his jaw, and she noticed that he hadn't shaved. She liked the stubble. It was more than a shadow and kind of sexy.

"Well, I'll show you anyway. Not show," she corrected herself, "but tell you what I have."

He sighed. "It was so peaceful when you were gone."

"Yes, well, now I'm back," she spoke in a bright, chipper manner, refusing to indulge his black mood. "Get used to it," she said pleasantly.

Sam got off his bed, lazily walked over to them, sniffed her leg, then sat down, resting his head on Brent's bare foot, keeping one eye on her. Smart dog, probably recognized the insincerity in her voice. Probably knew she was a fake too. Just like Brent, she'd been trapped in darkness and had a really hard time seeing her way out of it. She understood his depression, having lived it herself, but she couldn't sit by and let him sink deeper into it. Her job was to help him, whether he wanted it or not.

Brent flopped back on the couch. "Could you please turn off that horrible noise?"

"You don't love opera? Who doesn't love opera?" she asked with a bright smile. "It transcends the soul."

"If you must play music, how about Carrie Underwood or Beyoncé? Some hot dame, with a hot body, whether she can sing is unimportant. At least I can envision something sexy."

"A singer is supposed to be able to sing, not just look good." She glanced at him. "Men can be such pigs; all they think about is a shapely ass." She sighed. "Guess you can't help it. You're only a few pathetic steps away from being a primal beast." She clicked her fingers. "Hey, that reminds me. I should get your guitar. Why don't you fiddle around with that while I rearrange a few things here?"

"Like what?"

"Like your shirt's on inside out. I want to check your drawers and make sure everything is lined up correctly and not wrong side out."

He felt his shirt at the neck and found the tag she was talking about. "Why didn't you say anything sooner?"

"Why bother? You refused to go outside so it didn't matter." She watched him pull at the shirt. He looked angry. Upset. So he did care about something. It was important to him to look put together even if he wasn't inside.

"It does to me," he answered, struggling out of his shirt.

"Let me help you," she spoke more gently. "Put your arms up and we'll fix it."

She raised the shirt over his chest, up and over his head and through his arms. He had powerful shoulders, tight abs, but was so skinny that he looked as defenseless as a baby. Yet, defenseless or not, she knew better than to get too close. A kind word, a simple caress could turn into a slap in an instant. She'd learned that too, the hard way.

Quickly, she turned the shirt correctly and placed it back over his head. His face was inches from hers and seeing him so vulnerable tugged at her heart. Such a handsome face—strong, good features, a rugged warrior's body, and yet so fragile inside.

She pulled the shirt down over his shoulders, over his chest, and leaned in to tug it down his back. Her breasts lightly touched his chest, and she sucked in her breath. Waiting. Fearful. Thankfully he didn't seem to notice.

"There. Now you look perfect."

He ran a hand over his buzz cut. "Do I?"

"Uh-huh." Changing the subject and moving away, she asked, "Are you familiar with talking software for your computer? The librarian told me about a free screen-reader for Windows computers. Said it was really easy to use and can give you hours of enjoyment. Like having an entertainment center on your computer. Movies, music, news reports."

"I used one at the rehab center, if it's the same thing you're talking about."

"Probably. But give me a few minutes to install it, and then you can see for yourself. Whatever you're interested in, you should be able to find here."

"That does sound good." He stood and stretched. "It'll help time go faster. Now, a day seems endless."

"I brought home tons of books in Braille, and one for me so I can learn too. That way, anything you don't remember, I'll be able to help you with."

"You've been very thoughtful," he said in a false kind of voice. "Thanks." It set her teeth on edge.

"Stop being so polite. It doesn't sound sincere." She took another step back and folded her arms under her chest. Carl would do that just before an explosion—his voice would get all soft and nice, and then he'd let her have it. He wasn't Carl, she told herself. Brent wouldn't hurt her. Yet, even telling herself this, nervous butterflies floated in her stomach.

"What do you want me to say?" He shook his head. "I thought you liked me being nice."

"I don't know. Just be yourself. Don't creep me out." She gnawed on her bottom lip. She knew she sounded a little crazy, but maybe she was after living with Carl. Why hadn't she escaped sooner? Why had it taken her so long to gather her spirit and flee?

"Now you want me to yell at you? Thought you hated being yelled at."

"I do, but this personality switch is just as scary. Usually, when a person is pretending to be overly nice, hell's about to break loose." She gave a shaky laugh. "Sounds crazy, I know."

He frowned. "Not crazy, but that sure is a strange way of looking at things."

"I'm just saying. It's not natural, and it's not sincere." She rubbed her arms, as goose bumps appeared. "Inside you something is lurking, and you're getting ready to erupt." Prickles of fear ran up and down her spine, and she used all her mental strength to combat them. She was safe here. No one wanted to hurt her.

"No, I'm not." There was heat in his words, but his expression was kind. "I had my eruption today over the music. That's about as wild as I get."

"I've seen you simmering. Your anger is just below the surface," she added sullenly.

"What the heck do you know?" He sighed, clearly frustrated. "You're not a mind reader or a psychologist."

"I know tension when I see it, and you're hanging on by a thread."

"Go fix my drawers," he said quietly, "and stop trying to analyze me."

"Okay." She stopped for a second, knowing she should apologize, but afraid it might open the door for questions. "Just have to say one thing before I leave."

"Now what?"

"For a skinny guy, you've got great abs."

He chuckled and she left, confused by her mixed emotions. This job was certainly more interesting than the last one with the poor Alzheimer patient. She'd had to bathe him and help him dress, even change his underwear, and that hadn't been pleasant. Other times he'd cursed at her and accused her of taking his belongings, but most of the time he slept or just stared out the window.

Brent was damaged too, but he provided more interesting challenges. For the short duration she was here, she'd like to improve his mental condition, and her own as well. She didn't want to take up her new position as a tutor to three little French children if she was the one hanging by a thread.

Natalie found his guitar and took it in to him, then went back into his bedroom to reorganize his drawers. She could hear him strumming a chord or two, and was pleased that he had something to do.

Tomorrow, she'd insist that he go out and get some exercise beyond a swim at the pool. He needed to re-enter the world, socialize more. She understood his terror and that he was depressed and afraid. She knew from experience what it felt like to be both, and was still working on those issues.

She had had quite a few friends when she first met Carl, and they had gone on dinner dates with a few couples that she'd introduced him to. But it wasn't long after, perhaps three to four months into their relationship, when he'd started to question why they needed to be with her friends instead of spending time alone. Her mother had just died and she had been needy, and Carl had fed that need in her.

Six months after meeting him, they were engaged. His controlling got worse. He didn't like her going out to the gym at night, seeing her friends, or chatting on the phone. She had stopped doing anything that made him angry, and her resentment grew.

The first time he hit her, she'd been so shocked she'd run out of the house, down the street, without a thought in her head except to escape. She didn't have her keys, her handbag, not even her shoes.

He'd come looking for her and found her on a park bench, sobbing into a tissue that a stranger had lent her. Carl had knelt down beside her and taken her in his arms and begged her forgiveness, then he'd gently led her back to the apartment they shared. Things had been good for a while, but only as long as she didn't rock the boat. His moodiness turned uglier and he began to pick on her for every little imaginary thing. The attacks grew worse, moving from verbal to physical. She'd threatened to leave and in return he'd put her in the hospital with a split lip and a fractured leg.

She'd been black and blue, but when she refused to testify the doctors couldn't do anything to help. She had been released into his care. And then the nightmare began.

Natalie emptied her brain, refusing to give Carl another thought, or more power than he had. She returned to Brent. "So how's the guitar? I heard you playing and it sounded pretty good."

"It was crap." He got up. "Look, I know you mean well, and you've got to do what you've got to do, but I'm just tired, that's all."

"You sure? I thought you'd be interested in the screen-reader."

"I'm tired. And I've got a pounding head."

"You want some Advil?"

He shook his head. "Don't like medicine."

"Why not? Sounds like you need it."

"Got something called SSID. Short for symptoms, signs, and ill-defined conditions. Just a long way of saying combat stress." He stretched and yawned. "Medicine doesn't make it go away, so why bother?"

"How does this condition affect you, and what do you do for it if you don't take meds?"

He shrugged. "Not much. Drugs sugar-coat it but they don't fix the underlying problem, so I would rather deal with it than medicate myself."

"Tell me more about SSID, so I know what you're dealing with."

"Okay. It's not that big of a deal. The common symptoms are chronic fatigue, muscle weakness, insomnia, headache, back pain, muscle aches, just to name a few."

"Ouch." That was a lot of physical discomfort. "Well, you definitely need medicinal support for all that."

"Look, if it makes you feel better, I'll have two Advil."

She got up to get it, wishing she had an easy cure to help with his stress, which she knew was worse than his physical ailments. Emotional and mental problems were far more challenging. She wasn't sure what the best treatment for a guy like him might be, but letting him do nothing wasn't an option. She had to push him to help himself or he'd never be independent.

She handed him the pills and a glass of water, and waited until he knocked them back. Then she took the glass out of his hand and returned it to the kitchen.

He was halfway to his bedroom when she stopped him. "Brent? Can I have a word?"

"What now?"

"Look, I know you got frustrated this afternoon, tossing your books aside. I understand your feelings, but I'm here to nudge you. Sorry, I know you'd rather I disappear, but that's not going to happen. I'm going to stay right here and keep on nudging."

"No you're not. I'm going to bed. And you're not invited."

"After your nap then. I'll still be here."

He scratched his head. "What do you want from me?"

She stepped towards him. "Nothing tonight. Go and rest. But I want you to know that I'm here to help you." She stopped for a moment, unsure if she should go on. "Thing is, you have to help yourself. Nothing's going to come easy anymore. You're going to have to work hard to be the man you used to be. But isn't it worth it?" She softened her voice, not wanting to be judgmental, only helpful. "You're young and strong. Fight, Brent. I promise you it will be worth it. Don't give up."

"I'm not. But how the hell would you like to be blind?"

"I wouldn't like it at all, and I completely empathize." Her voice cracked a little, and she took a step back and straightened her shoulders. She wanted to fight for him, but she couldn't push until he was ready. "Rest now and we'll take another step tomorrow."

Without another word, he disappeared.

Natalie sat down, wondering how she could break through the wall he'd built around himself. He was hurting deeply, and was more frightened than she had ever been.

She took out her Kindle and tried to engross herself with the romance novel she'd been reading, but her concentration was all over the place, and she had to reread the sentences twice.

After an hour, Brent stalked into the room. He didn't look rested, only more disturbed. He'd scratched his face, perhaps in his sleep.

"What's your story?" he demanded, his mouth a grim line.

"Told you."

"Yeah, yeah, yeah. A bad relationship. How bad?"

"It doesn't matter now. It's over." She gnawed on her bottom lip. "But at least I had the gumption to do something about it and move on with my life. Not that it was easy, and I'm not saying for you it is." She swallowed hard. "You might be fighting the biggest battle of your life, but just remember that I'm here to help. I'll support you in every way I can." She knew she had to be strong for him, but she'd been through the wringer too. "We will do this together. Both of us are survivors."

"Okay, okay, I get it," he grumbled. "Why don't you download that software you were talking about, instead of giving me a sermon?"

She felt a ray of happiness. Maybe she could help him after all, leave him better than he was before. "I could do that." She found the website and followed the instructions on the screen for a free download. It surprised her that the other caregivers hadn't already done this for him. Obviously they'd not stayed long enough or cared.

While she made dinner, an easy chicken piccata with steamed basmati rice and a Caesar salad, she listened to the latest news in Afghanistan. Brent had chosen to entertain himself with a report from the official US Army website.

She would have preferred he indulged himself in something other than the reminder of war, but at least he'd found something for the moment to be interested in.

After dinner they settled onto the couch and watched *NCIS* together. "I love Abby, don't you? She's such a character. I wonder why they don't give her a love interest."

"I don't know the show as well as you. Never watched much TV the last couple of years. Too busy shooting down the Taliban."

"Of course. Silly me. Obviously, you didn't have time during your deployment." She was silent for a few moments. "Want me to fill you in?"

"No, not necessary. It's fine. I'll just listen and pick it up from here."

"Okay. But if you want me to give you a blow-by-blow description of the action, then I'm your girl."

"Why don't you just sit and enjoy it, so I can listen?"

"I could do that." She folded her arms, and stared at the TV. After a little while she couldn't contain herself. "Did you watch any TV in Afghanistan? Do they have it on the bases?"

"The big bases, yeah. Not the outcamps, which are temporary posts."

"I see. So you did get to watch some American shows?"

"British and American, yes. Now can you please be quiet?"

"Just one more question, then I won't say another word."

"You promise?"

She laughed. "It's a big one. Are you ready?"

"Shoot."

"Here goes. Drumroll please…"

"Get on with it."

"Don't be so grumpy." She nudged his arm. "Okay—do you want to know what I look like? It doesn't seem fair that I can see you, and you have no idea who you're sharing the house with."

She glanced at him and wondered how it must feel. She could see everything, every facial expression, every hair out of place. He couldn't hide from her, and she must be this big mystery to him. He had no idea if she was big or small. She could look like a sumo wrestler and have a huge honker and hairy armpits and he wouldn't know. It didn't seem right.

"Go ahead," she said when he remained silent. "Ask me anything."

He snorted, a half laugh. "If you were ugly, would you admit it, or tell me you're a raving beauty? I would probably prefer to think the latter."

"I'm neither. If you want, I can give you a brief description."

"I'm not interested, but if you want, give it a shot."

She stayed quiet for some time, a little hurt that he didn't seem to care. But then she'd be leaving in a month, so as long as she kept out of his way and treated him fairly, what difference did it make if she looked nice or not?

"Okay. Tell me. I know it's eating you." He glanced in her direction, at the other end of his couch.

"It's not eating me. I don't care, either."

He chuckled. "Okay. I'll tell you how I see you, and you can tell me if I'm right or wrong."

"All right. How tall am I?"

"Medium height—maybe five six or seven."

"Pretty good. I'm just under five-six."

"And slight of bone. Probably weigh around a hundred and ten—twenty tops."

"What makes you think that? I could be a porker."

"Your walk is light. When I've brushed past you, I knew you were small."

"All right, I'll give you that. What color hair? Eyes?"

"Well, I'm not sure, but I think you might have mousy brown hair and big brown eyes. Like Bambi."

"Oh." She felt deflated. He thought she was mousy looking. "My hair is highlighted, or was. Haven't had the time lately or the money. And my eyes are hazel, but more green than brown. And I don't resemble a deer." Although there had been times when she'd been skittish and had wanted to run away into the woods.

"Okay. I'm close then." His lips curved in a teasing smile. "You're not mousy at all. I know Shane, and he hired you. Probably thought a good-looking woman around the house would cheer me up."

Her spirit lifted and so did her chin. It had been a long time since she'd received a compliment. "Shane's very thoughtful. If he wasn't married..."

"His wife would put a dagger in your heart if she knew you were thinking like that."

Natalie laughed. "More like a scalpel, and I wouldn't blame her. Is she nice?"

"Yes. She's gorgeous, so I'm told. Didn't meet her until I got back so I'm only going by what Shane says. I do know that he's a lucky son-of-a-bitch and adores the ground she walks on."

"That's sweet. I'm glad." She settled back in the sofa. "Okay, back to me. What else do you see?"

"A turned-up nose. Twinkling eyes, and a pretty, sexy mouth."

She laughed. "Dream on. I don't want to bust your fantasy." She jumped up, suddenly uncomfortable at how this conversation made her feel. She had a yearning low in her belly and felt heated both inside and out, which was completely out of place, considering he was in her care. "You want some popcorn?"

"Sure. Want me to get it?"

"If you'd like." She knew it would be much simpler for her to toss the packet in the microwave, but if he wanted to show his independence, she had to let him. Plus, it gave her time to cool down and get her blood pressure under control.

Sitting down again, she watched him blindly poke around the cupboard until he found what must be the right box, then took the package out, found scissors next to the knives, and cut a corner. She nodded her approval.

"How can you do that?"

"I was in an intensive one-on-one training program at NFB. I stuck it out for the first two months. I'm not a complete invalid you know."

She didn't say another word, knowing that to praise him would be a mistake, and to take matters into her own hands would be infinitely worse. She had to let him stumble and make a few mistakes in order for his confidence to grow.

Five minutes later he handed her a bowl of warm, buttered popcorn and she felt emotional tears fill her eyes. She'd been through hell the last couple of years, and little things could set her off. She'd even cried changing the diaper of her Alzheimer patient.

"Thank you." She popped some in her mouth and forced it down, fighting the urge to cry simply because she was proud of him. "Killer popcorn," she said when she could.

"Told you I was a hotshot chef."

They watched *NCIS Los Angeles*, and she filled in the gaps. Later, she turned off the lights, and walked him to his room. "Goodnight, Brent. I hope you sleep well."

"Me too. Don't need any more nightmares."

"I'm sure you don't. I'll see you in the morning." She turned and walked across the hall. Her room was very close to his, but she didn't lock the door. She hadn't felt safe in the cheap hotel, or since she left her friend's house. Now for the first time in years she could sleep without fear.

CHAPTER SEVEN

The following morning the smell of fresh coffee had her nose twitching. She stumbled out of bed and, wearing only a light nylon knee-length robe, went in search of the coffee.

"Good morning," Brent said. He was sitting at the table, wearing his morning attire of sleep pants, his chest bare.

She ogled him for a moment, knowing it might not be part of her job description, but was certainly one of the perks. Not only did he have superb abs, but a nice matting of chest hair, with a fine tickle that trailed down into... Whoa. Stop right there. No peeking below the waist.

"Good morning back at you." She smiled, keeping her eyes on his face, which would need a shave within a few days. She wondered if he'd want her do it. Maybe after breakfast she'd ask.

She added cream to her coffee, stirred, and sat down at the table opposite him. "I didn't hear you last night. You slept well?"

His lips curved in a smile. "Well enough. I heard you snoring up a storm early this morning. Might have been what woke me up."

"I don't snore. Do I?" She sipped her coffee, enjoying the normalcy of the occasion. Someone looking in would see two young people, a couple, having a very normal conversation over their morning coffee. Not a blind, wounded veteran terrified of his future, or a woman hiding from her past.

"Like a freight train." He seemed to be enjoying teasing her, and she decided to play along.

"Do freight trains snore?" she asked and playfully stuck her tongue out at him knowing he couldn't see.

"Not sure, but you do." He raised his toast. "Want some? I make the best toast in town."

"Well, that being the case, I sure do." Silently, she applauded his actions, glad to see that he seemed in a positive frame of mind.

Watching him, she took a big swallow from her coffee cup, and was pleasantly surprised at the strong flavor. "This is delicious. Starbucks?"

"Naw. Dunkin' Donuts. I buy whatever's on sale."

"Well, you make excellent coffee and the best toast in town. What else can you make?"

"Any microwavable meal on the planet."

She laughed. "Uh-huh. And I bet you can whip up a mean peanut butter and jelly sandwich."

"Not to brag, but I can also handle a grilled cheese." He brought over two slices of buttered toast on a plastic plate. "Want some raspberry jam?"

"Don't mind if I do."

When he got the jar out of the pantry, he nearly put it on her plate, but she managed to move it in time so the mishap was avoided. "Thanks. I didn't expect to get served breakfast. Thought I was the hired help around here. But a gal could get used to this. Sure could."

"Don't get too used to it—you'll be leaving soon. Right?"

"Right." She noticed he had a little jam on the corner of his lip and wanted to wipe it away. Or lick it. She felt a little flash of heat coil in her belly at the thought, and was startled by it. She'd thought Carl had cured her of ever wanting a man physically again. But Brent moved her and stirred her emotions.

He was a big teddy bear kind of guy. Could be a little rough on the outside, but gentle underneath. "Are you in a hurry to get rid of me?" She bit into her toast and swallowed a sudden lump. "What about that fantastic music we were going to make together?"

"No time for that. I was thinking about it this morning and decided we should hire a tutor. She could come in and teach us both, then you could help me."

"Brent, there's no need for that. I'm a teacher and your aide. Save your money. I'm quite capable of teaching you myself." And the more people who knew she was living here, the more danger she'd be in. "I have to earn my keep. And I know five languages, for heaven's sake. How hard could Braille be?"

"All right then," Brent said. "I did some thinking last night and early this morning about what you said. You're right, and I give you permission to nudge me all you want. After all, I might never see again, and I have to accept the truth of that and prepare myself."

"I hope that won't be the case, but I'm glad you want to move forward." As she studied his face, she felt another wave of compassion. What courage it would take to accept such a fate and be willing to embrace it.

"I was a damn fool to leave the program I was in. Just couldn't face it." His hand trembled as he held the cup. "Now I've got to. It's been a year since the crash and most people who sustained similar injuries would be seeing by now."

"You're better than most people," she told him, adding, "On top of that I think you're being very brave and smart." She kept her voice steady, although it was an effort. Tears pricked the back of her eyelids and she wanted to give him a hug. "When can we start?"

"As soon as possible."

"Good. I have enough books to begin with, and the library has plenty more." She jumped up and cleared the table, excited now that they had a plan for the day. He was right behind her and she bumped into him.

His hand reached out and covered her breast and she froze, hoping he didn't know what he was feeling. An awkward silence fell between them.

"What are you wearing?" he asked.

"Not much. Just my nightie." She still didn't move and his hand still held her breast. It felt warm. Nice. In spite of herself, she felt tingly, even slightly aroused.

"Is this what I think it is?"

"Yeah, I'm pretty sure it is." She lifted his hand and put it down by his side. "I'll make sure I'm properly dressed in the morning."

He grinned. "No need to do that on my account. I can't see a thing. And I'll try not to feel you up either."

"Oh, okay. Good idea." Her heart hammered, and her pulse raced. Putting some needed distance between them, she stepped into the kitchen. Sam left his spot under the table near Brent's feet to follow her. His wet nose nudged his empty bowl.

She tossed him the crust on her toast, which he devoured in one bite. "Has Sam been fed yet?" she asked Brent, hoping her voice sounded normal.

"No. Wasn't sure where you put the dog food."

"It's at the bottom of the pantry in a big large bag."

"Fine. I'll find it." He glanced in her direction. "What color is it?"

"The bag? What does it matter?" Then she saw his sweatpants had a tent in them. "Oh, you mean..."

"Yeah. I mean what you're wearing."

"Pink." She could feel her cheeks turn the same color. She should stop this conversation. Like now.

"I like pink. You should wear that more often. Actually, I think it should be your in-house uniform."

She laughed. "In your dreams." She put the dishes away but couldn't wipe the smile off her face.

"Oh, it will be. Don't worry."

She put a cup of kibble in Sam's bowl, washed her hands in the sink, then skirted past Brent. "I'm going to shower and dress and then the two of us are going outside to walk Sam. You want to change or you want to watch?"

His leg moved fast and barred her path. "I haven't had a reaction like this in a long, long time." His voice lowered to a sexy whisper, "You better be careful that it doesn't happen too often."

He was very close to her and her mouth went dry. "Or what?"

"Or I might want you for more than babysitting." She felt the warmth of his breath against her cheek, but didn't move.

"Don't say that." Her heart beat rapidly, like a bird's wing. Her tummy knotted and she felt a familiar flutter of excitement that was a prelude to sex. What did she want? For him to let her go, or kiss her right here and now, and make her feel protected and cared for?

"Sorry. But I can't help the way you made me feel." He moved away and she was free to go. "Like a man again," he said in a disgusted voice.

She closed the door behind her and leaned against it. She released a long, shuddering breath. What had she been doing? What was she thinking? Cared for? Crazy girl. He didn't care about her—he was just horny, that's all. And why was she flirting with this poor man who had more worries than she did?

She knew better than to play with fire. But there was something about him that got her pulse racing like a thoroughbred. When his hand cupped her breast, she hadn't wanted to push it away. And neither had he. Damn, it had felt good. So had the tingling between her legs.

She walked into the bathroom and turned on the shower, letting the water grow warm. The nightgown slid off her body, and she was still aroused.

This attraction had to stop. She needed to end it now—after all, she'd be leaving in a month. It wouldn't be fair to him. But oh, how she wanted it. His hands, his mouth on hers. To be swept away with passion just for an hour or two. To forget what a brutal man could do to a person's soul.

Sex with Carl had been a cruel punishment in the end. It brought her no pleasure, only pain. When they'd first met it had been romantic and wonderful, but as soon as Carl had put a ring on her finger the game was over and he let his cruelty be known. She had started to hate sex and dread any sexual banter, knowing it would lead to a night of misery for her and gratification for him.

Stepping under the shower, Natalie scrubbed her body and lifted her face, wanting to erase not only the memory but every trace of Carl from her body and soul, and yet she knew she couldn't scrub deep enough.

EPISODE THREE

CHAPTER EIGHT

When the door shut in his face, Brent turned and went into his own room to dress. This would be his first walk since he'd left rehab the previous month, and it was a really big deal, but he was determined not to let it show. After all, he wouldn't be alone. He had two companions, a pretty lady and a smart service dog. What could go wrong?

Since he couldn't color coordinate his clothes, he decided to keep it safe and put on a pair of jeans and a golf shirt. He could still hear the shower and Natalie singing in Spanish, so he decided to wait for her outside.

It was late June and after stepping out on the balcony he knew it was a warm, sunny day. He fought back the acid bile in his throat, telling himself not to be a wuss. He had no reason to be apprehensive. He couldn't see, but that was only a minor inconvenience—after all he had both legs didn't he? Helluva lot more than some of the poor fellows he'd met in Walter Reed.

He needed to bury the attitude and be appreciative of what he had.

Perhaps Shane had been right to hire an attractive woman—his mood did feel lighter. Or it could simply be the fact that he was taking his first steps outside. He'd been holed up too long—his fault of course—but it would feel good to stretch his legs and then get down to some serious studying.

He'd been a real prick during his training with the Wounded Warrior program. It was an intensive one-on-one course, but he'd been unwilling to put any real effort behind it. And to stay confined for a duration of six to nine months—no way in hell. In hindsight—which he was getting good at—he realized Operation Freedom Bell was a terrific program, with a group of guys going through the same shit as himself. But he'd clung to the belief that his condition was temporary since he could see fuzzy shadows once in a while. Still, it would benefit him to do something positive while he was waiting.

He also needed to prepare himself for the worst scenario, just as he would have when given a dangerous mission while trying to carry it out with a minimal risk of lives. He missed that the most. Flying around, putting out fires that threatened people's homes and their existence. The search and rescue missions had given him the same thrill. He and his team had been responsible for saving a great many lives. Now he couldn't even save his own.

Natalie was taking her time getting ready and he was anxious to leave before he could think of a dozen good reasons to stay. He got up and nearly knocked into her. "Oh, here you are. I was just coming to get you."

"I'm ready if you are," she said in her soft voice. "I'll just get the leash and a doggie bag and off we go."

"Okay. Just don't expect too much."

"I won't. We'll only go as far as you're comfortable with—around the block will do."

He grabbed his white cane and felt like a complete idiot, but he didn't think he could manage without it. He tap-tapped the way down the hall, counting his steps to the elevator. Sam was right next to him, if only for moral support.

Natalie punched the down button and a few seconds later the elevator arrived and the door slid open. "Here it is. I'll hold the door. You and Sam can step inside."

He nodded. "I'm okay with this part. I've used the pool several times—it's just the street that I'm worried about."

"Sam will take good care of you. Won't you, Sam?"

Sam barked in agreement.

When they reached the lobby level, Natalie held the door again, and waited until he and the dog were out. When they got to the sidewalk, Natalie linked an arm through his.

"It's a great day. Low seventies, and a cool breeze."

"Maybe we can make it as far as the beach," he told her. "I'd like to smell the ocean breeze."

"Now you're talking. It's only a couple of blocks. Let's see what happens."

They started walking down the street, and Sam stood still at the crossroads, as though waiting for a signal to cross. Being a residential area there were street signs but no light signals to guide them along.

"We can cross now," Natalie said. "There're no cars coming."

He felt a moment's panic, and turned his head to listen. When he didn't hear any traffic, he swallowed hard and stepped out. Natalie kept her arm linked with his and he knew she'd never let anything happen to him, but still perspiration coated his skin.

"You all right?" she asked.

"Fine." He breathed deeply. "I'll be all right. Lead on."

"Okay. The beach is right ahead. Another couple of blocks. Can you make it?"

"Not sure. We'll see." He began to relax, knowing he had both Sam and Natalie by his side. He couldn't do this alone, but he didn't need to—not until Natalie left, and he was no longer in such a hurry to see her go.

He sniffed the salty air. "I want to put my feet in the sand."

"Me too." She squeezed his arm. "You're doing great, Brent. I'm so proud of you."

Her words of praise made him puff his chest out and walk with his head a little higher. This getting-out business was not so bad after all. Instead of anxiety, he felt a growing excitement to be so close to the beach again. He loved the sand, the surf, hot, sunny days—and the scent in the air brought back a flood of memories of Shane and himself, young and carefree, surf boards in hand, roaming the beach like some golden sun gods.

The memory made him smile.

"What are you smiling about?" Natalie asked.

"Thinking back to all the good times that Shane and I had down here."

"I can only imagine. You two were what—eighteen or so when you moved to California? Bet you had the time of your lives."

"Was pretty good, come to think of it. Didn't have any money, but when you're that age who needs more than a cheap bed and a cheap meal?"

"What did you do before you signed on with CAL FIRE? I'm sure they didn't hire you right away."

"We got odd jobs. I worked in a car wash for six months, and Shane waited tables. We were waiting to be discovered by some big Hollywood agent. Us and maybe five million others."

She laughed. "What about your family? Your dad didn't turn his back on you, did he?"

"Naw, he showed up and tried to drag me home, but I was of legal age to live on my own, and he couldn't do a darn thing about it. We had a scuffle and he left me with a black eye and a fat lip. It wasn't until a year later that he helped me get into flight training."

"Sheesh. You had a fistfight with your Dad?"

"And lost. That was kind of demoralizing." He laughed and grabbed her hand. "All this talk has brought back some good memories. Come on." He gave her a tug. "I have an idea. Why don't we make this a real event and go down to the shore? Celebrate my first big step." He grinned. "We could even grab an ice cream on the pier."

Belmont Shore was a seaside resort, a residential town more than a tourist haunt, but it had a healthy, happy lifestyle, with a boardwalk that was busy every day of the year. People would bike, skate, walk, run, or take the kids and enjoy the rides and arcade.

"You sure you want to do that? It'll be noisy and busy. This might be enough for your first time out."

"Come on. Be a sport. I haven't felt like doing anything in a long time, and now you're wimping out on me?" He glanced in her direction. "I never asked you, but do you have a car?"

"I do, but it's small. Can we take yours?"

"Sure. No problem. The keys are on a hook in the kitchen. Let's go back and get them."

When they got back to the apartment building Natalie told him to wait in the lobby, and she dashed back upstairs. A few minutes later she returned.

"You're not just trying to get out of studying, are you?" She asked with a smile in her voice.

"No," he grinned. "When we get back we'll hit the books, I promise. I'm not trying to ditch the hard part."

They took the elevator to the underground parking and Brent clicked the remote to unlock the doors, which helped direct Natalie to his car. "Nice," she said, showing appreciation for his BMW convertible. It had a small backseat, and Sam jumped in.

"You trust me with this?" Natalie asked.

"It's eight years old, with 75,000 miles on it. Hell, yes." He got in the passenger seat and fastened his seat belt. "You know your way around, right? It's about a ten minute drive. I'll show you where to park."

"Got it. No problemo." She climbed in, started the car, and backed out of the parking spot. "Hey, Sam," she called. "Buckle up."

Brent chuckled. "Hope he knows that command."

"You mind if I put the top down?"

"Go for it." She put the car in park and waited as the top folded into the trunk. Then they were on their way, and the breeze felt good on his face.

Natalie played with the radio dial until he handed her the remote for the Sirius XM that he'd installed shortly before enlisting with the Army. He'd taken the Beamer to

Ft. Rucker with him, and the convertible had scored him a few dates, although the training had been rigorous, with little time to spare for pretty girls.

"What's your favorite station?" she asked him.

"I like country, some pop. None of that ghetto stuff."

She laughed. "Oh, this one's nice." It was a love song by Elvis.

He still knew how to roll his eyes, and did so. "Are you lonesome tonight?"

"Nope. I got you and Sam."

He didn't answer that, but they listened to the radio station all the way to the beach. He didn't mind it too much, especially when she sang along with the music. She'd forgotten her shyness about singing in front of him, he noticed, and was glad. "So what kind of music do you write?"

"A little more contemporary than this. I love Adele, but then who doesn't, and like her and most musicians, I write from my own past experiences."

"Give me an example."

"No. I'm not going to do that."

"Come on." He turned her way. "I already know you have a nice voice. You were singing with Elvis."

"Okay. Okay." She hummed a few notes.

"I'm not hearing you."

"You're a pest." She turned off the radio, parked the car in a lot across from the beach, and sang very softly, "You hurt me once, you hurt me twice, and now you better play nice. Come on, baby, you know what's right. Give it to me baby, and I'll be yours tonight."

He nodded with approval. "Hey, that's not bad."

"Why, thank you, sir." Brent heard her car door open, and as he unfastened his seat belt, she opened his door. "Here, take my arm." She guided him to the sidewalk. "Hang on until I get Sam out."

The dog jumped out of the car, nearly knocking Brent off his feet. "Whoa, boy. I know you're excited. I am too." He realized he was. Twenty-four hours ago she'd have had to drag him out of the house, kicking and screaming all the way, but he'd woken up this morning with a new attitude. And it had nothing—not one damn thing—to do with her.

Everything to do with Captain James kicking his dream ass, maybe. Or the quick feel of Nat's breast. But that was it—as personal as it got.

He lifted his head and listened to the sound of the ocean waves, the sound of laughter and activity coming from the boardwalk. "Here," she said, and handed him the dog's harness.

"Okay, Sam, lead on." The retriever stopped at the crosswalk and they waited for the audio signal, indicating the light had changed. Sam knew when it was safe, and led him forward across the street.

Natalie had not interfered, wanting to see how the man and dog did together. "Good boy," she said. "What a wonderful accomplishment to teach a dog to be of service. I hear they're training greyhounds now, after they retire from the track."

"Not much of a life is it? First they gotta race for years, then instead of kicking back with their feet up, they need to work in their old age. Should be in Florida, drinking Arnold

Palmers next to a pool." Brent stumbled on a crack in the sidewalk but quickly gathered his composure.

She laughed. "I can just picture that. But on the other hand, I think it makes them special, not just a run-of-the-mill mutt."

"Like poor Sam," Brent said. "Working for your keep. Aren't you boy?"

"Woof, woof," the good dog answered.

"He's so clever too," Natalie said. She took Brent's arm and they strolled along the boardwalk, enjoying the sounds and smells coming from the vendors, the hypnotic rumble of the rolling surf.

After a while they stopped for their ice cream and sat on a bench to enjoy it. "This was a good idea," she said. "Can we do this again soon?"

"Sure. Don't see why not." He licked his cone, thinking how much better it tasted with the salty air, the sound of people and laughter, and feeling the press of Natalie's knee next to his own. It wasn't so damn scary being outdoors. Better than staring at walls and counting the minutes go by.

"Perfect. The exercise will do us all good, and then we can spend the afternoons working."

"Sounds like a plan," he agreed.

The ice cream was rapidly melting and Natalie used her napkin to wipe a dab of chocolate from his chin. "Thanks," he said, licking his lips.

"Welcome," she replied, and then he heard her sharp intake of breath, and felt her tense. "Brent. Put your arm around me. Kiss me. Right now. Please?"

"What the hell? I'm not going to kiss you. Why would I do that?"

"Just do it." She threw her arms around him and kissed him hard.

He could taste the ice cream on her lips, the sweetness of her breath, the way her mouth opened almost unwillingly. He was close enough to feel her heart racing, and sensed her fear. He didn't want to let her go, but after a few dazed seconds, he shook her off. "What was that for?"

"We have to leave." Her voice shook. "Now."

CHAPTER NINE

Heart thudding, Natalie peeked over Brent's shoulder. Carl? She was sure it was Carl. But how had he found her?

She lowered her head and stood up, pulling Brent to his feet. "I'm sorry, but we have to go back."

"Why? What's got into you? I thought we were having a nice time."

"Can't explain right now," she said, dragging him along.

As she sent another furtive glance over her shoulder, an attractive, smiling woman came into view, swinging a young girl's hand. She joined the man she'd been so sure was Carl, and watched as he swung the little girl—possibly three or four with bright blonde curls—onto his shoulders. The child laughed with joy.

Relief made her weak, and she expelled her breath, feeling limp as a rag doll.

"Are you okay? What's going on?" Brent's head jerked around as if searching for something he couldn't see. Having been to war, the man could probably sense danger a mile away.

"What is it?" he asked again. "What frightened you?"

"Nothing." She squared her shoulders, forcing herself to breathe normally. Her pulse still raced double-time. "I'm all right now. I just thought I recognized someone that I'd prefer not to see."

"That man from your past? The one who broke your heart?"

"No." She gave a shaky laugh. "Someone else."

Sam nudged her leg and to cover her confusion, she bent to pet him. "Hey, Sam, buddy. Yes, we can continue our walk. But not for long. We have a lot planned this afternoon, and it's nearly noon." She put an arm through Brent's. "Let's just go a little farther down the boardwalk, then head back. Is that all right with you?"

"Whatever you want." He stared straight ahead with a scowl on his face.

They walked past several vendors, but Natalie couldn't shake off her nerves. The back of her neck prickled with fear as though she were the target of unseen eyes. "Want a hot dog or some popcorn?" she asked Brent, hoping to sound casual. "It smells good."

"No," he said, his voice subdued. "I'm not hungry."

"Okay, we'll have lunch at home. Are you ready to go back?"

Without commenting, he stopped and turned, and they headed back down the boardwalk the way they'd come. She didn't speak a word until they reached his car.

"I'm sorry for the kiss," she muttered, taking a deep breath. "It must have seemed pretty crazy to you."

"Cut the crap. Something had you scared. Or somebody."

"I was trying to avoid someone, but not because I was scared. I owe the person money," she lied. "I couldn't afford the lodging and I skipped out." She rushed on, "This is not something I should be telling you, but I can see you're not going to let this go."

"You don't seem like the kind of person who'd get herself into a situation like that." There was some heat in his voice, and his jaw was set, but it wasn't scary like with Carl. Brent's smoldering appearance was downright sexy.

"You don't know me very well," she answered in a soft voice, wondering how she was going to get out of this without seeming like a complete flake. "And it wasn't really my fault. The guy I told you about, the one who broke my heart, well he ran up some bad credit and I bailed him out, then he left me hanging with the debt." The lie came easily, and she wondered how an honest person like herself could simply let it roll off her tongue. Like she'd been doing it most of her life.

He cleared his throat, and frowned. "If you need money, why don't you just ask? I can pay you up front and you can settle your debt, then you won't have to go around avoiding someone for the rest of your life."

"I don't want your money. I won't be staying long, and how could I repay you?" She gave a fake laugh. "Don't want to be dodging two people, now do I?"

She used the remote to unlock the doors and waited for Sam to jump in the back. "Here," she said and took his arm to guide him. "Let me get your door."

"I've got it." He brushed her off, slid inside, and shut the door, then busied himself with the seat belt. His mouth was a grim line and Natalie could see he was pissed off. The fact their first outing had been cut short? The kiss? Or could he see right through her stupid story?

She got behind the wheel and turned on the engine. "Okay, we listened to Elvis coming here, your choice on the way back."

"I don't give a shit about a music station." His jaw was clenched. "I don't know why you're lying to me but I can tell you are." He glanced in her direction. "You're not very good at it."

She darted him a quick look. "Really?"

"Yes. Really." His right hand was fisted, running up and down his thigh. "My sight might be dimmed, but my senses sure aren't. I'm aware of a lot of things. You were frightened and you were lying."

"Frightened of what?" She bluffed. How could he sense these things? It wasn't fair that he could see inside her. She wanted to hide from everyone, including him. What a pair they both were—each hiding from the world for two very different reasons. "I wanted to kiss you. So, big deal."

He shook his head, still frowning. "Good try, but another lie. You're not attracted to me." He stared straight ahead. "You pity me, and that's worse."

"Not true." Damn, she might pity his circumstance, but that had nothing to do with the fact that she liked him as a man. He needed to know this. The kiss under different circumstances would have been extremely nice. It had heated her blood even in her moment of utter panic. She was physically attracted to him, which was wrong on every level.

With that thought in mind, she jammed the car in reverse and backed out of the parking spot. "Maybe you don't see as much as you think." She stopped to pay the attendant for the two hours, then hit the main road again.

He seemed to mull it over, then eventually replied, "I see plenty."

"I'm sure you're very intuitive, but not when it comes to me."

"I know that when you make teasing remarks or flirt a little, you feel guilty afterward."

"Why would I? I have nothing to feel guilty about." Her hands tightened on the wheel, and she kept her eyes on the road. How could he know these things? It was like he read her thoughts aloud.

"Because you're my aide and work for me. You probably think it's a conflict of interest, or something." He turned his head slightly in her direction. "I think you have a happy nature but it's been suppressed. I only see flashes now and then."

She laughed. "That's a stretch." She pretended to yawn. "Besides, I don't flirt with you. I like you fine, but I wouldn't flirt."

"What about this morning?" He looked straight ahead, as he spoke. "You didn't move my hand."

She nearly choked. "Oh my gosh," she sputtered. "I was hoping you wouldn't know where it was. That's why I left it there." At first, that was the truth. She'd hoped he'd move his hand and they could go on as if nothing happened, but then the warm feel of it on her breast had felt so incredible, she'd not wanted to move it away. Did he know that too?

"You think even a blind man could forget a thing like that? I know the shape and feel of a woman's breast."

"Okay, then why did it take so long for you to let go?"

"I'm not stupid. It felt great." He grinned. "I had a hard-on, didn't I?"

She remembered the good size tent in his pants, and felt a flash of heat. "Yeah, no big thing," she answered, striving for a casual tone. "It happens to a lot of guys in the morning."

She felt her cheeks grow warm, and knew it wasn't from the sun. The image of his hard-on flitted through her mind. She hoped she wouldn't have to face that every morning. Too much temptation for a temporary aide.

"I'm explaining my physical reaction to you so you don't throw yourself at me again."

"Throw myself? I didn't throw myself! I kissed you, and I told you why. Because I didn't want that guy to see me."

"Yeah. Whatever." He stared straight ahead. "Living together could get difficult. You know, men and women can never be friends."

"Who said? Sure they can."

"Did you ever watch the movie *When Harry Met Sally*?" Brent cleared his throat. "Billy Crystal said it. When they parted ways after he gave her a ride at the beginning of the movie."

"Yeah, I know the part, but he proved himself wrong. They were great friends for a long time before they fell in love." She darted a quick look at him, trying to read his face. It didn't reveal anything. "Still, thanks for the warning. I'll make sure it doesn't happen again." She turned on the music, glad to have something to fill the unnerving silence.

"I didn't mind your kiss."

"What? I didn't hear you." She turned down the blaring music.

He shifted uncomfortably. "I said I didn't mind your kiss."

Her heart did a little Congo beat. He had enjoyed her kiss. So had she, but that was something else she dared not share. So many secrets. Well, it was best that way. She turned the volume on high, and shouted, "Still didn't hear you."

He grinned and leaned his head back, eyes closed, his face relaxed. Natalie would have enjoyed watching him like this, but her eyes were needed on the road. The thought also occurred to her that if she didn't need to run, and didn't have dreams about to come true, she might want to linger and stay.

Once they were home, she made them both sandwiches and took hers over to the desk. She flipped through a book on Braille and wondered how in the world she'd teach him that. Hopefully, he'd remember most of it, and it would come back to him quickly.

She ate in silence, thinking about his sacrifice to his country, and the thousands of young men and women who gave up so much in the fight for freedom. Some returned outwardly maimed, while others had battle scars that remained hidden. Like Brent, the tragedies probably manifested in nightmares and stress disorders. Such bravery and heroism was beyond comprehension but only to be applauded.

She swallowed a sudden lump. "So how can you afford to pay me? Do you get a disability from the government, or something?"

"Yeah, and I have a little savings too." He ate his last bite of sandwich and carried the empty plate into the kitchen. "Operation Bell was a free service for veterans. If I hadn't been such a moron, I'd have remained as a resident and learned all the skills I needed. But you already know that story."

"You could probably go back, right?" She entered the small kitchen too. "If I left you wouldn't need to pay me. You'd be cared for and given the tools you might need in the future. I read about their program and they teach you skills to find employment. Don't you want that?"

"I do, but I want it this way." He put their plates in the dishwasher. "Maybe I'm an arrogant ass but I don't want to live with a bunch of men in a dorm. I like having my own space."

"I get that." After living under the thumb of a man like Carl, she could certainly appreciate being alone and not having to answer to anyone. "I like having my own space too."

"Have you given any thought as to what you'd like to do in the future?" she asked.

"I haven't a fuckin' clue. It's going to be pretty damn limited if I don't get my sight back."

"That's not true. I'm sure there're plenty of jobs that with a little training you'd be qualified to do."

"Yeah. Maybe I could be a dish washer or a piano man." His chin jutted her way. "So when did you skip out on your rent?"

"Uh…" She hated lying, but telling the truth was dangerous. Lies could protect the innocent. "After I left my friend's house, my old college roommate. I stayed there for two weeks, then I found a place I could rent on a weekly basis. It wasn't very nice, but it was all I could afford."

"And the landlord, he was down at the beach this morning?"

"No. Not the landlord. It was the apartment manager." Again, she felt the need to expand on the story. "He hit on me, and I got nervous and left in the middle of the night."

"The guy hit on you, so that's why you didn't pay your bill?"

"Yeah, something like that." She looked out the plate glass windows, not wanting to lie to his face.

"I wish I could see you right now, and then I'd know for sure if you're telling the truth or not."

"Why wouldn't I?" She wished he'd get off the damn subject.

"You might be hiding from something that you consider much worse."

Ah, he had her there.

"Look, I have some secrets," she told him, "and I'm sure you do too. Why don't we agree to keep them to ourselves since I'm not going to be a permanent fixture in your life?"

His face changed. He turned away from her and put his hands out to feel the wall as he left the kitchen. "I'm going to lie down. The walk tired me out."

"Brent...I didn't mean that the way it came out. I'm sorry."

"No need to apologize. You're right. Let's keep it real." He ran his hand along the sofa and found the corridor to his bedroom. She heard the door slam behind him.

She didn't move, knowing it had to be this way. Becoming too friendly would not do either one of them any good. She needed to keep her emotional distance, and not get comfortable. She could certainly care for Brent, but not get romantically involved. That was the sensible thing to do, and if nothing else, Natalie was a sensible woman. Tutoring children on a country estate in France would be her safe haven. Until she got there, she had to keep her heart intact and not give it away to anyone who'd give her a reason to stay.

CHAPTER TEN

Brent lay down on the bed and closed his eyes, wondering what secrets were so bad that Natalie couldn't share. Hell, didn't she know everything about him? Way more than she needed too, that's for sure. She knew about the incident in Afghanistan, but not about the terror of hearing everything happening around him but unable to see. It had taken him what... hours... days to realize why it was so dark. He'd had a concussion and when he came to, he'd thought it was the middle of the night, and knew they'd crashed and were stuck on some fucking mountain terrain. He hadn't panicked then, nor when he discovered insurgents had them surrounded. He could hear his comrades shouting to each other, screams of anguish as if they were being burned alive, mortar fire, enemies speaking in their harsh dialect, the scent of gunshot as they emptied shell after shell into what he presumed were his crew.

He waited, listening in the dark, expecting the next shot would be his own. Time passed. Still his vision never cleared. He could rub shoulders with someone next to him but he didn't know if the man was one of his own, or if he was cowering behind a dead or dying enemy soldier. That had been when his real terror began.

So compared to that, what could a woman like Natalie be hiding? If someone was stalking her, he could get her protection. If she trusted him.

Nothing about this morning made any real sense.

Unless she'd done something to protect herself, like kill the guy. That would be a motive to keep the truth to herself. He might be harboring a fugitive, a woman being sought by the authorities for murder. Although he considered himself a good judge of character, and if she'd killed some creep, he probably damn well deserved it.

Curiosity got the better of him, and he left the bedroom, hoping to learn more about her circumstances. If she needed help, he'd do his best to see that she got it.

"Natalie?"

"I'm here, Brent. On the sofa."

He followed the sound of her voice, and bumped into her knee. He took a seat next to her, but not too close. "What are you doing? Reading? Knitting?" He teased, "I don't think you're old enough to knit."

"I'm not knitting. Reading, yes. Nothing exciting, I assure you." She put his hand on the book. "It's a book on Braille."

"You going blind now?" he asked dryly.

She laughed. "No, but I need to learn if I'm going to be of any help to you."

"That's true." He looked toward her. "I actually enjoyed getting out today, in spite of the fact you got spooked, and I thought it would be a good idea to do something fun tomorrow. Maybe we could take a picnic down to our local beach."

"Really? That's a great idea. I'd love that."

"Cool. Let's plan on it." He was about to say more when the phone rang. "Is that Shane?" he asked. "He calls me every week and tries to get me to come over."

"It is." She handed him the phone and left the room, probably to give him privacy to talk.

He got off the phone a few minutes later and called out, "Natalie. Change of plans. Shane invited us to go sailing with him and Josh. Told him he was crazy at first, then he convinced me that a day out on the ocean would clear the fog in my head. Can't be worse than it is, and hell, if I fall over and drown? So what?"

"Are you kidding me? You want to go sailing? Geez, Brent. You're really moving full speed ahead. I'm impressed."

"Well, it's time. It's been more than a year since the accident, and all I've done is feel sorry for myself and wallow in my misery." Before she could say anything, he hurried on, "Figured you might also want to have someone else to talk to besides me."

"I don't mind talking to you. Actually I enjoy it."

"That's nice of you to say, but I'm sure hanging around here with a blind man is kind of dull."

"You're not blind, and you're not dull."

"Lauren wants to meet you. They've been bugging me about going over there and I can't keep putting them off." Brent hoped that Natalie might open up to another woman, since she obviously couldn't or wouldn't with him. "You'll enjoy Lauren. She's a sweetheart."

"Sounds great. If you want to go, then I do too."

A thought occurred to him. "Their son Josh has ADHD and had some problems at school. Maybe you could help him a little this summer. Make some extra money. Then you could pay that apartment manager the money you owe him. Right?"

He sniffed the air. She was wearing a fruity scent again. What was it this time? He shifted a little closer, wanting to find out.

"I won't have the time," Natalie answered. "When I'm not working with you, I still have plenty of things I need to attend to. My friend, Lori, is helping me to find a place to live and a secure job."

"I see. Well, we could still socialize, couldn't we?" When she didn't reply, he added, "Come to think of it, Lauren has a lot of connections in the community and she might be able to help you with a teaching position."

She stood up quickly and he could hear her roaming about the room. "I might move on this fall. I've never traveled and there're a lot of places I haven't seen. Not sure where I'll end up."

"You've come a long way already, and southern California is tough to beat. Once you spend the summer, you'll agree." He leaned his head back and closed his eyes. "Do you like sailing?"

"I've never been," Natalie answered. "But I love the ocean. When my sister and I were young, my family always took us for a summer vacation to the shore."

"You think you might end up living close to your sister or your dad?"

"Not likely, but who knows?" She was silent for a moment, then said, "Dad moved to the west coast of Florida and remarried. I'll probably make my way to Sanibel Island to see them this fall. I haven't met his wife, but I know that she's younger by ten years and they golf every day."

"Do they know you're on the run?"

"What?" She coughed like she was choking. "I'm not on the run. That's a ridiculous thing to say. I just left Washington with some debts—that's all. I'm getting my act together, and will have everything figured out soon."

"Glad to hear that." He changed the subject. "Wonder if I could still rig a sail? Probably, as long as I didn't fall overboard."

He sniffed Natalie's scent and knew that she stood near him. He felt a magnetic pull her way. "I need to find some activities to do again. What do you think? Maybe if I were tethered, I could sail around the world."

She laughed. "You think big, don't you?"

"Why not? No point in thinking small. Hell, there's got to be lots of things I can do." He let out a long sigh. Who was he kidding? He'd said those things to impress her, but he knew he couldn't do any of the things he'd once loved. His life would be constricted to a colorless square box and she wouldn't be in it. "In my dreams anyway. I used to be a big adventurer—loved all sports, the more dangerous the better. Bungie jumping, parachuting, river rafting, it was all an adrenalin rush."

"You could probably still do that, if you wanted. People ski, jump, do all kinds of things in tandem. And you have Shane."

"He's a little busy these days, with med studies and a new baby on the way."

"True, but what about the Wounded Warriors? Don't they have all kinds of events and volunteers doing stuff like that?"

"They do, and I had them visit me in the hospital. Tried to get me interested, but I decided I'd just wait until I got my sight back. I'm a stubborn fool, what can I say?"

"A cute stubborn fool," she said, and touched his arm. "We'll find you a companion, don't you worry, and before I leave you'll be doing all those things. I promise." She laughed. "You'd have to blindfold me to jump out of a plane. Holy crap. Wasn't it scary?"

He smiled and wished she'd touch him again. "At first, but then it was such a rush I couldn't get enough."

"I suppose you've done a lot of sailing?" she asked.

"Sure. Dad had a big yacht in southern Florida, and we'd sail to the Bahamas or Bermuda every summer. Mom loved it too."

"That must be a nice memory for you."

"It's one of the better ones, not that I should complain." He shrugged, almost embarrassed to admit how lucky he'd been. "I had it easy growing up, although my father could be quite a tyrant, and my older brothers were a pain in my ass. But we never lacked for anything. Had a huge home on the beach, boats, new cars every couple of years, the best schools."

He felt a flush rise up his neck, and was glad for his faint beard. "I drove my dad batty. I was in an expensive private school, which was okay until Shane's family moved into the neighborhood. After we became friends, I got myself kicked out so I could go to the local high school Shane attended. I stopped the military academy that I used to go to each summer and spent the days surfing. Dad threw a fit and tried to ground me, but I snuck out at nights."

"Did your father find out?"

"Eventually." Brent grinned. "Shane and I got into all kinds of trouble, nothing serious, just kid stuff. But what really got my father riled was when I gave up a football scholarship to Notre Dame. He threatened to disown me and I said go ahead." He shook his head. "I wasn't so smart in those days."

"I guess not. So that's when you and Shane hitchhiked here?"

"Yup. Right after graduation." He shook his head. "Can't believe we did that. But I didn't know what I wanted to do or wanted to be, and college seemed a waste of time." He chuckled at the memory. "We were going to be surfer dudes, and get bit parts in the movies. When that didn't work out the way we planned, we did those part-time jobs I told you about, before we got on with CAL FIRE."

Natalie gave a soft laugh. "So things worked out in the end."

Brent froze for a moment. "If you mean, being close to blind is working out, then I guess you're right."

She touched his arm. "I didn't mean that. But it was your decision to go off to war. Do you regret it, Brent?"

"The war got personal for me. I did what I had to do." He thought about all the shit that happened overseas, some good, some bad. "And no. I have no regrets."

Natalie sighed. "I'm glad. What's the point of having regrets? It doesn't change anything. It can't erase your past."

She got up and he heard her stumble, and Sam growled.

The dog came up to Brent, putting his head into his lap and rubbed up against his leg. "You all right, boy?" he said, leaning down to scratch the dog behind the ears.

"I'll take him out for a quick walk, then come back and start dinner."

"You want company?" he asked quietly.

"Sure. That would be nice."

He had suggested going with her, not knowing what the danger was, but he knew that it did exist. If only in her mind.

CHAPTER ELEVEN

After dinner, they worked for an hour on Braille, and Natalie could see Brent losing patience. He smacked the book shut, stretched his arms and yawned. "That's enough for a beginning session," he said.

"Okay, sure." Natalie stood up. "You want me to turn on TV, or listen to something on the computer?"

"Not really. I might just rest. Why don't you read or do something that you like."

"I could but I have a better idea. The librarian told me there're some games for the blind on the PC. Would you mind if I take a look? Might be something you'd be interested in."

"Help yourself. I might just snooze on the couch."

She opened up the laptop and found a website for the blind that was created by someone who was visually impaired. Excitement flowed through her veins. How cool was that? Maybe that would motivate Brent to think outside the box. He was smart and an adventurer. Perhaps he could get inspired and do something equally wonderful.

"Brent! This is so awesome." She told him about the guy who'd invented it. "They use a voice synthesizer to describe what's happening to the player. You can control the game through the keyboard or mouse. Come over here and give it a try."

"Not interested. I'm snoozing."

"They've got Battleship! And Blackjack. Solitaire, Scrabble and a whole lot more." She glanced his way, and he had his eyes shut, but she knew he was listening.

"If you don't want to play, maybe I will." He didn't budge, so she decided to try a game to see how it worked. Keeping it simple, she downloaded Blackjack and kept her eyes half shut to see if she could perform the tasks. Not too shabby. The games were designed for players who had any range of visual impairment, and she bought the package of eight games, figuring that if he didn't like them now, he might one day.

"Last chance. Want to try a game or should I shut it down?"

"I'm not in the mood right now," he mumbled.

"Okay. What are you in the mood to do?"

"Doesn't matter. How about you?" Brent stood up and walked over to the patio doors, looking out at nothing.

"Well, now that you ask..." She hesitated, then blurted, "Since you didn't laugh at me in the car, I was kinda thinking about working on a song."

He turned. "Why would I have laughed? You're good."

"My ex didn't think so." She shrugged, pleased by his comment. "But then, he didn't think I was very good at anything that didn't involve him."

"Your ex was a jerk."

"Agreed." It was nice to have someone on her side for a change. "And that's putting it mildly." She jumped up. "Hey, you want to strum your guitar?"

He agreed to please her, she was sure. Everything about him was so un-Carl-like that she couldn't help warm feelings from pooling inside.

After she retrieved his guitar, she hummed a tune, and he played to it, then she added a few words to the music. After several false starts she had some lyrics and a pleasing melody.

They worked on it for perhaps an hour, then he put the guitar aside. "Not bad," he said. "It's got potential."

She laughed. "You've got potential." She bumped his shoulder. "You're pretty good with that guitar. It must be nice to play again after you haven't bothered with it for years."

"Let's just say that it's nice to have company again." He was silent for a few seconds than spoke again. "Can I ask you something?"

"Sure. Fire away."

"You love music and seem talented enough. How come you didn't pursue it before? Or did you always want to be a teacher?"

"In college I was actually part of a girl band. Not the lead singer, but a backup. Had purple hair, and all three of us got tattoos." She got off the couch and he could hear her moving around.

"I'd let you see it," she said, "but you'll just have to trust me. It's a heart with a rose across it. Kinda girly."

"Where is it?" he asked, raising a brow. "Ankle, shoulder? On your hip?"

"Uh... none of the above. It's actually above my left breast."

"Nice. Since I can't see it, maybe you could let me feel?"

She laughed, and her heart fluttered. "Good try," she said and sat back down. "I quit after about a year. It was just a phase. Nothing serious."

"Thing is, you never know when that lucky break will come." He stretched his hands over his head and cracked his knuckles.

"Well, it was never that important to me. I really wanted to use my language skills and get a great job doing something internationally. But then Mom got sick and I had to stay home. Music's just an escape of sorts. Something I do for myself."

"I see. Well, I still think you've got talent."

"That's nice to hear. Especially since my United Nations job is permanently on hold." She was warmed by his comments, and felt her confidence lift. "Now that those dreams have turned to dust, maybe one day I'll take this seriously. Be the next Susan Boyle."

"If you believe in yourself, anything can happen."

"You need to remember that too." She touched him again, a small pat on his thigh, but suddenly everything changed. The silence lasted longer, and she felt the oxygen leave her lungs. The atmosphere had become sexually charged and she was pretty sure that he didn't need eyes to know that.

His hand reached out and grabbed hers. She tried to pull it away, but he only tugged her closer.

"What?" she asked, knowing full well that he wanted to kiss her. Damn but she wanted it too.

"Nothing, Natalie. I just wanted to hold your hand." He linked his fingers through hers. "Only for a moment. Do you mind?"

Mind? No—she could practically feel his hot lips on hers, his tongue... "I guess we shouldn't," she squeaked out. She didn't move her hand away, but neither did she return his pressure. "You don't even know me. And I work for you."

"Forget that for a second. I know enough about you, and I don't want anything other than companionship." He lifted her hand and kissed the palm. "That's all. Nothing to be afraid of. I can't see you, and I would never hurt you."

"I'm not afraid. Not of you." Her voice rose. "Not of anything." That wasn't exactly true, but she was working on it. She'd never give in to fear again.

"Just the guy you owe money too, right?" He said it lightly, but she knew he really wanted to get to the bottom of this story. Perhaps she should just tell him the truth, but she was ashamed to admit how weak she'd been—how she'd stayed so long in that abusive relationship. Lori was the only person who knew. She'd never told another soul, not even her sister. How could she? That was not the person she wanted to be, but it had been the person she'd become.

She scoffed, "That's right." Much better for him to think she was a flake or a liar than a victim of abuse. It was her private shame.

He let go of her hand and sighed. "I wish you'd confide in me."

"I am confiding in you. That's what we're doing. Talking."

"Okay. We'll keep it casual, the way you like it."

"Perfect." She was silent for several minutes, thinking how even now her life with Carl had damaged her and destroyed her chance for a happy, healthy relationship. At least for the time being. One day perhaps she'd meet another nice man like Brent and be able to open her heart. That day was a long way off. "Are you angry?"

"No, I'm not angry. I just feel that I have an unfair disadvantage, because I can never look at you and see what you're thinking or feeling. Words are all I have."

"Ask away—I'll do my best to answer. But there are some things I don't want to discuss. If we get into a gray area, I'll say so. Okay?"

He closed his eyes, and looked toward the ceiling. "That's okay. Another time." He lifted her hand again. "Your veal marsala tonight was excellent, by the way. I'm a lucky man. Could have some old dragon taking care of me, instead of you."

"Thank you. It's nice to have someone appreciate my cooking."

"Don't tell me. Your ex again?" He made a face. "That guy was a moron."

"You have no idea."

"Why did you stay with him then?"

"That's the million dollar question, isn't it?" She sighed. "When I finally had enough of his bullshit I took a hike. And here I am."

He squeezed her hand. "I'm glad you found your way here."

Her breath hitched and her heart rate speeded up. He was a special man, so sweet and gentle, and she was so vulnerable. It would be easy to cave in to him and stay here, safe and cared for, but she couldn't. She didn't want to be needy anymore. Wasn't that why she'd run away? To be strong, independent, and prove that she didn't need anybody? "I'm glad too."

"I know I said I only want your company, but I was wrong. I really wish I could kiss you. Am I being too pushy?"

"No, not pushy, but Brent... we shouldn't go there. I'm attracted to you, but I just got out of a bad relationship and it's too soon for me to commit to anyone right now. There are some things I have to do. Plus I need to heal from that unhealthy relationship I was in."

"How bad was it?"

"Gray area, Brent. I don't want to discuss it."

He didn't say anything, seemingly processing her words.

"I understand. Problem is, you have made me feel things again and I don't want to go back into my cave and feel useless. I'm only thirty-four and my love life isn't over yet. Not by a long shot."

"You're right. Of course it isn't. You'll meet someone wonderful and everything will work out for you, Brent." She blinked away a tear, wishing things could be different, and that Brent had walked into her life once she had her own problems solved. "You just need to be patient, that's all."

"Right. That was a stupid thing for me to say. I'm sorry if I made you feel uncomfortable." He stood up. "I'll see you in the morning."

She wanted to jump up and grab his hand. Put it over her beating heart, and curl into him. She wanted to hold him, kiss him, share his bed. Only not now. Remaining seated, she cursed Carl once again.

He'd taken a few steps, when she called out his name. "Brent. Under different circumstances I would have enjoyed it too. You're a very attractive man, and it would be easy to care for you more than I should."

"Don't worry. It's better that we don't mix business with pleasure. I've got a feeling that if we did we'd end up more messed up than we are now."

"So right." Disappointment, mixed with relief, made her swallow hard. This was best, she told herself. The way it had to be. "Glad we both agree."

∽

The following morning Brent woke up early and wandered into the kitchen to make coffee. He took the bag out of the freezer and noticed it felt light. He squeezed it and didn't feel the grounds except for a smidgen at the bottom. Picking up the scoop, he counted one, two, three, and then it was empty.

He knew how much Natalie looked forward to her coffee and wished he'd been more observant the day before. Dammit! There might be enough to squeeze out two decent cups and he could go without. Or she could run down to the store as soon as she got up. It was only a ten minute walk and he could have breakfast waiting for her when she returned. Then again, he could work on that confidence building/independence thing and go himself. What was the worst thing that could happen? He might trip and fall or get run over by a car. Hadn't he said often enough that he didn't want to live this way?

Of course, that had been before Natalie entered his life. Now he didn't mind sticking around so much.

Sam sniffed around his feet, obviously hoping he'd get his morning nibbles.

"What do you say, ole boy? You up for a walk? There's a store not more than three blocks away." He grinned and ran a hand over his head, feeling ridiculously proud of his independence. "Won't she be surprised?"

He put the harness on Sam, grabbed the house key and forgot that he was wearing his sleep pants. He grabbed a fleece jacket and put it over his head, and found the dreaded white cane that he loathed with every ounce of his being. "Guess I better take this," he told Sam before they stepped out the door. He turned right and walked the twenty steps to the elevator, and found the button to punch.

"This is going to be quite an adventure, but I think we're up for the job. Don't fail me now, you hear?" The door slid open and he and Sam stepped in.

He and the dog were alone to face the unknown together. As soon as they reached the sidewalk, panic seized him. What in hell had he been thinking? He knew where the store was, but the dog didn't. Well, hopefully Sam had more experience in this than he did. Times were rough when he had to rely on a dog's intelligence rather than his own, but he'd had dogs as a youngster, and knew just how smart they were.

"Come on, boy. We can do this." He turned to the left and walked to the end of the street. He knew it was the end because Sam stopped. There wasn't a light and the three blocks were residential, but still his heart pumped with adrenalin and sweat trickled over his backbone.

Brent listened for the sound of cars and swallowed hard as bile rose in his throat. He had to cross the fucking road and trust that this animal would keep him out of harm's way.

Since he hadn't been the lead pilot during his Afghan tour, he'd never had to depend on someone having his back. Now he did and it was a damn dog.

"Let's go," he told Sam, not hearing anything coming in either direction.

The dog led him across the street, and Brent's heart began to pound. Every nerve end in his body stood on high alert. He fought for control, knowing a panic attack was fast approaching. Breathe, he told himself. Breathe nice and slow.

Walking slowly, they carried on to the next corner and Sam stopped once again. The moment Brent stopped walking, his ears began to ring, his vision clouded like a thick gray fog. The usual shapes and shadows he would occasionally see were gone. His breathing came fast and hard. He froze, unable to cross the road.

He pulled Sam away from the curb, and stumbled onto the grass beside the sidewalk. He slumped down and put his hands over his face.

He heard footsteps running toward him and didn't know if it was someone who wanted his wallet or was eager to help. He kept his face buried, as waves of shame rolled over him. So mortified, he hoped it was a mugger, rather than facing a helpful citizen who'd look on him with pity.

CHAPTER TWELVE

Natalie saw him and slowed her steps. She had never seen a grown man humbled like this. Her chest ached, and she bit her lip to hold back a sob.

This courageous man... sitting on a sidewalk, hiding his tears...

It was too much. She sucked in a couple of quick breaths, needing to compose herself. She walked briskly forward.

"Hey, Brent, what are you doing here by yourself?" Natalie put a hand on his shoulder and sank down on the grass next to him. "You planning a picnic without me?"

Sam barked, then jumped on her and nipped at her ankle.

"Get down." She spoke firm to the dog. "Don't bite me. You're in my bad books just like your master here. Why didn't you wake me if you wanted to go for a Sunday walk?"

Brent still had not raised his head. She got to her feet and took him by the hand. "Come on, you big, brave soldier. I'm glad you waited for me but we don't have all day. Shane and Josh are expecting us soon and we still have so much to do."

When he didn't answer, she gentled her voice. "I woke up and came into the kitchen, and you guys were gone. I threw on my clothes and came running out to find you. Sheesh. I haven't even brushed my teeth or hair. Can't believe you two went without me, knowing how much I love to walk."

"Go away," he mumbled, not looking up.

"I'm not going anywhere." She wrapped her arms around him and kissed the top of his head. She needed to gather her emotions and keep them in check. Last thing she wanted was for him to see her cry. "Next time, wake me up so I can come too. Okay?"

"I was going to the store to buy some coffee. I tripped over the damn dog." Misery etched his face. "Told you I didn't need a fucking companion. Nothing but trouble."

"Did you hear that, Sam?" She rubbed the dog's head. "You made him trip."

Brent got to his feet, his jaw set, his mouth an angry slash. "It's only three blocks. I couldn't even make it three fucking blocks."

She kept the sympathy out of her voice as she answered. "You only had one block to go."

He snorted with a half laugh, half cry. "Shoot me now. Once I was fearless, now I'm nothing more than a pathetic wimp."

She took him by the shoulders. "Stop that right now," her voice was fierce. "I won't have you talking that way. And don't you dare feel sorry for yourself. Don't... you... dare."

He sneered. "How're you going to stop me?"

"Like this." She leaned in and kissed him softly on the lips. The kiss was to ease her own distress as much as it was for him. Not only did he have her worried sick when she woke and found him gone, but seeing him so completely undone made her ache to the core. "You could have gotten killed out here today. I don't want anything bad to happen to you. Not on my watch."

He did laugh this time. "What's going to happen when you leave? Who's going to hold my hand then?"

"When I leave, I'll make sure that you're able to fully function on your own. I'm not going to leave until that happens. I promise." As soon as the work permit came through she'd be free to go, so she had to get him independent quickly.

"You can't promise. What if your past catches up to you?"

She sucked in a breath. "That won't happen. Besides I'm no longer running from my past as much as I'm running toward my future." She now had something positive and exciting to look forward to, and damned if she was going to miss it. This was her time, and she'd waited long enough. No matter how much she cared for Brent and how easily she could lose her heart, it couldn't deter her from her plan. She'd made too many wrong decisions in her life, and now she had to make smart choices.

"What are you afraid of? I know you have something you're not telling me."

"Nothing—just you getting hurt." She let out her breath. "Come on, let's go." She grabbed his arm and started walking. When they reached the store, she stopped and looked at him. "You're wearing your sleep pants, by the way."

He felt his legs. "Hmm. Guess I am." He turned his head. "What are you wearing?"

"Nothing interesting. Just gray sweats and a black tee."

"What's underneath?"

"A lacy pink bra and matching undies."

He shook his head. "Oh, that's just cruel."

She smiled. "We're at the store. Let's get that coffee and go back home. We still have a picnic to take care of and a date to sail."

"Don't tell Shane about this. Okay?"

"It'll be our little secret. But we can tell him you're working on your Braille. He'll be pleased about that."

"That's true."

"Okay, back to our shopping list. I should pick up a rotisserie chicken and some other things for the picnic lunch. Anything in particular that you'd like?"

"I'd really like to see you right now." He stopped and pulled her to face him. Lifting her chin, he used his hands to feel the shape of her face.

She stood still, even though other people were walking around them with curious glances. She didn't care what people thought. It had been a long, long time since she did.

"I pray for that to happen. Hopefully, one day it will," she whispered, "and I want to be around when it does." Saying the words aloud made her realize how much it was true. She might be in France, and would never see the look of wonder on his face—never witness that magical moment when the world would open for him again. It hurt to think she might miss all that.

"Enough about that," she said, purposely shoving it to the back of her mind. She had learned to deal with unpleasantness by refusing to think about it. "Do you want to come with me or just wait here until I'm done?" she asked, stopping at the entrance to the store.

"You go ahead and get what you need. Besides, running up and down aisles doesn't exactly thrill me."

"Fine. Stay put and wait for me."

"Okay, Mom. I'll be a good little boy and won't move."

She laughed and helped him take a few steps back so he'd be out of the way as people walked through the door.

When she was done with her shopping, he was right where she'd left him. "Hey, good-looking," she said, slipping her hand through his arm, "you going my way?"

"Lead on." His face brightened the moment she took his arm.

As they neared the apartment building, she slowed down. "I have a question, and it's not to be mean, but how can Shane be a doctor with one hand?"

"He's got two," Brent joked. "No really, he'll be great. That mechanical hand of his can do anything. He's going to be a GP, and wants to help with the Wounded Warrior program. I'm sure he won't be doing any surgical procedures, but who knows? Everything's becoming robotic these days."

"I see." She picked up the pace again. "I'm looking forward to meeting his wife. What does she look like?"

"You ever seen the TV show, *Bones*?"

"Yes. I like the guy in it."

"No surprise there. Well, according to Shane, Lauren looks like that Bones lady. Big blue eyes, same kind of hair."

"Wow. She's beautiful."

"Nice too."

They were back at the apartment, and Natalie punched the elevator button. "You sure were brave coming out here this morning, and now going sailing too." She hugged his arm. "You're moving fast, Warrant Officer Harrington."

"Not sure about that, but there is one more thing I'd like to do today."

"What's that?"

He pulled her into his arms and kissed her on the side of her lips.

"You missed," she said and kissed his chin. "Oops. So did I. Perhaps we should try that again."

Taking her face into his hands, he trailed gentle kisses all over her cheeks, her forehead, the tip of her nose, and then found her lips and stayed. The kiss became less gentle as he parted her lips and slipped his tongue inside. He tasted minty and sweet and delicious, and she wrapped her arms around him, holding him close.

"Oh, that's better," she whispered, kissing him some more. "Now you got it right."

"Know something?" He put his arms around her back, and her heart did a triple flip.

"What?" Her voice was husky and she could feel her pulse racing.

"I didn't want you around, and now I'm going to be sorry when you're gone."

Her heart lurched. "Oh, Brent." She pushed away, eager to stop the feelings that shot right through her. Need and want swamped her like a tidal wave, taking her to places she couldn't go. She had a wonderful, exciting future ahead of her. Sure, it wasn't the dream job that she'd anticipated and worked toward, but it was an adventure just the same. And she would leave him, ready or not. She had to—until she did something on her own, she'd never know if she could.

"In a month or so, you'll learn enough tools to be self-reliant. We are going to work on those together." She fought back the strange urge to cry. There was so much churning and yearning inside of her. Emotions that she didn't understand, or want to if she did. "You won't want me then."

"I want you now. Guess sex's out of the question?"

She laughed. "Glad to see you're in a better mood. And yes, it is."

EPISODE FOUR

CHAPTER THIRTEEN

With Brent's directions, Natalie drove the BMW to Lauren and Shane's house. It was only about six blocks from the beach and the boardwalk, and a few miles south of where Brent lived. Natalie had expected they'd live in a nice home, but was immediately charmed by the painted pastel blue and white shingled house. It was not much more than a seaside cottage, with a lovely fenced in yard in the front, some nice landscaping with flowering bushes, and potted plants on the stairs. Even at first glance, she could see it was a little dream home wrapped in love.

She parked in the driveway and noticed a basketball hoop over the small one-car garage, and a couple of bikes still needing to be put away. She was just getting out of the car when the front door opened up and Shane called out, "Need any help?"

"No. We're good," she answered back and took Brent's arm, leading him toward the stairs. A second later, a beautiful woman appeared next to Shane. She was exactly like Brent had described her. A stunning brunette with a warm smile and high energy.

Before they reached the top of the stairs, Lauren moved quickly and offered her hand. "Hello, Natalie. It's so nice to meet you."

"Nice to meet you too," she answered. "What a sweet home."

"Thank you." Lauren grabbed Brent and kissed him on both cheeks, and linked arms with him. "So glad you called yesterday, wanting to do something besides sit in your apartment and count the seconds going by." She laughed, taking any sting out of the words. "Josh is excited to go sailing, and it's such a perfect day."

Shane gave Brent an affectionate punch on the arm. "Hey, buddy. Good to see you out. High time too."

Natalie felt like a total outsider as she watched them fuss over their friend. The love they had for each other made her throat close tight. She choked on envy of what they had, what she could never have.

The thought of the French countryside beckoned. Would she at last be free? Could she find peace and love, and maybe one day have a family of her own?

"Natalie, I haven't seen Brent looking so happy in a long time. You must be doing something right." Lauren took her hand and led her into their home. "I've been eager to meet you, and I hope you don't mind if I quiz you a little at dinner."

Shane gave her a sympathetic look. "She can be a hound-dog when she wants information, but I told her to go easy."

"I just want to get to know you. That's all." Lauren's bright blue eyes swept over Natalie's face, and she was sure that Lauren was taking her measure. "Shane is a great judge of character and I respect his opinion. Glad to see he was right about you."

"Thanks. I like it here and working with Brent," Natalie said, wishing she'd stayed home.

"I'm sure we're going to be very good friends." She gave her husband a teasing glance. "I'm not going to rake you over the coals. It's Shane's job to do the grilling." She laughed, making a weak joke. "But we're not grilling tonight. I'm making lasagna. You like pasta, don't you?"

"Sure. Sounds great." Natalie shot Brent a look. What had he told his friends about her? Had he mentioned the landlord she supposedly owed money to? Surely not. He wouldn't betray her trust like that.

"Nat's a little shy," Brent said, and put a hand on her back. "But I haven't fired her yet, so she must be all right."

She wanted to punch him in the arm for that remark, but kept her voice upbeat instead. "I don't have anything too exciting to tell. But I want to hear all about working the ER," Natalie told Lauren. Then added, "Why don't you come with us so we can get to know each other better? You won't get seasick, will you?"

"I've had morning sickness, but it's over now. Still, I don't want to chance it."

A skinny, coltish boy, with long strawberry blonde hair and the same bright blue eyes as his mom came bounding into the room. "This must be Josh," Natalie said, with a relieved smile. She had a feeling tonight she might need a diversion, and this young man might save the day.

He rushed up to Brent and threw his gangly arms around his middle, darn near knocking him over in his exuberance. "Uncle Brent! We're going sailing. You're coming too, right?"

"I sure am." He rubbed the boy's hair affectionately. "Wouldn't miss it for the world."

The boy looked shyly at Natalie. "Hi."

She moved forward. "Hi. I'm Natalie, and it's nice to meet you."

He grinned and she saw a dimple flash in and out. "You take care of Uncle Brent, don't you? When's he gonna see again? Dad says he will, but that he's stubborn. Then he called him a name. Can I say what it is?"

Shane put a hand on Josh's shoulder. "No. Brent is hopeful that he'll regain his sight, and knows he shouldn't have left rehab before learning all the stuff they could have taught him. We don't need to rub it in. Do we?"

Lauren touched Brent's arm. "Ignore them, Brent. You can learn the skills you need on your own time. This isn't a race. Speaking of which, I know you guys are in a hurry to go boating, and I packed a lunch. Josh, will you go get it?"

Natalie glanced at the two men. "Didn't Brent tell you I was bringing food?"

Lauren answered, "Shane didn't mention it, but you know men. Next time, you and I will talk." She shrugged. "Oh, well. Better to have too much than not enough."

Josh ran into the kitchen and returned with the picnic basket. He handed it to his mother. "Fried chicken and homemade potato salad. Mom and I made it," he said proudly.

"Thanks, hon," his mother said with a fond smile.

"We've double upped. Sure you don't want to come?" Natalie asked, thinking it might be a more relaxing way to get to know each other than over dinner.

"No, I better not." She made a face, and put a hand on her still flat belly. "This little one has given me all kinds of grief, and he hasn't even arrived yet. Wait till he does."

Shane kissed her, took the basket, and told her to rest. She waved them good-bye at the door, and Natalie relaxed. If Lauren pried too hard, she might not like what she discovered.

They took Shane's SUV to the marina and the boat was ready for them. It was a 29-foot Catalina sloop, a beauty of a boat as far as Natalie could see. "Wow. This is great. You guys can sail this thing? Look at all the rigs."

Shane laughed. "We grew up in Florida, don't forget. And Brent's dad had several boats over the years."

"Good, because I've been on a ferry and a water-ski boat when I was a kid, but never sailed." She handed Josh one of the two picnic baskets and stepped on board, then reached over for him. "It's a big step. Careful."

"I can do it." He refused her hand, and the boat moved fractionally as he took the long step, and for half a second he was straddling the pier and the boat.

Natalie grabbed the basket out of his hands just as Shane pulled the boy back to safety. He started to cry.

"What happened?" Brent asked.

Shane picked Josh up and lifted him safely onto the boat. "Boat shifted. Nearly lost my son," he told Brent.

Josh sniffed. "I'm okay. You better take somebody's hand," he told Brent. "It's safer."

Natalie smiled. "Can you put the basket in the galley for me?" The boy took the larger basket and with two hands, swung it toward the steps leading inside. She knew it was heavy and awkward but it gave him something important to do, and time to compose himself.

"Here, Brent. Take my hand." She reached out for him and guided him forward, not minding when he bumped into her. She stood there for a fraction of a second, feeling the warmth of his body next to her own. His linebacker body was big, hard, strong. She closed her eyes, imagining what it would be like…

Shane jumped on board. "Hey, you two. You going to help me here, or stand there all day?" he said with a wink and a grin.

Natalie felt her face flush. "I'll get rid of the other basket and give you guys some space up here." She quickly disappeared downstairs, and helped Josh put a few items away in the small fridge. The galley area had a small stove, a table and two bench seats, a small TV, radio and CD player, and a bunk in the rear. It wasn't luxurious, but clean, comfortable, and spacious for an afternoon outing.

"Do you like Uncle Brent?" Josh asked.

"Sure I do. He's very nice, and I hope he gets his vision back real soon."

"Yeah. Me too. I tried it once. You know… I closed my eyes and tried to find my way around my room just to see what it was like. I bumped into a wall and got a bruise. It was scary. Have you tried it?"

"No, I haven't. But it's a good idea. Maybe I will when I get home."

"Why don't you try it here?" He sat down on the blue covered bench seat to watch. "Go ahead."

"I can't. There isn't any room. Besides, we have stuff to do."

"Like what?" He jumped up. "Are we going to fish?"

"I don't know. Why don't we ask your daddy that?"

"He's not my real daddy, you know. My real dad died when I was only three."

"I'm sorry. That must have been hard on you." She remembered Brent saying that he'd only met Lauren recently, after his return from war, and Natalie hadn't connected the dots. Lauren had been married before. She was so young to be a widow—how fortunate that she'd met a wonderful, loving man like Shane.

"Naw. I don't remember much. Anyway, I love my new daddy more. He's got the coolest hand. Did you see it? It's bionic. Like superman or something."

"Yeah, that is extra cool." She wasn't sure about his mother, but Josh was a great kid.

She found the sunscreen to apply to her face and arms. She was wearing a T-shirt and a pair of jean shorts, and although it was only in the low seventies she knew that out on the water even a minimal amount of sun could result in a burn. "Have you got your sunscreen on?"

"Yeah, Mom doesn't let me go outside without it."

"Smart mom."

By the time the two of them went on deck, the men had the sails up and the boat in motion, and they were headed for the open sea. The sky was blue, with a few scattered cumulus clouds, and the white sail flapped in the breeze.

Shane called Josh over. "Here, son. You can help me steer." He shifted over so the boy could have the wheel. "See that buoy in the water?" he asked, pointing. "You need to head the boat right of that."

Josh beamed with pride. "I'm doing it. I'm driving the boat. Wish Mom could see me now."

Brent lazed in the front of the boat, and Natalie scooted along the edge and plopped down next to him. "How're you doing, sailor? Enjoying yourself?"

He tilted his head back, and lifted his face to the sky. "Feels good. Glad we came out."

"Me too, but you're going to get fried out here. Mind if I put some lotion on you?"

"I'm okay. Haven't been in the sun for a while, and I could use some color."

"Your head is bare and you don't want to get a bad burn." She squeezed some lotion into her hands and without asking permission, dabbed some on his forehead, his cheeks and nose. "There. Rub it in."

He did as she asked, then grabbed the bottom of his shirt and lifted it over his head. "Might as well get my chest tanned too."

"Okay. But you asked for it." She liberally applied the lotion on his chest and back, and because she had an excuse to touch the strong, broad chest that she'd glimpsed every morning, she took full advantage of the moment.

She spread the lotion up and over his shoulders, down his arms, and massaged it in with quick, brisk movements. Her hands strayed to his chest where she lingered a little longer.

His muscles tensed under her strokes, which sent her internal temperature soaring. He had a matting of fine, silky hair on his chest, and she ran her fingers through it, glad that Shane and Josh were seated well behind them, half hidden by the billowing sail. She didn't want anyone to see her taking advantage of her charge. But wicked girl that she was, she didn't let a thing like guilt stop her either.

She slid her hand lower, eager to feel the rock hard abs that had enticed her since the first time they'd caught her attention. He quivered under her touch, and she felt an answering need low in her belly. She massaged the cream into his warm flesh longer than was necessary and heard the sharp intake of his breath. Clearly, he enjoyed it too.

She murmured, "You probably should have left your shirt on."

"What? And missed this?" He sucked in his stomach muscles and gave her a sinful smile. "You think I'm an idiot?"

She laughed softly. "How long do you think we can keep this up before they catch us?"

He chuckled, and she felt his abdominal muscles contract. "All day, I hope."

After a few tantalizing minutes, she told him to lean forward, then started on his back. Her mouth was close to his ear. "You have a nice bod, Mr. Harrington. I hope you don't mind if I appreciate it in the mornings." She knew she shouldn't be encouraging him this way, but after everything that had happened today, she was feeling deeply emotional and deliciously warm and sexy. She hadn't been excited about a man in years, and now here he was... This sailing business was serious fun. She could grope him and have a perfect excuse.

He coughed. "You do?"

"Uh-huh."

"Well, I appreciate you going braless too."

"I have one on right now." She leaned in close and brushed against his back. "Can you tell?"

"Pink?" he asked.

"Yes. Lacy, pretty, and pink."

"Hey, you guys," Josh yelled. "Whatcha doing?"

Shane lifted off his seat to see and caught Natalie in the act.

His eyes widened, then he grinned, and she blushed.

"You two getting warm up there?" Shane called out. "Want a cold beer or soda?"

Natalie reluctantly got up, feeling a little tingly all over. "I'll get us some beers. Josh, you want a juice?"

Shane said, "Juice for Josh and a soda for me. I don't drink."

"I can help," Josh said, getting to his feet.

"You stay," Brent answered. "I'll give Natalie a hand."

Shane laughed. "If you want, you can use mine." He made a claw with his mechanical hand, making his son laugh.

While Shane entertained his son, Brent stood and carefully followed Natalie to the aft of the boat and down the steps into the galley below.

"Nice work getting us alone," she said, and turned into him.

He cupped her face, and kissed her hard.

Heat flashed through her, and she clung to him, aware that it had been years since she'd felt this way. When she and Carl were first dating, the sex between them had been hot, but that seemed a lifetime ago. After the first exciting months, it became a painful ordeal, and she'd had to pretend to please him, pretend an orgasm, pretend to smile, pretend to be a woman in love.

"Brent..." She breathed his name, then her mouth opened up under his.

That was all the invitation he needed. His tongue swept in, tasting her, plunging in as though he couldn't get enough, wanting to go deeper. She clung to him, not just accepting his hungry kisses, but matching him as their tongues mated and dueled.

His chest was warm and inviting, and she pulled her own shirt up so as to feel skin on skin. She broke away from his lips and kissed his neck, running her tongue over his shoulder, taking little nips of pleasure.

His hands covered her breasts, and he teased the nipples until they grew hard under his fingers. She felt herself grow weak and leaned into him for support. His hips moved against her and she felt... everything.

Knowing she had to stop this before it went any further, she forced herself to push him away. "You can't...," she whispered. "We mustn't..."

He stood still, breathing hard. "You're right... but this is to be continued. Later. Alone, back at our place."

The "our place" sent a thrill through her, one she tried mostly to ignore. It wasn't their place, and it never would be. She had to leave soon, before Carl had a chance to follow her trail. Whether she was ready to go or not, Europe waited and this time she had to answer that call. Nothing, and no one, would make her give up on this dream again. It was time to have her own adventures, and not put her life on hold.

Pushing that reluctant thought out of her head, Natalie busied herself with the food while Brent surrounded her in the tight quarters. He pretended to help, but mostly bumped into her, using his hands to feel his way around her and the counters. Then they both returned upstairs after another hot, fiery kiss, flushed and happy.

"Josh, could you run down and grab the paper plates and napkins for us?" Natalie asked. "We ran out of hands."

He giggled. "I've got two."

He dashed off, and Natalie placed a plastic tablecloth down on the seat behind the wheel, and laid everything out as best she could. She knew they could anchor and eat downstairs but it was too nice of a day to do that.

Brent handed Shane a soda, and her a beer. "Cheers," he said, and raised his can.

"Cheers," she replied, eyes glued to the chest she intended to graze on tonight.

"Looks like you two are getting along," Shane said with a smug smile. "Didn't I just know it?"

Brent plopped down beside her and took her hand. "You don't know shit. I brought Natalie along today, thinking that perhaps she might want to tutor Josh for the summer, and make some extra money. Figured it would give Lauren a break too."

Josh popped his head out of the stairwell. "I don't need tutoring, do I Dad? I'm doing better at school."

"Well, you've made vast improvements all around, but a little extra help never hurt anyone." He winked. "Your choice, son. This is your vacation after all."

Josh glanced at her, his eyes narrowing. "I don't want a tutor, Dad. I don't like school. Besides, I'm going to be a fisherman when I grow up. I can be on a boat way bigger than this, and do nothing but catch fish all day." He clapped his hands in excitement. "Can we fish now, Dad, can we?"

"Not yet. We're going to have a picnic first, then we can throw out a few lines."

Josh kicked at the basket on the floor, and it skidded across the deck.

"Josh. Pick that up and apologize," Shane said, eyeing his son. "That's no way to behave. You know better."

"You promised me we could fish," he said, and pouted. "And I want to. Now."

Natalie glanced at Shane, a question in her eye. When he nodded, she spoke gently, "Josh, come sit down and have some chicken and potato salad. As soon as we eat, we'll pack this stuff away and fish. Okay?"

He folded his arms. "Uncle Brent. Do you want to fish first, or eat first?"

"Eat. Aren't you starving? It's well past noon."

"I'm a little hungry, I guess. Okay, eat, then fish. I'm sorry, Dad." Josh ran over and hugged him.

Shane kissed the top of his head. When he glanced up, he shouted a warning, "Heads down. Crazy fool is coming right at us."

He switched tack, and the boom swept from one side to the other just as Brent moved to protect Josh. The boom smacked the right side of his head and Brent went down.

CHAPTER FOURTEEN

So this was what death was like. Bathed in warmth, rocked gently as a baby. Peaceful. Beautiful.

"Brent! Brent," an angel's voice called. The Pearly Gates opened for him? After all his mistakes, he was grateful—but not in any rush to leave. He liked it fine right here. Why was he here? How had he died? He didn't feel dead, just at peace.

As he tried to remember, his head ached and the floating feeling popped like a bubble having reached maximum density. A bright light seared his eyes.

"Shane, quick, I saw his eyelids flutter." Then the same voice softened with worry. "He won't wake up."

Shane? What was he doing in heaven? And that voice—so familiar. Last he remembered, he'd been out on a boat. And he'd kissed Natalie. That's who the angelic voice belonged to. Had she killed him? Why would she do an awful thing like that?

His head hurt, and if he were in heaven, he shouldn't be feeling any pain. He'd be playing a harmonica in the clouds or some dang thing. Fuckin' head felt like it was split open. Probably shouldn't swear either, just in case the guardian angels could read his mind.

He winced. Maybe he was in that transitional place between heaven and earth, and both beckoned him. Heaven was full of light, and earth was dark and had no future for him...

Slowly he opened an eye, and the blurry outline of a face swam before him. He caught the glitter of a tear off a sunbeam around her face. Don't cry, he tried to say. He didn't deserve an angel's tears.

"Brent, come on," she whispered. He recognized the voice. It wasn't an angel, it was Natalie. Yes, Natalie was worth waking up for. An overwhelming surge of emotion that felt like love settled around his heart.

Shane's face appeared over Natalie's shoulder. Even fuzzy, his best friend's facial features were imprinted on his brain.

"Get up, you lazy slug. It was just a little bump on the head." Shane knelt down and Natalie moved away. He felt Shane's rough hands on his shoulders, shaking him. "Come on, buddy."

Brent tried to open his eyes. Tried to mumble something. But it was so peaceful here. Warm and light. If not in heaven, where was he? He thought hard. The boat. Sailing. That's why they were all together. Something happened on the boat, something about Josh.

With great determination he opened his eyes. "Shane? Where's Josh?" He shifted and tried to sit up, but his head spun and his belly felt ready to heave-ho.

"You okay, bud?" Shane's face peered closer, and then he heard Josh shout his name.

"I'm here Uncle Brent, here, here." Josh flung his arms around Brent's shoulders and it was all Brent could do not to hurl. The movement rocked his head and sent his vision twisting. "You can't see me, but I'm here."

Funny thing was, Brent could sort of see him—like looking under water, but ten times more convoluted. He blinked, looking around. Natalie, yes, smiling now, but fractured like a prism. He rubbed his eyes.

"I got you, Josh." He kept one arm around the kid's skinny body, anchoring himself. "What happened?"

Shane pulled Josh back, while Natalie stepped forward. "You hit the back of your head. You're bleeding. Let me see."

Brent felt the sore spot, and his hand came away wet and sticky. Blood. Felt like a nasty gash.

"How do you feel?" Natalie said, softly, close to his ear. Her breath, watermelon sweet, her skin like sunscreen. He couldn't focus on her features, but he'd know her scent anywhere.

"You okay?" Shane asked. "Going to be sick?"

Brent gave a careful, slight nod. "Yeah."

Shane grabbed him a pail used for collecting fish. "You look a little green around the gills," he said, checking his head. "Not a bad injury, but you were out, buddy. A concussion means we should go back."

"But what about our lunch? And fishing?" Josh asked in a petulant tone.

Brent felt his stomach heave, and breathed deeply, determined not to ruin the boy's day. "I'm all right. I think. Help me up?"

Natalie slipped her arm around his waist. "Shane's got the sailboat under control. Rest a little longer." She gave him a slight squeeze and he remembered her tears. "You took a big hit to the head. It knocked you out for a few minutes."

He attempted to stand, but the sky and boat and the fuzzy images swirled. He sank back down. "I do feel a little woozy." Was his vision going to stay this way? He closed his eyes as tightly as possible, then opened them wide. Dots fragmented into light, but he couldn't focus on any one thing. It was different from the distorted fog he'd come to know, clearer in some ways, but like seeing through splinters of glass.

"Are you all right?" Natalie put her hand on the back of his neck. "Need the bucket?"

"Don't think so." Brent sighed. "What a screw-up this turned out to be."

"Not your fault, man," Shane quickly said. "Some idiot in a speedboat was going way too fast. He was to blame. Not you."

The picnic basket and the lunch had been tossed across the deck. Josh looked at his dad. "I'm sorry. I didn't mean to ruin lunch. Mom will be so mad."

"You didn't, son." Shane answered. "But we need to head home."

"I'll be fine—just give me a second or two." Brent tried to speak normally, but it took great effort. "We still have food to eat and fish to catch. Right?" His stomach gurgled.

Natalie covered his hand with hers. "You should probably go to the ER and get checked out."

Brent blinked again, hoping to clear his vision, but it was a fractured mess. Would it eventually clear, or remain like this? "Shane's a medic. Lauren's a doctor. If I feel bad, I couldn't be in better hands."

Shane clapped a hand on his shoulder. "I'm turning the boat around just the same. Lauren wouldn't forgive me if

I let anything happen to you." He gave a short laugh. "Not that I would care, but you know how she is."

"Does it hurt, Uncle Brent?"

"Only a little. I've got a hard head."

"Guess we can't fish," Josh said sadly. But then his voice brightened. "Hey, can we do this again tomorrow? Please, please, please?"

Shane saved him from answering. "Sorry, Josh. Not tomorrow. Maybe some time next week you and I can go fishing together."

"Okay, Dad. Hey, how about a cookie?"

Brent smiled at the easy way Josh accepted Shane in his life, and how great Shane was at being a father.

"How about some lunch first?" Shane countered. "Are you trying to get me in trouble?"

Josh giggled.

"I'll fix a plate," Natalie said, standing up with a last squeeze of Brent's hand. "But first I'm going to get Brent some ice for his head."

When she returned, she cleaned his wound gently with the damp towel, then handed him the icepack. "The bleeding has stopped," she told him. "But this might help prevent swelling."

She moved aside and he heard her collecting the food.

"Who wants to eat?" Natalie asked.

The men declined, but Josh said he was starving.

"Well done, Josh," Natalie said when the boy finished eating. She kept him company and chatted to him about school, his friends, and favorite sports.

Brent stayed quiet, preferring to sit and stare out toward the sea.

He didn't mention the fact that he could make out shapes and see bright light, and the sun glimmering on the water. His vision wasn't clear, and it might be fleeting. He just wanted to savor this alone and enjoy it for all it was worth. It might be taken away from him again, and he didn't want to get their hopes up, or his own.

∼

When they docked at the marina, Natalie heard Shane on his cell with Lauren, explaining they were on their way home. She admired how quickly he put his wife's fears to rest. "No, Josh is just fine." He told her about the speedboat, tacking quickly, and the boom that hit Brent in the head. "Hope it knocked some sense into him," he said not too discreetly.

Natalie chuckled, understanding that the comment was Shane's way of letting Lauren know Brent was okay too.

"Shotgun!" Josh yelled as they neared the car.

"I guess that means you get to sit in the back with me," Natalie whispered, taking Brent's hand in hers.

Brent grinned. "Lucky me." For a brief second their eyes connected, and Natalie's breath hitched. Awareness flared. Could he see her? She shook her head, biting her lower lip. That was foolish, of course. If his sight had come back, he'd have told them immediately. Wouldn't he?

She bumped shoulders with him and opened the back door. "How're you feeling, soldier boy?"

He slid inside. "Head aches, but that's no surprise. And my stomach's better now we're back on land."

"You sure were quiet on the boat coming in. I'm glad we're staying with Shane and Lauren for dinner. Just in case."

"Not me." He lowered his voice. "I kind of like the plans we made on the boat."

Her belly curled at his seductive tone. "Plans? What plans? I don't remember making any," she teased. "Maybe that bump on your noggin put some ideas in your head. Ideas of things that can't happen."

He slid his leg against hers. "You remember plenty, and believe me, so do I." The back of his hand brushed her thigh. "And I don't believe in can't."

"Oh yeah? What about all the times I've heard you say, 'I can't do this or that,' before listing your one reason why."

"Oh, you really know how to hurt a guy."

"You have no idea." She rubbed her fingers against his.

"I have an active imagination." He sat in such a way that his shoulder was against hers. He had linebacker shoulders, but his body was still too frail to fill them out. Before she left, she wanted him to be all that he had been before. Strong in body, in spirit, and in mind. Those were the best gifts she could give him, not the physical pleasure they both craved.

A short time later they pulled into the driveway, and Lauren rushed out of the house to greet them. After a kiss for Shane and a hug for Josh, she glanced in the back. "Guess I should have come along this afternoon after all. Who knew you might need a doctor on board? Though my darling Shane is just as good."

"Not yet. Working on it, though." Shane grabbed Lauren for another kiss.

Natalie stepped out of the car and reached in for Brent's hand, though it was more for the sake of touching him than his needing help.

Brent slid out, wearing a sheepish expression. "Sorry to ruin your free afternoon, Lauren. I know you don't get many."

Lauren inspected the red spot on the back of his head. "The blood's already drying, but I can always give you a stitch or two to make it pretty."

"No. That won't be necessary," Brent responded, stepping closer to Natalie as if she could keep him safe. "Keep your stitches to yourself. My head's beginning to look like a patchwork quilt."

She laughed. "Fair enough." Lauren checked his pupils and asked him questions regarding a possible concussion, and seemed satisfied by his response.

"You'll live," she said with a smile, then took Josh's hand and led the way toward the house. "Let's get some ointment on my patient here. A little dash of iodine never hurts."

"Doesn't hurt you, but what about me?" Brent said, making a face. Josh giggled.

Natalie was drawn into the family dynamic, and against her will, wondered what Brent would be like with a child of his own. He was so natural around Josh that she could only imagine he'd make a great father. Tamping down unwelcome thoughts, she hooked her arm through Brent's and they went inside.

They all played Yahtzee, Josh's favorite game, and then the guys went to watch baseball, while Josh took off to his room to play on his Wii. Natalie followed Lauren into the kitchen and watched as she checked on the lasagna.

She offered her help, knowing this would likely be where the gentle interrogation began.

"So what did you do before meeting Brent?" Lauren asked the question as she opened the cupboard, taking down the salt and pepper. "Shane said you're a Spanish teacher, from Kelowna, Washington. Correct?"

Nice. Casual, but direct. Natalie nodded. "Uh-huh. I taught middle school kids. French and Spanish." She glanced at Lauren. "Languages are my specialty. I also know a little German and Italian."

"Very impressive," Lauren said. "Shane also mentioned that you love music?"

She nodded in agreement. "Yes. It's a hobby. But I helped with the school play this year. The kids did *Oliver*. They were very good too."

"You write your own songs, Shane said. What kind of music do you enjoy?"

"Anything with lyrics." She laughed and settled in to chat. With Lauren asking the questions, she told her about her dreams as a young woman, and how they had never come to pass. After telling Lauren about her mom, Natalie guided the conversation to her sister. "She's the creative one in my family."

"Each family is only allowed one creative child?" Lauren's eyes brightened with suppressed laughter.

Natalie smiled. "Well, she was always so gung-ho about everything. Went after whatever caught her interest. I was more the sitting back kind of girl, waiting to see what would fall into my lap."

"I assume nothing did. Is that why you moved here?" Lauren put her back to the counter, crossed her ankles, and drank from her glass.

"I needed a change of scene. I'd been in that small town too long. Figured if I didn't make a move, I never would."

"That's a good reason," Lauren said, putting her glass down, and turning to her. "You like Brent, don't you?" She didn't wait for an answer. "He likes you. Maybe you should think about putting roots down here."

"How about we start that salad?" Natalie walked to the washed pile of veggies stacked by the sink, choosing a cucumber. "Peeler?"

"Here." Lauren paused. "I don't mean to pry."

"Yes, you do," Natalie said softly, slicing the cucumber. "But I get it. You're protecting your family and friend. You don't know me."

She was tempted to confide in Lauren, but she'd done that with her friend Lori, and that had turned into a disaster. And the fewer people who knew about Carl and her plans to go to France, the better.

Everyone thought the police could protect her. Natalie would have thought so too, had she not learned the hard way. No one could protect her but herself.

Natalie finished slicing the cucumber, then picked up a tomato. "I can't stay, Lauren. I've been tied to one place all my life, and I need to spread my wings a little and see where they fly. Don't know where I'll end up."

"I see. Well, that is too bad. I think Brent will be disappointed when you leave."

"I know—it will be hard for me too." Natalie slid the chopped tomatoes, crumbled feta cheese, and pitted black olives into the salad. She stood up straight and looked Lauren in the eye, determined to appear strong even if she jumped at shadows in the dark. "Right now we're growing close but for the wrong reasons. I need him and he needs me."

"You don't think it's more than that? That perhaps you could be right for each other?" Lauren took the garlic bread out of the oven and didn't look at her as she spoke. "This past week, you've really put a spring in his step, that's for sure. And I would hate for him to be hurt again."

She didn't like making excuses, but the truth was too dangerous for her to share. "I may be back one day, but right now, I need to see a little more of the world around us. I've never been to the Grand Canyon, Hawaii, or anywhere exciting. Never been outside of the United States." She swallowed a lump in her throat, thinking of Brent. "Trust me. Brent will be fine." She wasn't as afraid for him as she was for herself. How could she leave him—already he meant so much to her. She was falling too fast, too soon. As she had with Carl, and look how bad that had turned out. She couldn't let that happen—not again. She needed to learn to stand on her own two feet.

"Enough said," Lauren said, and brushed her hands. "Are you done with that salad?"

Natalie nodded, and Lauren drizzled a light olive oil dressing over the top then put it on the table. The lasagna had been sitting on top of the stove to set, and she now carved generous squares and slid them out.

"Shane, Brent, dinner's ready." Lauren poked her head into the family room. "Tell Josh to wash up before he comes to the table."

The five of them sat down to dinner, and Natalie learned more about Brent in that hour than spending a week in his company. The men talked about their escapades during their "wild" youth; the skateboard competition that knocked out Shane's front tooth; the time they'd played hooky to go to a Lakers playoff game, and had been captured on the televised screen during halftime. The night they'd taken Brent's dad's vintage T-Bird out for a joy ride and wrapped it around a tree.

"We had mild injuries, just some cuts and bruises," Shane said, chuckling at the memory. "We were just sixteen, and I'd only had my license for a couple of weeks."

Lauren glanced at the two men and shook her head. "Brent's dad was so mad he made the two of them do lawn work for a year to pay for the repairs on the car."

"That's true," Brent said seriously. "And he grounded me for six months too. No phone. No TV. No dates. I was sixteen years old, and I was stuck in the house for half a year. It was painful, but we learned our lesson, didn't we, Shane?"

"The hard way. So, Josh, don't do what we did. Learn from our mistakes."

Josh was wide-eyed as he looked at his father and his friend. "You stole your dad's car?"

"No, we didn't steal it. Borrowed, is more like it." He got up and collected some plates. "Actually, the story doesn't sound so good in the telling of it." He stacked the dishwasher and came back to the table. "Hey, Brent. Remember that time when your mom and dad were away for the weekend and you and I were down at the beach . . ."

"Sweetheart, haven't we had enough stories for one night?" Lauren asked pointedly. "And since you're in the kitchen, mind grabbing the pie from the oven?"

"Sure. But it was a good story. We were surfing and there was a kid in trouble and we managed to use our boards and bring him back to safety."

"Yeah, the tide had changed and he got caught in a rip current," Brent remembered.

"I gave him CPR. Didn't even know how to do it properly back then, but I'd seen enough shows on TV and didn't have time to waste." Shane glanced at his wife. "Used my finger to clear his airway and gave him mouth-to-mouth. Kid was ten, and he puked all over me, but it was the proudest moment of my life. Probably part of the reason I became a medic."

"Have I told you lately that I love you?" Lauren said, getting up and putting her arms around her husband. "You make me proud, hon."

He kissed the top of her head. "Ditto, baby."

"Knock it off, Mom, Dad," Josh said. "It's embarrassing."

"I think it's rather sweet," Natalie replied with a smile.

Brent sniffed the air. "Is that apple pie I smell?"

Lauren laughed. "It is. I'll slice, and Shane, darling, you can use your magic hand and scoop the ice cream." She glanced around. "Anyone want coffee?"

They lingered over coffee and dessert, and the evening was completely enjoyable. Natalie found her tension melting away. Normal people, normal conversation, was not something she'd enjoyed in the past few years. Living with Carl she'd always had to be on guard. At Lori's too. And with Brent she couldn't feel completely safe either. He stirred feelings in her, and she was there to protect him from hurting himself, but what if Carl found her? She couldn't protect them both.

Before they left, Natalie escaped to the kitchen to clean up, but Lauren stopped her and told her about the music therapy department at the hospital and how they were always looking for volunteers.

"It's just a thought," she said. "But the sick kids love it when someone new comes in and sings or plays an instrument. They have so very little to look forward to in their day. If you're here for the summer, and you're interested, I can set you up."

"I'll think about it, Lauren. But, once again, I'm not sure how long I'll be in California." The idea did excite her though. She loved children, part of the reason she'd become a teacher, and this would bring a little comfort to them.

"It would give Brent something positive to do while he's recuperating," Lauren said. "It'll get him out of the house instead of lying around thinking about himself."

"Oh. If he'd come with me, that would be cool." Natalie glanced at Lauren and grinned. "He plays the guitar and is very supportive about my music. It might help to motivate him."

"You see? We think alike."

"Thanks for everything, Lauren. It's been a great day, all things considered. And it was so nice to meet you."

"Well, here's my card with my cell phone number. Call me if you decide to do this and I'll set it up."

"Will do. That's a promise."

She told Brent about the hospital idea on the way home, and as expected Brent didn't show much enthusiasm.

"I'm all for helping out Lauren, but we don't have time to spend at the hospital." His shoulders tensed and she watched his jaw tighten. "We have a busy enough program as it is. Need to be completely independent before you leave. If you leave, that is."

"You know I have to go eventually, but this might be something nice for you to do even after I'm gone. If you don't enjoy it, you don't have to go again, but it would be fun for us to give it a try. I'm really excited about it and hoped you'd be too. If we suck—we quit."

"Not interested." His body language remained stiff as he stared sightlessly out the passenger window.

"What's wrong? Is it the hospital experience? If that's the reason, I totally understand." She felt her cheeks warm, realizing how insensitive she'd been. "You've spent enough time there." She could only imagine the difficulties he'd endured. "Why would you want to volunteer more time? Sorry, I was being selfish."

"No, not at all." He didn't say anything for a moment, then sighed. "Might as well tell you, I suppose. For a few minutes, back on the boat, I could see more than light and shapes. Everything was fragmented, like looking through broken glass, but it gave me a brief moment of hope. For the past hour, things have gotten darker and more muddied again."

"Well, it's nighttime now, so it is darker," she said quietly and touched his leg. The idea that he had been able to see more clearly sent ripples of excitement through her. Goosebumps popped out on her arms and she shivered, and tried to remain calm. "I'm sorry, but I'm also thinking that this could be really good news. You must tell your doctor."

"I'll call him in the morning, but unless it comes back it doesn't mean anything."

"Well, speak with him anyway. Maybe he'll want to run some tests." She gave him a quick look. "I wish you'd have told us when it happened."

"I didn't want to get everyone's hopes up. Now I'm glad I didn't."

She was silent for several minutes as his words settled in. How awful it must be for him to have had a fleeting glimpse of light only to be plunged back into darkness. Her spirits dipped too.

"Brent, we don't have to do this music thing. It's all right."

"How do you feel about it?" he asked. "Is this important to you?"

"No, not really. But it is for the kids." She thought about what Lauren said, how it might be therapeutic for him to get out and help others. Others worse off than being blind.

"I'll think on it, okay?" He turned in her direction. "Which reminds me, didn't we also have plans for tonight?"

"Those plans were put on hold when you hit your head and almost suffered a concussion. Last thing I want is to have you overexert yourself tonight." She checked the rearview mirror, her heart skipping as red lights flashed behind her. It was only an ambulance, she realized, and pulled over to let it pass. The emergency vehicle sped by and her breathing eased.

Brent continued, in a low and sexy voice, "How about if I just lie there, and you can do all the work?"

"In your dreams," she answered sweetly. "Besides, it was not a well thought out plan. We can't have sex." But oh, how she wanted to. Yet she knew it wouldn't be fair to him, not when she planned to leave. It would also make it difficult for her to walk away. She had feelings for him now and if they made love and it was as wonderful as she imagined it to be—well, she might change her mind and endanger both him and herself. "I won't be staying for more than a month or two. It would just mess things up, and I like what we have now."

"Don't be logical. I like it better when you're not thinking clearly."

"That's some answer." She reached over to touch his arm. "I really enjoyed the day, and your friends are great. They love you dearly and want only the best for you. Just as I do, want the best for you, I mean." Her cheeks flushed, realizing that she'd almost told him she loved him. Oh, my gosh! Her feelings weren't that serious. She just liked him a lot. Too much, in fact.

"Sex is the best for me." A smile slid across his face. "It would be great therapy. Better than singing to kids in the hospital. And I know that you want some loving too. Come on, be honest. Wouldn't you like to play around a little before you move on?"

"What? And leave us both with broken hearts?" She laughed. "No way."

"Who said my heart would get involved? I take my relationships casual, remember?"

"So you say. But I'd rather we didn't go there, okay?"

"Yeah. Sure." He returned to staring out the window. "Not much I can do to sway your mind."

She left him to stew, knowing that he preferred the idea of having wild sex with her than being the blind man in her charge. Yet that's what it was, and for the time being, the way it needed to be.

Once they arrived home, Brent led the way from the underground parking to the apartment door, his fingertips brushing the rail. He knew exactly when to stop and found the lock on the door. Well, he'd gone up and down the elevator when he'd go for his swim, so he had that part down. They had to work on getting him to the store and back, down to the beach, a place where he could catch public transport. There was a lot of work to be done.

Sam barked once in greeting, then spun in circles to welcome them home.

"If you wait a second, I'll walk him with you," Brent said, heading toward his back bedroom. "I'm getting a Tylenol."

Poor guy. He'd hit his head pretty good. It must be throbbing. "Don't worry about it, Brent. I'll take him. You've had a long day, and Sam could use a nice walk. Don't you, boy?" She scratched his neck, then clipped on his leash, not needing the harness.

"You sure?"

"Of course I am. Your head is probably feeling like it's split in two. You've been a trouper all night."

"All right then."

Natalie let herself out, and Sam dashed to the elevator, dragging her with him. Obviously, he was in need of his walk.

When they reached the street, she checked out the surroundings. The well-lit street made her feel safe enough walking Sam at night, but Natalie knew to remain on guard despite appearances.

The boogeyman was real, and she could never forget for one moment that she was not safe.

They'd walked a couple of blocks in the quiet neighborhood and Sam found a spot to squat. She had the plastic doggie bag out when she looked up and saw a police cruiser inching by. He flashed his lights and lifted a hand in greeting.

Her blood went cold. She held her breath, barely able to nod in return and watched until the cruiser continued past and rounded a corner. Did Carl know people here? Had he planted someone to watch over her? Her paranoia spread like a brush fire in the Santa Ana winds. Air rushed out of her lungs and she stood there for a second, watching, waiting to see if it returned. He'd looked at her. Waved. Was it a warning? Or just a friendly neighborhood greeting?

Inaction could get her killed. Run, her mind screamed. *Run, Natalie, run.*

She jerked on Sam's leash, and the two of them raced the few blocks home. Sam, sensing her tension, stayed by her side.

When she got in the elevator, she leaned against the wall and took several deep breaths. The cruiser had done her a favor, reminding her how easy it would be to think that she could live a normal life, with normal people, and that nothing bad would catch up to her. The moment she got comfortable and let down her guard might be her last.

CHAPTER FIFTEEN

Brent woke up, head pounding, nerves tight. He'd had a piss-poor sleep last night, mainly due to the knock on his head, and concern over the fact he could see a little but not enough. What did that mean? He was getting his sight back, or this would be it? He'd live the rest of his days seeing things like a TV set having technical problems, a large gray fuzz.

Shit. He rolled over and looked at the wall. What color was it anyway? Damn if he could remember. It wasn't beige, but something darker, like mocha or something. Well, it looked gray now. He would make an appointment with the eye specialist and try to get in right away.

Hell, if his sight came back in the next few days, he wouldn't need Natalie anymore, and she'd be free to go. That should please her. And him. He wouldn't have anyone nagging him, telling him what he could or could not do. Sam could find another home too. Then he'd be alone, the way he liked it. He should be up doing a jig instead of moping in bed, but he didn't feel very damn enthused.

He got up, testing his eyesight, but it was still like seeing in a thick fog. Slightly preferable to the darkness though. Using his hands he found the window that faced the partial water view, and stood before it. Lighter than the walls. He tried to squash his excitement, but that tiny glimmer of hope crept in just the same.

Leaving the window, he went in to shower, letting the warm water run over him. He stood there for several minutes, breathing deeply, trying to kill the hope that leaped inside of him. It was better to live without any expectations, because then you weren't crushed when they didn't work out. It might be a sad outlook on life, but he'd discovered that truth along the way. No hope. No bitter disappointment.

He turned off the shower and toweled himself off. He squinted in the mirror, wondering what he looked like now, unsure if he'd even recognize himself. He'd lost weight; he knew that by his clothes. Jeans were hanging low on his hips. Khakis were a size too large. Not that it mattered. He didn't go anywhere special, if at all, so it was immaterial whether his clothes fit or not.

He rubbed his jaw, no longer liking the feel of the rough stubble. His hair should be on his head, not on his face. Hell, maybe he had hair growing out of his ears and nose for all he knew.

He grabbed his electric razor and decided to shave it off.

"What are you doing?" Natalie stood next to him. He hadn't heard her come in, but he could smell her scent again. Like some damn fresh fruit. Tempting you with sweetness, but could be sour to the taste.

"What does it look like? I'm going to shave."

"Uh-huh. I can see you've attempted that a few times, and if you don't mind me saying, it hasn't been that successful. You usually miss a patch or two." She took the shaver out of his hands. "Your eagerness to do everything yourself is commendable, but just this once—would you mind if I did it?"

He wanted to tell her that, yes, actually he did, but she was standing so close to him and his body was reacting to her, in ways that it shouldn't. Shane had been wrong to hire a young, attractive aide—an old biddy would have tortured him less.

"Turn to face me," she spoke calmly, seemingly unaware of the action that was going on under his towel.

He turned around, knowing his arousal must be evident by the way the towel was being stretched. Hell, let her deal with it. He hadn't invited her into his bedroom, or his bath. Or his life, for that matter. He hadn't made love to a woman since he'd returned, and if he got an erection now and then, good for him.

She gulped and took a step backwards. "Uh—why don't you sit on the commode, so I can reach you better? You're half a foot taller than me," she told him, although he'd already figured that out. Blind or not blind, instinctively he knew certain things. Like he had a pretty good idea that she had perfectly formed breasts, more than a handful, but firm and perky. He could almost see the high, round butt and her slender calves.

He didn't want to sit. He wanted to reach out and pull her close, let her feel his desire. To hell with common sense. Where had it ever gotten him? What was wrong with just doing what would feel good and to hell with the consequences? He liked being horny and thinking about making love to her. It sure beat lying around, feeling depressed.

"Sit, if you want me to give you a clean shave."

"I can think of other things I'd like more."

She laughed. "I'm sure you can, but we discussed that last night."

"That discussion hasn't ended."

"Shelve it or shave yourself."

He sat down. "Okay. You win. Do it. I want the damn thing off."

"Sit still. It will only take a minute." She took his chin in her hands and lifted it. "I've never shaved anyone before, but it can't be too hard. Right?"

"We'll see. If you nick me, I get to take revenge."

"Like what kind of revenge?" she asked, sounding out of breath.

"The kind you don't want to discuss."

"Well, in that case, I better not nick." She put her hands on his cheeks, and he didn't know what she was thinking, but he hoped she might kiss him.

She didn't. Instead, gently she put the shaver to his face and moved it around. "Wait. Let me kneel. I can't get under your chin." She knelt between his legs and continued shaving him, taking her time, it seemed to Brent.

"Okay. Perfect. You look good," she told him.

"Can I get up now?" he asked, his voice a little gruff.

She stood and pulled him up, and he bumped into her, hard-on and all.

She didn't move, but he could hear her breath quicken.

"You okay?" He held her elbow, not wanting her to leave. "You're breathing heavy. Like you've run a mile. Or did fifty quick push-ups."

Her breasts were against his bare chest and he could feel her laughter as well as hear it. "Oh, yeah, I'm more than fine. Seems like you are too."

"Morning erection. I'm sure you've seen it before."

Her hips were very close to him, and although he couldn't be sure, he had a suspicion that she moved a little closer.

"I'll remember that from now on." She stepped away, and he felt a sense of loss.

"I came in to say your coffee is ready. You ready for some breakfast?"

"Sure. I could eat something." He let the remark stand alone, knowing that what she planned on serving up was not what he hungered for.

"After breakfast we can take Sam for a walk then take you to the doctor's. Why don't you give them a call? Set up an appointment for later today." She touched his face. "Can you see anything this morning?"

"Not much. It's like a heavy, thick fog."

"Hmm. Better than nothing, anyway. It's a start, Brent. I'm taking it as a positive sign."

"Take it any way you like, but I'm not getting my hopes up."

He looked at her and could almost make out the shape of her face. He wanted to see her so badly—it was frustrating as hell.

She stepped back. "I'm making blueberry pancakes. Sound good?"

"With mango sauce?"

"We don't have mango sauce. Just syrup."

"What do I smell when you're near? Peaches, mango, something fruity."

"It's my body lotion. I change it every day." She laughed. "Tomorrow it'll be strawberry."

"That's just cruel."

"I want to stimulate your senses. It's healthy."

He grabbed her hand and pulled her toward him. "It's healthy all right."

She didn't fight when he bent down and found her lips. But she didn't kiss him back either.

"Mistake?" he asked.

"I thought we both agreed…"

"You did." He ground his teeth. "I didn't."

"It's best this way." Her small hand touched his chest. "You know that as much as I do." She lifted her hand and stroked his cheek. "This is hard on me too. I know what we should do, and making love is not it. But, believe me, I want you too. So you see I'm really, really trying to do the right thing here and I could use a little help!"

"I like kissing you, dammit! What the hell is so wrong with that?" He ran a hand over his face, feeling totally frustrated by her, by every damn thing in his life. "You want me and I sure as heck want you. I know that it'll be good."

"Maybe so, but I am trying to keep this professional between you and me. Now why don't you call that doctor? Maybe we can get in right away."

∼

Natalie made them the blueberry pancakes, then they both took a walk to the park. Brent had set up an appointment to see the ophthalmologist at four o'clock, so they had plenty of time to get some exercise and studying done.

Once she got Brent settled on a park bench, she tossed a ball to Sam and let him run around. She'd been pleased that Brent had agreed to come. It was a nice day, low seventies, a slight breeze, but after living all her life in the state of Washington, when most of the year was dreary and gray, this weather couldn't be beat.

If she didn't have an exciting job offer in Europe, she'd be highly tempted to stay. But Carl knew she was here in southern California, and if he came looking, she'd best be gone.

"Here, Brent. You toss for a while. My arm's getting tired." She plopped down beside him on the bench.

"What if I hit someone?" he asked.

"You won't. And if you do, they'll just get mad at me." She hugged his arm. "See, there's some advantage to being visually impaired. No one's going to give you a left hook, but me, that's a different story."

"I hope not. No one's ever hit you before, have they?" He turned in her direction, his face etched with concern.

Dammit! Why had she joked about something like that? Opened the friggin' door for questions, that's what she'd done. And she hated to lie to him. She only did it out of necessity.

"Of course not. Don't be silly." She nudged him. "Go on. No one is near. Give it a good throw."

"Okay. If you're game." He took aim and sent the ball flying through the air. Sam leaped with joy and pounded the turf after it.

"Hey. Did you ever pitch for the Dodgers?" she asked. "Pretty impressive for a guy who's been laid up for some time."

"Glad to see my arm still works. Got a few good parts still left in me."

She studied him for a moment, wondering how his aim could have been so good, and why he seemed interested in everything around him today. Did he see more than he let on? She'd love to be in the room when the doctor examined him, but likely she'd have to remain outside the door.

Sam barked and nudged Brent with the ball. He took it out of the dog's drooling mouth and tossed it again.

Natalie stood up. "I'm going to buy a bottled water. Want one?"

"Sure. Want some money?" He reached into his back pocket. "Take what you need."

"That's trusting. I could rob you blind."

He laughed. "Of course I trust you. Shouldn't I?"

She could take his wallet and just disappear into a new life. But of course she wouldn't, and he knew that. "You should. Thanks. I took a five and will bring you the change."

"Don't be long." He bent over to pat Sam on the head when he felt him nudge up against his leg.

"I won't." She headed for the vendor who sold cold drinks, hot dogs, and sandwiches out of his truck. A few people waited in line, and she glanced back at Brent and Sam. He was still tossing the ball, and quite well in fact. But then, he had played football in school.

"Two bottled waters, please." She took the five out of her pocket, and tucked the dollar change back in her jeans, then, feeling as carefree as a kid, she hurried back to where Brent sat on the bench.

She watched Sam drop the ball, then using his nose he pushed it closer and closer to Brent. He barked and jumped around in excitement, his tongue hanging out, a happy grin on his sweet face. Such an ordinary scene, except for the fact his master was visually impaired and couldn't see the ball that lay at his feet.

Natalie must have been about twenty feet away from Brent when she felt a pair of eyes on her. She glanced around and saw nothing unusual, just children and families enjoying the day. Still, a chill ran down her spine. She looked to the left and to the right. Why was she spooked? It was mid-morning with dozens of people milling about. An ordinary day.

She was about to call out to Brent when from out of nowhere someone grabbed her arm and pulled her hard up against him. Every nerve end stood on alert, and without even turning her head, she knew—she should have kept running.

Carl had found her.

She opened her mouth to let out a scream, but his hand clapped over her mouth. She could smell his familiar scent, a nauseating combination of Old Spice and swagger. Her throat tightened and she gagged. "Don't say a word," he whispered. "Walk with me."

She twisted and tried to break free of his grasp, but his iron grip held her firmly against his side. "You're a clever girl. Don't do anything stupid now."

Fear raced through her, but she knew if she cowered to him now, she would never be free. Raising her foot, she stomped on his as hard as she could. His grip loosened and she screamed and pushed at his chest. He stumbled back and she called to Sam. A second later, Sam bounded toward her, just as Carl reached out for her again.

Sam jumped on Carl, snarling, holding him in place. The dog had the cuff of Carl's sleeve in his mouth and was tossing his head back and forth, growling. A crowd gathered near, and Carl yelled, "I'm a police officer making an arrest. Someone get this dog off me."

Natalie knew she had to get away. Now. Before he could show his ID and convince people that he was what he said. The silver spooned tongue that he possessed could charm anyone who didn't know him the way she did.

She took off at a sprint toward Brent. Sam followed. "Brent—get up now! I'm in trouble. We have to go." Grabbing his hand, they darted down the path, back toward their home. Without knowing anything, Brent supported her, running so fast he nearly dragged her along.

The apartment was still five blocks away, and she was out of breath. "Please," she gasped, "not so fast."

Brent broke her hold and stopped running. "What the hell is going on?"

"I have no time to explain, but we have to go. Keep moving, just slower. I can barely breathe."

She could hear Carl behind her, gaining ground. She saw a group of young guys playing basketball, and headed for them. "Help me! Guy behind us—" she panted, "—is after me. Got a restraining order," she said, between gulps. "Please help me."

A young guy with big shoulders, baggy pants, and tats up and down his arms staggered over. "Is that the asshole?" he asked, arms crossed, legs spread, watching Carl's approach.

"Yes. Yes. My ex-boyfriend. He'll kill me."

"This guy blind?" he said, pointing to Brent.

"If I weren't blind, we wouldn't need your help." Brent answered. "I'm ex-military and happy to do what I can. Guy's dangerous."

Sam barked ferociously, and Brent put a restraining hand on him. "Down boy."

"Police officer," Carl shouted, waving his badge. He headed straight for Natalie. "I'm taking her in," he said, as the basketball players gathered in close.

"No, you're not," the tattooed guy said and lunged, striking Carl in the face. He went down. "Run, you two. We've got this dude."

"You like hitting women, do you?" the husky kid said and kicked him hard. His buddies joined in. Brent put an arm around Natalie and dragged her away.

EPISODE FIVE

CHAPTER SIXTEEN

Brent, fearing for Natalie's life, didn't linger, and this time he pulled her along. He could hear Sam panting as he loped along beside him. When they reached the apartment building, he pushed her inside, relaxing a little when he didn't hear footsteps from behind. Obviously the basketball players were keeping Natalie's ex occupied.

They stumbled into the elevator and Natalie collapsed beside him. He could hear her sucking in painful breaths, and knew she was bent over, gasping to fill her lungs.

He allowed her a few moments, struggling to control his anger and worry. It was not happening. "What the hell was that all about? Why didn't you tell me you had a lunatic for an ex?" he yelled once her gasping subsided.

"Soon as we get inside," she said, still breathing hard. "I'm sorry." She touched his arm, and he jerked away. He didn't want to be touched or placated right now. He wanted the fucking truth.

"I'll tell you everything," she whispered. "I promise."

He took the keys out of his pocket as soon as the elevator door opened and marched toward his apartment, without waiting for her or Sam. He had the door opened in seconds and glanced back in her direction.

"I'm fed up with your lies. Don't even think about making something up."

"I wasn't really lying," she answered. "I just didn't tell you the whole story."

He slammed the door behind her and made his way to the sofa. He put his head in his hands, rubbed his face, and tried to gain control. From what he could hear, she'd been frightened to death and could have been killed. Someone had been a real threat to her and he couldn't do a damn thing to help.

"Who is this guy? You said your ex? He's the jerkface you've told me about?"

"I'm sorry. I've not been completely honest with you, but I didn't want you or anyone to know that I was in real danger." She took a moment then continued, "Carl, my ex-fiancé is a sick bastard, and after putting up with his beatings for damn near two years, I finally escaped." She released a long shuddering breath. "It's humiliating to admit that I stayed with this man. Anyway, that's why I'm here."

The truth was worse than he'd expected. He felt a rage inside of him and wanted to smash something. Preferably the asshole's face. "You don't have to be ashamed. He should be. Fucking nutcase."

Brent wanted to wrap his arms around her and hold her tight, but he still needed some answers. "How did he know where to look?"

She swallowed. "When I first got to California I stayed with my friend Lori. She told her husband about the abuse and he told someone he knew." Her voice had a hitch in it when she said, "That's how he found me. Lori's husband, John, told a narc about me, who then told his supervisor.

When Lori told me this, I left her house and went to a hotel. Then I took this job with you." She whispered, "Guess the supervisor called Kelowna, Washington. So the trace got back to here."

She sank onto the sofa, next to him. "I would have told you but I couldn't. If you'd known, you'd have wanted me to call the police. Or to leave."

"I wouldn't have wanted you to leave. I would want to protect you."

"How?" Her voice was pitiful when she spoke, "You couldn't do anything. No one can. He got away with this before and likely will again."

"That can't happen," Brent said, confused by her attitude.

"Yes it can, and does. I was hospitalized once and told the police about his abuse and they protected him. Not me."

"You should have gone over his head. Someone had to listen."

"I would have thought so too. Now I know better," she said stubbornly. "Look, I'm sure it's not like that here, but there it is. It's a small town, and it's an all-boy's club. They protect each other."

She sighed and put a hand on his leg. But he wasn't in the mood to be cajoled. He shifted his leg and stared straight ahead, thinking about what she was telling him, and trying to make sense of it. He didn't believe that the whole police force could be corrupt, but he knew she believed it.

"I hate this," Natalie said softly. "Always watching my back, moving around, afraid to stay too long in one place."

"You should have told me," he said, with a little less heat. "We could have done something to keep you safe. Now that he knows you live around here, he won't stop until he gets to you."

He heard the sharp intake of her breath. "I know."

"You have to move again, don't you?"

"Yes. Yes, I should." She told him about the police cruiser the night before. "That could have been totally innocent, or he might have someone keeping an eye on me. He did that in Kelowna. Had people watching over me. Carl is cruel and likes to play with my head."

"How would he know anyone here?"

"I don't know." Her voice rose with frustration. "Maybe he doesn't. If he knew specifically where I lived, I think he'd have been here already. But hell if I know. Twisted bastard."

"We need to stop this and get you a restraining order. It's the only way you'll be safe. And free." Brent cursed. "This isn't Kelowna, Washington, and nobody here gives a crap about him. He won't be protected."

"I don't trust the system and besides, you saw what happened today. I was grabbed right out in the open in the middle of the day. He flashes his badge, and everyone steps aside."

"The guys playing basketball didn't. They protected you, and most people, including law officers, will." Brent pulled her close. "He can't get away with it. If he attempts to harm you, he'll be arrested." He kissed the top of her head. "You must believe that."

"I don't." She slipped free of his embrace. "I can't."

He let her go, although his arms felt empty. "I couldn't protect you today. But with Sam here, maybe... If you won't let me call in my friends, then I don't know how to keep you safe. I don't want you running for the rest of your life."

"You got me home safe," she whispered. "You nearly dragged my ass back when I couldn't run another step."

"Natalie. Don't cover for me, it only makes it worse."

She sighed. "I'm not. You're twice the man Carl is, and if you could have gotten your hands on that bastard, you'd have pummeled him good."

He didn't laugh. "Operative words. If. If I'd been able to see him, yes, then I might have been able to help."

"Well, we can't change that, can we?" She added softly, "We still have a little time before he finds us. I'll have to be careful about going out. But I promised I'd stay until you were confident in your independence. We'll just have to rush the process a bit."

"You're still in danger, now more than ever. If you want to stay, and I'm not sure that's a good idea, then it means you don't leave the apartment. Not to walk Sam. Not for a second." Helpless anger threaded his words. "I don't want you to go, but neither do I want you to stay."

"I was a prisoner of his long enough," she told him. "And I'm here to take care of you, not the other way around. I can go out with Sam if I don't go far. I won't get caught. I know his tricks too."

He could hear the tremor in her voice and knew to go easy on her. Poor girl was terrified, but determined to remain strong in spite of the personal danger. "I can walk Sam. He's trained to lead the blind, remember? That's his job. To walk me."

She touched his shoulder. "He's seen you now, and so you're a target too. But we have the underground parking. We could take the car and get out of this immediate area, and go for as many walks as we like. At least we won't be locked in here like prisoners. The way he wants us."

"Better just for us to remain inside," he said and reached out, pulling Natalie's head down to his chest. "Did you give Lori my address?" he whispered, brushing her hair back and caressing her cheek. He twiddled with her ear and continued lightly stroking her face.

"She knows I'm working for you, but I didn't tell her where. She didn't want to know." She clung to him and murmured, "Lori was so angry with her husband. It wasn't his fault. He thought he was helping me, but it backfired. Carl must have learned that the call came from Belmont Shores when he was questioned."

"So you knew he was coming here," he asked, "and yet you stayed?" He pushed her back from him. "Are you crazy?"

"I didn't know for sure. And I promised I wouldn't leave you until you were ready. Besides, I'm not ready to go. Not yet, but I'm working on it." She sucked in a breath and lifted her head. "Lori's trying to get me a work permit for France."

"France? You don't need to go to fucking France." His chest heaved, and a deep fury rose from the pit of his stomach. His neck flushed, and he felt himself choking. Unable to breathe. She'd put herself in danger just to stay and take care of him. What if something had happened to her? He couldn't bear it if she was hurt. The thought of this maniac coming all the way here to find her made him queasy. The guy would probably kill her given the chance.

He had to make her go. She wasn't safe. Not with him. "You should have just left. Gone to the Florida Keys or someplace. Instead you stayed here." He got up and began to pace. "I'm not an invalid, you know. I took care of myself before you got here, and I can do it again. I just can't take care of you." He cursed. "I want you to leave. Now. You have to protect yourself. Go pack your bags."

"I'm not going anywhere. I'll say when I'm ready to leave." She stood. "Not you, and not Carl."

"This is my place, and you work for me. Or did. I'm firing you." He put his hands on his head, wanting to tear at the hair that wasn't there. Frustration made him crazy. "You aren't safe and I don't want you here."

"You're not firing me and I'm not quitting either!" She shook his arm. "I don't take orders from you. Or anyone. I'm staying until you can do without me."

"You are the most stubborn, foolish woman I've ever known," he shouted back. "I have Shane and Sam. I sure as hell don't need you."

He heard her suck in a breath, and knew he'd hurt her. He wanted to apologize but didn't. He couldn't bear the thought of something happening to her. She mattered to him. More deeply than she should.

"You do need me. I know you do." She stomped off, and he heard her slam the bedroom door.

Problem was, he was starting to believe that he did need her. Not to survive. But to be happy.

Without considering his actions, he went after her, opened her door and grabbed hold of her. She trembled, her breaths coming quickly and he knew she wasn't afraid—never of him.

His mouth found hers and he kissed her long and hard, until there was no fight left in her. His knee felt for the bed, and pretty sure he was on target he pushed her down and fell on top of her.

She didn't push him away so he continued to kiss her, softer this time. His hand felt underneath her top and caressed her breast. She quivered, but didn't move his hand. She arched her back, pushing her breast farther into his hand, and moaned his name. He bent his head and suckled her breast over the lacy bra.

She held his head, keeping his mouth where it was. He snaked his hands around her back and undid the bra, giving his mouth better access. Licked the tips until they hardened and peaked, and then sucked gently until she squirmed under him.

"Brent, oh my God. Please, please don't stop." She kissed his head, "I need you... want you... so much."

"That's good, baby." He continued to fondle her breasts and his hand found her jeans' zipper and slid it down. His hand slid inside to her lacy undies. "I'm not going to stop. Not tonight."

She gasped, and he covered her mouth with his own, rubbing his hand over the warm center of her. He slid a finger under the edge of her lacy underwear and pushed it aside, then touched her lightly, slowly, letting the moment build between them. She moved to his caress, and he slipped two fingers in, finding her wet and hot.

He slid down on the bed and used his tongue, tasting her essence, taking his time, reveling in the pleasure it gave her and him. God, it had been so long, and he was so hungry. For this. For her.

"No," she moaned. "Not like this." She pulled at his shoulders "I want you inside me. Now, hurry."

He didn't need to be asked twice. He quickly slid his own jeans down and kicked them off, then removed hers over her ankles. Within seconds he had her naked, and wished with all his might that he could see her properly. He could taste her soft, sweet skin, smell her tantalizing fruity scent—pineapple?—and ran his fingers through her thick, lush hair. He tried to focus but her perfect body was still only a gray blur, a blur that he could touch and enjoy and make love to.

He entered her quickly and filled her deep. With slow, sure strokes, he met her thrust for thrust, sinking into her soft, female form, with effortless ease and immeasurable pleasure. So long since he'd felt a woman beneath him, legs tucked around him. He wanted it to last and to savor her for as long as he could. So close to peaking, he slowly withdrew, and when she whimpered he gave it to her again. Sliding in as deep as he could, then gently pulling out, he gave them both time to settle into a natural rhythm. He continued to kiss her, his tongue plunging inside her mouth, matching his movements, throat deep, then giving her a chance to breathe. Their bodies were slick with sweat as he slapped his thighs and hips against her, wanting to drive so deep he could never find his way out.

Natalie had her nails dug into his hips, and he relished the pain as he moved them both closer and closer to the climax. Her breathing hitched, her body went still, then she bucked once, twice. He picked up speed, reaching the top of the pinnacle, while bursts of light exploded in his brain, his vision floated, his ears began to ring. The blood pumped into his groin faster and faster as his chest heaved and shuddered, then, tumbling down on top of her, he found his release and they fell over the edge together.

~

She sighed, content. It had been everything she'd hoped—and everything she'd feared. He filled her body, he filled her heart, and he could easily fill her soul. He was everything she'd ever wanted, ever dreamed of, the prince charming she'd hoped to find. But she was a great big noose around his neck. He didn't need a troubled person like her. She was dead weight and he had enough problems figuring out his own life, let alone protecting hers.

Yes, she had to go, but not yet. Not until her papers came through. And leaving Brent? How could she? He'd wormed his way into her affections. Did he feel the same?

"Now what are we going to do?" she asked quietly, her emotions subdued.

He kissed her shoulder. "Well, we can't take it back, so why don't we just rest awhile and enjoy the moment?" His hand roamed over her ass, and tucked her in closer.

"No. We have things to do."

"Like what?"

"I don't know. Prepare ourselves."

"What? Right this minute?"

"Well, it doesn't have to be this very second." She smiled and kissed his neck, and let her hand trail down his belly. She knew they should get up but she just wanted to revel in the moment for a little longer.

"Good." His voice deepened with supreme male satisfaction. "Want to do it again? I'm still hard as a hammer."

She giggled and stroked him. "Yes, you are. But no. Body does, but unfortunately for you, my mind is being sensible." She pushed at his chest, but he didn't budge. She kissed his neck, then tried to slip away, but he wasn't having it. "We shouldn't have done what we did in the first place."

"I disagree." He rubbed up against her. "We needed this, and I firmly"—his rock hard penis nudged her again—"think a second round is in order. It's been about eighteen months since I had a woman in my bed. Well, not my bed, but you know what I mean."

"Since you had sex. Yeah, I know." She ran her fingers down his cheek and put a finger on his lips. "You're an amazing lover and totally sexy. And a sweetheart of a guy. I'm sure that when I leave there will be many women in your bed." She tried to keep the hurt out of her voice, but just the idea of another woman touching him, kissing him, loving him caused her heart to ache.

"I don't want other women. I want you." He leaned on an elbow and lightly touched her face. Then he smiled. "Why am I a sweetheart?" He scoffed. "No woman's ever called me that."

"Maybe you weren't before. The war probably changed you. Made you a nicer person. Someone who didn't drive across town to get over a broken heart." How long would it take, she wondered, before he forgot all about her? A day, a week? Maybe less than that.

"You still remember that comment?"

"Yeah. It rankled."

"Huh. I guess it did. Why?" He stroked her back, and kissed her neck. "No reason for it to bother you. I was only joking."

"It didn't sound like a joke. And I just think a lot of men take relationships way too casually. Feel like they can do anything they damn well please. It annoys me, that's all."

"And what about women? What do they want? To nest, have babies, a man to pay their bills?"

"You don't really mean that. Do you? You're just egging me on."

"Tell me I'm wrong," he said with a smirk.

She sat up and hit him with a pillow. "You are so out of touch, you don't know your nose from your ass."

He laughed. "I know your nose from your ass." He smacked her lightly on the bottom. "Go take a shower if that's what you want. I do have some things to take care of, calls to make. You're right. We'll turn this place into a fortress."

"You mean a prison," she answered sourly.

"I mean safe."

"I can't live in a prison. Not again." She sighed. "I know we have to keep the bad guys out, but it shouldn't be like that. Burglars, rapists, murderers, they get away with terrorizing innocent people every day."

"No one will get to you, Natalie. I promise you that."

"But what about you?" she asked softly. "You won't be safe either."

"During my short military career they called me Eagle Eye. And it wasn't just because of my eyesight either. I developed a strong sixth sense. I could sniff out danger even before it became real. I'll keep you safe, but you have to trust me."

She nodded and touched his chest. She did trust him, and she knew that he would do anything in his power to protect her. That was good enough for her. "So..." She let her fingers walk up and down his flat belly, watching his stomach muscles contract. She kissed his tummy, then whispered, "Does that mean I'm not fired anymore?"

He took her fingers and kissed them one by one. Then he shifted his weight to the far side of the bed and sat up. "We'll talk about it later." He stood, took a step and bumped into a dresser, cursed, then found his way into the corridor. "Meet you in the kitchen in ten minutes. Don't be late."

She laughed. "Yes, sir. I'll report for duty."

"Smartass."

Smiling, she walked to her own private shower and rinsed off. Her breasts were tender from his mouth and she could smell him on her. She hated to soap the reminder of him away, because time was running out, and she might not get another chance with him again.

CHAPTER SEVENTEEN

While Brent spoke to home security companies that Natalie had looked up on the Internet, she went out to the balcony to call Lori.

"It's me," she said in way of greeting. "Guess what? Carl's here. Yes, in Belmont. He's found me. Maybe not my exact location, but close enough."

"Holy shit!" Lori sucked in a breath. "How could he? John promised me that his narc friend knew what he was doing, and that he'd keep you safe. You are safe, aren't you?"

"For the time being. He tried to grab me, right out in the open. A public park, can you imagine! I managed to evade him. This time." Natalie took a few steadying breaths. "Look, don't give John a hard time over this. He thought he was doing the right thing, and I would have too, before I knew better."

"I'm going to kill him. Not give him a hard time." Lori swore. "The person who questioned Carl must have told him where the call came from. How could this have happened?" she cried. "Didn't that person realize he'd put you in danger?"

"I'm sure Carl made up some story. He's very convincing when he wants to be. And he has a clean record, as far as

I know. Go figure." She gnawed on her bottom lip, wondering if he was here alone, or if he had "buddies" helping him find his crazy girlfriend.

"John and I had a huge fight over this. I'm so sorry." Lori sniffed. "Look, are you holding up okay? It'll only be a week or two at most. I promise I'll call the French consulate's office and try to speed things up. Okay?"

Natalie let out a shuddering breath. The sex had released a lot of her tension, but this conversation had brought it back on. "Yeah. That'll be fine. Hurry, okay?"

"I will. And you tuck in somewhere and stay safe."

"You too. If he's found me, there's a chance he'll go after you. I don't think I ever told him about our friendship, but who knows what stuff he dug up on me."

"I don't think I have anything to fear," Lori answered. "But you stay protected, you hear?"

"I will. Don't tell anyone I called, okay?"

"You got it."

After she hung up, she put her back to the wall and peeked over the balcony wondering if Carl could possibly have learned where the blind man lived.

They were in a semicircle of apartment buildings, theirs being the last one on the right-hand side. His apartment was on the sixth floor, and they shared common grounds with the other buildings and a resort size pool. A few palm trees, a couple of picnic tables, a bike rack, that was all her limited vision could see. She could hear people splashing in the pool, and the shrieks of kids playing, but no one seemed to be lurking about.

She returned indoors and Brent was still on the phone. She touched his shoulder and leaned down to kiss his cheek, then sauntered into the kitchen to make sandwiches for lunch.

She slapped mayonnaise on four slices of whole wheat, layered in some fresh turkey breast, cheese, and thin slices of tomato. She cut the sandwiches in half, placed them on two plates, adding a handful of potato chips. While she worked, she muttered under her breath.

She didn't hear Brent until he came up behind her and kissed her neck. "What language was that? Didn't sound like French."

She turned to him with a smile. "German. I like to use my languages whenever I can, or my skills will be lost. So I talk to myself a lot." She laughed. "As long as I don't answer myself, right?"

"Right." He put his hands on her hips and pulled her up to him. "I have some other skills that I want to teach you."

She kissed him lightly. "Maybe later. Or maybe not." She slipped an arm around his waist and leaned her cheek against him. "I'm not sure about this. You make me feel things that I shouldn't."

"Like what?"

"Like I really like you. A lot. And I'm worried that if we continue to have sex those feelings will grow. And this situation is just temporary. You know that."

"It doesn't have to be." His chin had a stubborn tilt to it and she knew this was not what he wanted to hear.

"Yes, it does." She turned away from him and grabbed the two plates. "Go sit down. I made us lunch."

"Why do you keep insisting that you have to leave? Now that Carl made a move against you, threatened you in broad daylight, we should be able to get him arrested. Then you'll be free. Which means you can do anything you want."

"But I have a job in France," she reminded him. "Or will once the permits get here." It was safer that way, she told herself. If Carl avoided arrest he would continue to go after her, and Brent too. The less Brent knew about her future whereabouts the better. "Please don't ask me anything more about it. Just know that I'll be safe, and be happy for me."

Brent frowned. "If he's caught, you can be happy right here."

"Can we talk about something different?" Natalie poured two iced teas and brought them to the table. "Please sit and eat."

Brent grumbled something but took the chair next to her. He took two large bites and put the sandwich down. "Who were you talking to outside?"

"Lori. I warned her that Carl was here."

"Well, maybe her husband could let his friend know that the asshole grabbed you this morning. He should know that Carl is crazy and dangerous."

"I don't know who we can trust. I told her not to say anything."

"The police here aren't going to protect him, not once you explain how he's abused you for years. Believe it or not, most police officers are on the straight and narrow and are here to protect us."

"So you say. That hasn't been my experience."

"Okay, you ran into a few bad apples, but that doesn't mean the entire crop is ruined."

"Enough about this. What happened with the phone call? Are we getting an alarm system installed?" she asked, changing the subject.

"We are. Someone is coming here in a couple of hours and will see what we need. Should have it installed by tomorrow morning."

"Good. I'll sleep much better once we have this place safe."

"Speaking of safe. I have a plan."

"Please don't tell me it involves the police. Target practice would be good though."

He polished off the first half of his sandwich, and downed some tea before speaking. "While we're holed up here, I thought I'd teach you some self-defense."

"How are you going to do that?"

He grinned. "I don't have to see to know what I'm doing. And I can teach you skills that will keep you alive."

She thought about getting into a physical battle with Carl and grimaced. "I need a gun," she answered. "I should have bought one years ago. But I was afraid that during the night when he was sleeping I just might use it."

"I'm sorry your life with him was so bad." He reached for her hand. "But a gun is a bad idea. What if he disarmed you and took your weapon? He's a trained officer, and you're no match."

"So, self-defense is a better option?" She didn't keep the sarcasm from her voice. The idea of getting that close to him soured her tummy and caused fear to sprout inside.

"It better be." He finished eating, wiped his face, then pushed the plate aside. "Are you done?"

"Yes." She put her plate on top of his. "I don't have much of an appetite."

"Okay. Stand up." He stood and reached an arm out to find her. "Face me."

She did as he instructed. "Imagine me coming at you. You attack. Hit me hard."

She punched him lightly on the chest.

"Hard, damn it. I'm not as feeble as I may look."

She punched him harder, and he laughed. "Is that all you've got?" Playfully he jabbed her a couple of times, and that was enough. She didn't like being jabbed at.

Making a fist, she hit him as hard as she could.

Sam had been sleeping, but now he raced to Brent's side, barking and jumping around in excitement. He moved from Natalie to Brent, unsure who he should protect.

"That's a girl," Brent said. "Again."

"I don't want to hurt you." She would have no trouble putting up a fight if Carl attacked, but smacking Brent was another matter.

"Hurt me. I can take it." He stood straight, pushing his chest out.

"You sure?" At his nod, she let him have it. As hard as she could in the middle of his fine chest. At his surprised look, she dropped her hand, instantly contrite.

Sam howled, then went down on his haunches. He made whining noises, his dark eyes darting from Brent to her.

Brent grabbed her hand and twisted it behind her back, then spun her around. Her back was to him, his mouth next to her ear.

"This is what I'm going to teach you. If some asshole attacks you, he won't be expecting you to strike back. You can't overpower him, but the element of surprise is just as good."

"I want to learn that." Her arm was twisted behind her back, and she couldn't break free, but still she felt safe. She knew that in Brent's arms she would be protected, but he couldn't always be around. She needed to empower herself. "Now."

∼

Brent felt a surge of pride. At least he still had a couple of tricks in him and wasn't completely useless. Although, of course, he'd have to see the fist coming. Well, if he couldn't protect her, he'd make damn sure she could take care of herself.

He placed his hands on her shoulders and had her face him. "If you're in a public place and someone grabs you, first thing you want to do is scream for attention, then push back as hard as you can. You'll only have a few seconds to gain control so you'll need to strike quick. Aim for their weakness—the eyes, ears, nose, neck, groin, knee, and legs."

"But Carl's six feet and two hundred pounds. Fat chance I'd have."

"Nat, your size won't matter if you do it right, and I'm going to make sure that you'll know everything you can to arm yourself." He stopped for a second, knowing that what he could teach her might mean life and death. Her death.

The responsibility weighed on him, but he wouldn't let her down. He'd just have to rely on his instincts. They'd served him well before.

"What if I don't see him coming?" she asked, her voice nervous. "If he attacks from behind?"

"We'll get to that in a minute. First, let me show you the basic maneuvers, and we'll go over them every day until they're second nature to you. Okay?"

She shrugged. "I'm not sure if I'm up to this kind of thing. Wouldn't a shooting range be better?" She didn't want to engage with Carl in a fistfight, not if she didn't have to. "Ever see *Dirty Harry* or *Raiders of the Lost Ark*? They used a gun and got the job done."

"No, no gun. He'd turn it against you."

"Okay—I'm not convinced," she took a couple of quick breaths, "but if you're sure."

"Good girl." He lowered his voice and stepped closer. "If Carl is near enough to you, you can gouge, poke, or scratch his eyes with your fingers, or better, your knuckles." He showed her how to do both, and then added, "Not only does it hurt like hell, but might allow you time to escape."

"What if I can't get close to his face? What if he grabbed my wrist like he did earlier? I couldn't get away."

"Then we have another trick for him." Brent spoke softly, "Everything depends on how close he is. His positioning will determine which part of his body you'll attack."

"How will I know?"

"By the time I've taught you well, you'll know instinctively what to do."

She sighed. "I sure hope so. I'd hate to get into a physical brawl with him, because I know who'd be the loser."

"Not after I get through with you." He pulled her close and kissed the top of her head. "I'm going to make a warrior out of you."

She lifted her head and kissed him softly on the mouth. "I like that. And I'm ready to learn. Can we start now?"

"Sure, babe."

Patiently, methodically he went over basic techniques of self-defense, showing how to kick and where, and ways to use the hand as a weapon.

"By doing this," he used the heel of his hand as a weapon, "you can aim for his nasal bones, putting all your weight behind it. And if he's behind you, you can also use your elbow to break the nose."

She remembered the times Carl had held her down and punished her with his fists. He'd broken bones, but worse, he'd broken her spirit. She would not allow him to do that again. "Excellent. If he ever puts his hands on me again, I'll make him sorry."

"I hope you do, but this is just a precaution. By tomorrow we'll have this place as tight as Fort Knox, and if you curtail your activity outdoors, we should be fine until the police pick him up. And I know you don't want to hear it, but we do need to alert the authorities."

"Brent..."

He put a finger on her lips. "I know what you're going to say, but you won't ever be until you have a restraining order against him. He threatened you in the state of California, and he needs to be arrested."

"I know. I hope it happens too, but just in case we're wrong... teach me more."

He gave a frustrated sigh. "All right. Make the side of your hand into a knife again." She did. "The side of the neck is a bigger target, and you need to attack the artery and jugular vein. Keep the fingers straight." He put a hand on hers to see that she got it. "That's right, and keep them tight. Your thumb needs to be tucked and bent out of the way. You can also use your elbow on his throat, and your forward body motion for maximum impact."

"Good stuff. You really know how to hurt a guy." Natalie tried both tactics on him, but gently, of course.

"The knee is also a vulnerable target, and can be assaulted from every angle. You can learn to kick his knee without getting your foot grabbed. Try for the side of the knee."

She gently kicked him in the knees, as he showed her.

He grabbed her wrist, and through his coaching, taught her how to break the hold. "Good work, Natalie. You want to try some more?"

"I do."

He was about to show her how to get out of a choke hold, when the buzzer from downstairs rang.

"Who's that?" she asked anxiously.

"Must be the security guy. He didn't waste time."

They identified themselves, and he buzzed them up.

The fellow that showed up at the door was a thin man in a suit, carrying a briefcase with brochures of his samples. He looked in every room and came back to the kitchen table, sat down with them, and told them what he would do.

"We have safe, and then we have impenetrable, depends on what you're looking for."

Brent said, "I want to make sure that not even an ant can get in."

He laughed. "We can do that. All our stuff is state of the art, wireless and easy to install and use. Every window will have sensors, and both doors. We have motion detectors for outdoor activity, and inside too. Got infrared motion detectors, glassbreak sensors, a hardware exterior siren. Whatever you want."

"The best you've got."

An hour later, the salesmen left, and Brent twirled Natalie into his arms. "Okay, babe. It's not ideal, but at least we'll feel safe starting tomorrow. Tonight, I think it's a good idea if you sleep with me."

"Oh, you do, huh?" She smiled and kissed his chin.

"Yeah. You got a problem with that?"

He pulled her ass in and nestled up against her, giving her a taste of what was in store. "Unless you want to call the cops yourself and get an APB out for his arrest."

"Are you forcing me to make a decision?" She knew he was right. The police had to be told and the sooner the better. Carl couldn't be allowed to run havoc and continue to destroy her life. Not without a helluva good fight.

"I wouldn't force you to do anything you didn't want to do," he answered, his two hands cupping her cute behind.

"Okay. I'll sleep with you. But only because you're so irresistible." She inched back and she immediately felt the loss of him. "And you're right. Tomorrow I'll make an official report. The sooner I get Carl off my back, the sooner I'll be able to move on with my life."

"There you go again," Brent said, sounding hurt. "Always talking about leaving. What's the rush? Don't you like it here?"

"Of course I do," Natalie hastily assured him. "But we've both got things we need to do, and one of them is teaching you complete independence, which includes Braille. So come on, let's hit the books for a couple of hours, and then I'll fix dinner. You must be exhausted."

"It has been an active day, I'll give you that." He yawned. "I want to be around tomorrow when they install all this stuff, and then maybe we could go out. Take the car and get away from here. I'll feel safer once we have this place locked down."

"So will I," she told him.

They got the books out and spent an hour honing their skills. Even Natalie was learning to spell out words, and she felt a little proud of herself too. She'd always loved studying languages, and now she could add Braille into the mix.

Later, she whipped them up a casual dinner—baked chicken breasts with a wild mushroom sauce, rice, and asparagus. He had a beer and she enjoyed a glass of chardonnay and then they turned on the nightly news.

Brent lay back on the couch and within fifteen minutes of the news report, he was snoring softly. She watched him for a few minutes, and her heart turned to mush. There was so much to like about this man, and if she didn't have to go, she might be inclined to stay. But her future beckoned her, and all the dreams she'd had that had been put on hold were within her grasp. She'd never forgive herself if she let this opportunity pass.

She was only twenty-eight years old. And the past seven years of her life had been about pleasing others and stifling her own desires. Of course, she hadn't minded when it was her mother. Although the situation had been dire, and her mother was in a pitiful state, it had brought them closer than they'd ever been.

Natalie had always been a daddy's girl, whereas her sister and her mother were two peas in a pod. Thinking back, she remembered her dad tossing a ball with her in the backyard, taking her golfing at a par 3 course down the road. She hadn't even minded getting up in the wee hours of the morning to go fishing with him. She'd loved every minute of their special times together. Happy days and happy years, then something changed. Her mom and dad started to argue, their fights more frequent and louder. She and her sister had woken up in the middle of the night to hear her mother accuse her dad of having an affair.

He'd left for six months, then came back home, but things were tense around the house, and her mother emotionally shut down. Still, Natalie treasured the earlier memories, storing them up inside to take out once in a while and polish up, like other folks do their precious diamonds. During her teenage years, she could see her father pulling away, and in rebellion she'd acted out, hoping to get his attention, but it had only carried her down the wrong path.

Nothing she did made anything better; it only alienated her and made her angry and sad. Melanie went off to college and her father left the house for good. Six months later, her mother was diagnosed with cancer, and Natalie had taken care of her. During that sad time, the bond between them grew strong.

It was around that time that she met Carl.

Brent blinked and yawned, breaking her reverie. "What time is it?"

"You've been sleeping an hour. It's only eight. Too early for bed. You want some ice cream, or something?"

He stood up and stretched his arms over his head. His shirt lifted, giving her a yummy picture of his lick-worthy abs.

"I can get it. What flavor do we have?"

"We've got chocolate almond or butter pecan. I like both."

"Me too. So it'll be a surprise to both of us which we get." He guided himself to the kitchen and she sat up to watch. She knew he could do simple tasks by himself but still, she couldn't watch him without worrying. Would it always be like that? What if his sight never returned? Not that being blind meant a limited life. She knew that, but she hadn't quite accepted it. Not deep down. Neither had he.

"Come and get it," he said, placing the plastic bowls on the table.

Sam jumped up, tail wagging and followed her to the table. She tossed him a couple of treats before taking her seat, and wondered how long the poor dog would last inside without demanding to be taken for his walk.

She pushed the spoon around the bowl, without taking a bite. She wasn't quite as hungry as she'd thought. Her mind was all over the place tonight, and her emotions were stirred up.

Brent didn't seem to be having any trouble. He was gobbling up his ice cream, looking ready to lick the bowl.

"What are we going to do about Sam? He's going to need to go out."

"Not tonight. He can do his business on the balcony. We can put some paper towels down for him. He'll be fine."

"Maybe I could dash out just for a few minutes. It's dark out now. We could go out back, near the pool. It'll be safe."

"No. If anyone goes out, it'll be me."

Sam ran to the door and tugged at the leash that was on a hook.

"Shit." Brent slurped up the rest of his chocolate ice cream, wiped his mouth, and stood up. "I'll take him out back. You stay here."

"I'll come with you."

"No, you won't. You hear me, Nat. Not one word out of you." She could hear the frustration in his voice, but it didn't stop her. Being unable to go outside meant she was Carl's prisoner again, and she wasn't having it.

"Now, you're bossing me?" She raised her voice, determined to prove that she could make her own decisions, whether they were right or wrong. It was the principle of it, and damn if she would allow someone to take away that right. "I am so sick of people telling me what I can and can't do." She heard her voice break and sucked back a sob.

"Get used to it. You're not leaving this apartment unless I say so." He softened his voice. "It's for your own good."

"Don't tell me what is good for me." She saw red. It was as if he'd waved a flag at the raging bull inside of her. "If I want to leave, I will. You can't stop me."

He grabbed her hand and pulled her up against him. "Want to make a bet on it? You leave here, then keep walking. I won't be able to save you."

"You'd kick me out?" A wave of pain shot through her.

"I wouldn't be kicking you out. You'd be leaving on your own accord." She was standing so close to him that she could feel the body heat emanating from him. His jaw was set, and there was a tic in the side of his face. Angry, he looked hot.

She didn't say a word for a full minute. Her breathing came fast and furious. She wanted to punch him, or the wall, or something—she was so damn mad. But she knew he was not the cause of her fury, it was feeling trapped again.

"I'm sorry, Brent. I'm just flying a little high right now. Can't stand the thought that Carl has regained his control over me."

He wrapped her in his arms. "He doesn't. You're with me now. Safe."

"Thank you." She stood on tiptoe and kissed him. "You don't need to go out."

"I'll be back in ten." He snapped the leash on the dog. "Lock up behind me."

She did as he said, then went to the window and stood there, deep in thought. Perhaps she should pack her bag and go. Brent would be furious when he returned and found her gone, but he'd be better off. It would be safer for him. Carl only wanted her and he'd leave Brent alone.

But she needed to be able to protect herself. Today she hadn't stood a chance. If it weren't for those young guys shooting hoops, she'd never have gotten away. The one lesson in self-defense had not been enough to arm her, not with a big guy like Carl, who was trained in that stuff. In spite of what Brent said, she needed a weapon. That would surprise Carl better than the heel of her palm up his nose.

Being a military man, Brent might have a gun hidden somewhere in the place. She had a few minutes to search. If he did, where would he keep it?

She raced to his room and did a quick check of his closet, the back of his drawers. She'd been in both, but maybe it was wrapped up and she'd not noticed. No, if he had a firearm, he'd have it where it could do some good. Where would that be?

She ran out of the room, glanced over the balcony, and spotted Brent and Sam heading back. She only had a few more minutes.

She went back into his room, and got down on all fours, reaching her hand under the bed. There was nothing on the floor, but some instinct told her to reach higher, and sure enough she felt something, a holster in a sling, tied under his bed.

She withdrew the weapon, holding it tentatively with two fingers, and carried it into her room. She'd never handled a firearm, and didn't like the look or the feel of it in her hand. She didn't even know if it was loaded. It had to be, she reasoned. What good would it be to have an empty chamber if you needed the gun in the first place?

Dear God, what was she doing? Why had she taken it, if she wasn't prepared to protect herself and pull the trigger? She shivered just thinking about it. Where could she stash it until she'd figured what she wanted to do?

She opened her underwear drawer and stuffed it in the back, just as she heard the front door open.

She froze. Of course it was Brent; she'd seen him only a few steps from the apartment building. And yet fear shivered down her spine. Sweat trickled down her breast. Logic didn't matter. It didn't make sense for Carl to show up in Belmont Shores, but he had.

She swallowed hard, and peeked out the bedroom door.

CHAPTER EIGHTEEN

"Natalie?" Brent called, cursing the gray fog that prevented him from seeing. Every so often it would clear a little, like a storm cloud passing, then come back again. The fragmented glass thing had slowly dissipated, and he was back to where it was before the boating incident. "Where are you?"

Sam barked and ran down the hall. He skidded to a stop, and Brent guessed he'd parked himself in front of the guest room door.

"I'm here, Brent," Natalie called, and he listened to her footsteps as she came near. Relief washed through him. He knew no one could get inside, but the silence had frightened him. Everything about the day had been a holy terror. He didn't want to lose her, not to France, and most definitely not to the lunatic, Carl.

"Hey, Sam, what's up?" Natalie scratched behind the dog's ears. Sam yelped with joy. "You enjoy your walk?"

Brent thought she sounded breathless, her voice pitched slightly higher than usual. She stopped a few feet away from him, and he waited to smell her fruity scent. He knew she was there, but instead of pineapple or mango, or any one of the dozen tantalizing scents he'd come to associate with her, this was different.

It was acrid and pungent, like human sweat and fear.

He knew his sensory powers were heightened now that he was blind. Temporarily blind, he corrected himself. From years of fighting dangerous fires, and his missions in Afghanistan, he knew that unmistakable scent. Had something happened when he was gone?

"You okay?" he asked.

"Sure. Why shouldn't I be?"

"Not sure." Her indifference didn't fool him. He knew fear firsthand—he'd felt it many times, and recognized it in men stronger than himself. "Were you worried about me?"

"Yes. Silly, wasn't it?" She gave a short laugh. "I'll feel safer tomorrow when we get the sensors installed."

He put his hands on her arms. "We could call the police right now. They could come and take our statements."

"No. I'm not up to it. The questions, the stories I'd have to tell." She shuddered. "Tomorrow will be better."

"Okay." He held her close and felt her tremble. "You're safe for tonight. I won't let anything happen to you, I promise."

"Good. Let's not think about him anymore. I don't want to give him that much power. It's just you and me—alone in your bed."

He kissed her cheek. "I like the sound of that, and tomorrow, after we have everything installed, we'll go to the police station and tell them everything. I'll be with you, supporting you. We can face this together."

"Okay. Our history—well, it's not pretty. I don't want you to think less of me."

"I won't. I promise. You were very strong and brave today." He chuckled. "Those fellows this morning hopefully roughed him up a little. Put him in the hospital with any luck."

"They went after him with a vengeance." She gave a nervous giggle. "It's possible," she concluded.

"Right. If he's still able to walk, he might have hightailed it out of here, gone home where he belongs. Either way, let's forget him for now." Brent slipped a hand behind her back. "Why don't you take a bath or a shower, unwind a little?"

"I might do that." She sniffed her clothes. "Yikes. You're right. After all the crazy stuff we did today, I never got around to cleaning up. Sorry about that."

He patted her backside. "Take all the time you want. And I promise not to do anything except hold you safe. Unless you want to, of course."

"Sounds good to me." She turned and lightly kissed him on the mouth. "Thank you."

Brent knew that for all her brave front, she was shaken up badly by the run-in today. And so she should be. Carl grabbing her at the park had been a gutsy move and it showed his cockiness and God complex. The man truly thought he could get away with anything. And that scared him most of all.

Taking Sam out earlier had given him a few minutes to walk around and listen to the sounds of the night. There had been no whisper of anything unusual, and he trusted his senses enough to know that no one had been lurking about.

They were safe until tomorrow, and then the place would be impenetrable. He worried about Natalie—she was so skittish, her emotions on an uneven keel and might put herself in harm's way, unwittingly. He'd just have to make damn sure she didn't.

While she was in the shower, he went to his room to check on his gun. He sat down on the bed and felt underneath. Instead of feeling the firm, solid edge of his revolver, the holster felt empty. He dropped to his knees and felt around some more.

It was gone.

Natalie came into the room. "What are you doing?" she asked, her voice quivering.

"I was looking for something." He stood up. "Were you in my bedroom while I was out? My gun is missing."

She was silent for a moment, then her breath came out in a rush. "Yes, I found it and I took it. I'm sorry. I thought I wanted the extra protection but it scares me even worse."

"Where is it?" Brent fought back his anger, knowing how fragile and desperate she must be.

"In my bedroom. Top drawer behind my undies."

He marched off and came back a second later with it in his hands. "What the hell were you thinking?" So much for controlling his anger. He had an urge to shake some sense into her, since words weren't enough. But that would make him no better than Carl, and he wasn't that kind of man. No matter how pushed, he'd never physically frighten her.

"I figured I should leave," she said in a low voice. "You're safer here without me. I don't want anything bad to happen to you."

He put the gun back in the holster, then said softly, "Come here."

She took two steps forward. "Don't do anything like that again," he whispered, and held her tight. He kissed her forehead and rested his chin on the top of her head. "We're in this together. I don't need protection, and I'm not going to let you run off and face this danger alone."

She gulped. "Okay," she murmured and nuzzled in closer. "Sorry about the gun."

He could smell the sweet flavor of her, feel her warm soft body melded into his, and it only heightened his own anxiety. If anything happened to her...

She disengaged herself and moved toward the bed. "I'll sleep against the wall. Come, Brent. I'm wearing the pink nightie."

"In a second. I want to check the doors and windows one last time." He walked away, saying, "Tuck yourself in. I'll be right back."

She slipped into bed, and he double checked the doors and windows, and made sure all the lights were off. They were on the sixth floor and it was highly unlikely that anyone could scale the walls or enter from the outside, but he was glad to have Sam watching over the place.

When he returned to the bedroom, he heard the soft sound of Natalie breathing and knew she was asleep. He slipped into bed beside her. She stirred and turned over. Her butt was next to him, and damn if it didn't make him hard. He shifted, moving up behind her, putting a protective arm over her waist.

She cuddled closer. "Brent," she breathed. "Touch me."

"Thought you were sleeping," he answered and nuzzled her neck. His hand slid under the covers and found her breast.

"I heard you come in. I want you close to me, Brent, keeping me safe."

"Is this close enough?" His throbbing dick ached to rest between her sweet cheeks.

"Oh, my. That's getting closer." She flipped over. "I really like you, Brent Harrington. You make me feel... oh, so many things, but right now, you just make me feel hornier than hell." She sighed. "I know it's wrong, but at this moment it's right."

He laughed and took her mouth with pleasure. He kissed her hard and deep. She matched him tongue for tongue, and her hot little breaths and soft whimpers made his ache infinitely worse. He wanted her too. Deeply, intimately, body, heart, and soul.

His hand slid down, touching her, stroking the most intimate part of her, as if he owned it and had every right to be there. She might think she was leaving, but oh, he so wanted her to stay.

"Is that good, baby?"

She answered by moving against his hand. Her breath caught, and he used his middle finger to flick back and forth against her sweet spot, which earned him a shuddering sigh. She pulled away from him.

"I've got to get your pants off," she told him and tossed the blanket aside. She knelt over him and pulled down his boxer shorts. He sprang free.

She sucked in her breath, and then a half second later, he felt her tongue and moist mouth sliding up and down his shaft. Holy mother in hell, being blind might have some pleasant surprises after all. His senses were heightened, and nothing had ever felt so good.

He reached for her breasts and tweaked one nipple until it tightened and peaked. When he'd had enough of that, he lifted her up and guided one into his mouth. He suckled that baby, lathering it with his hot tongue. She pulled away and straddled him, then a moment later she mounted him and he was inside.

He put his hands on her hips and pushed into her, feeling the frenzy between them build. His cock was buried into her sweet warm flesh, and panting, she begged him for more. He arched his hips and held on, driving himself deep, then flipped her over onto her back. With her under him, he was able to slow it down, sliding all the way in, and retracting a little.

She dug her nails into his back. "Don't you dare go anywhere," she murmured. "Now. I want it all."

Well, his mama always told him not to argue with a lady.

He drove himself to the hilt, and didn't stop until she whimpered, shuddered, and cried out his name. Then, and only then, did he find his own sweet release.

EPISODE SIX

CHAPTER NINETEEN

Natalie closed her eyes as the moment built. She could feel Brent in every inch of her, all the way past the rib cage, deeper into her heart and soul. Her mind exploded and she cried out for him, wanting to hold on to this moment forever before she lost him for good.

The aftershocks were stronger than she'd ever known. Her emotions were so fragile, so new, so wonderful, and yet they filled her with dread. She didn't want to lose him, but they were both struggling with their own demons, and lost in a fog. Until they could figure out their own lives they could never commit or be together.

She rolled off him. "Wow. That was hot." She kissed his neck, then put her head on his chest. "Guess you didn't forget anything in your year of abstinence." She put her hand down and found him still hard. "I think the rest did him good."

He chuckled. "Might have. And I'm glad I pleased you."

"You didn't please me," she responded. "You gave me a big whopping 'O,' and I can't remember the last time I had one." She kissed his chest. "You're an amazing lover and an amazing man."

She watched him smile, knowing her praise did a lot for his confidence. That had not been her ulterior goal, but it was an added benefit. He hadn't taken pride in himself for a long time, and he should. He was everything a man should be—courageous and strong, but still so gentle. She dropped little kisses all over his chest and neck, loving him for as long as she could.

She wanted him to be happy when she left. He probably wouldn't be at first; he might even hate her some too. How could he understand her need to leave if Carl was no longer a threat? It wasn't that she didn't care about him deeply. She did and always would, but her job in France was already arranged, and she couldn't disappoint the couple expecting her arrival, or Lori, who'd worked so hard to get her this position. More importantly, it was her personal choice as well.

She couldn't let go of her unfulfilled dreams and never have an adventure of her own. He had had plenty, but she had never done half the things she'd set out to do. She needed to grow and learn to be independent and strong, instead of leaning on others. She needed her own confidence to soar. Only then would she be able to give everything of herself and not hold anything back.

He rolled over and tucked her in beside him. "Sleep tight. We have a big day tomorrow."

"Thanks for everything, Brent. Especially for being you."

He kissed her shoulder, but didn't answer. A few minutes later, she heard his soft snores.

Natalie was unable to sleep, and her mind slid relentlessly from one thing to another. Why had she thought to take his gun? She didn't know how to shoot and probably wouldn't have been able to pull the trigger if she'd tried. Taking someone's life? As much as she hated Carl, she knew she couldn't do him physical harm, unless her own life was on the line.

She fell into a troubled sleep in the wee hours of the morning, and was awake again at dawn. She snuck out of bed early and took her shower and was dressed when he finally stirred.

"Up, up, sleepyhead," she said, ripping off his bed sheet for no particular reason except to enjoy the sight of his male body.

He stretched and yawned. "Did I dream last night?"

She dropped a kiss on his lips, then stepped out of reach. "No, it was real enough. And no, we can't do it again. Hurry up. Coffee's made, and I want to practice some more of those self-defense moves you showed me yesterday. Before the security guys get here. I don't want them watching me beat you up."

"You're pretty cocky this morning, aren't you?" He grinned. "I don't think you'll be getting the better of me, but I'm willing to give it a shot." He sat up. "Extra bonus points if you can take me down."

"Deal. But not on an empty stomach. Want an egg muffin?"

"Sure. I'll take a quick shower. Give me ten."

"You got it."

She left his room and headed for the kitchen. She took the frying pan out, grabbed the eggs and two cheese slices from the refrigerator, and poured her second cup of coffee. When the skillet was hot, she sprayed it with a coating and gently dropped two eggs into the pan. A pair of English muffins went into the toaster.

She leaned against the counter and sipped her coffee as she waited for the eggs to sizzle. She hummed under her breath. For someone with a sick, twisted ex-fiancé after her, and her life in jeopardy, she sure was in a good mood.

That was just wrong.

∽

When Brent came out of the shower he could hear Natalie speaking gibberish, another foreign language he couldn't make out.

"Coffee smells good." He kissed behind her ear. "So do you." He sniffed. "What is it this morning?"

"Watermelon." She poured him a cup of coffee, black, and handed it to him. "Eggs are almost ready."

"I like watermelon. Especially refreshing in the morning."

She punched his arm, making him splash coffee on the floor. "What?" he asked in an innocent voice.

"You know what." He heard her mopping the coffee from the tile floor. "Don't even go there. We've got a zillion things to do today and that's not one of them."

"Just saying."

"And I'm just saying that the men will be here in an hour or two, and I want you to teach me stuff." She put the breakfast plates on the table. "Come. Let's eat."

He took his usual seat and bit into the sandwich. He wiped at his mouth where he'd dribbled some cheese.

"You're a good cook. Probably will make somebody a darn good wife."

She laughed. "Are you really as old-fashioned as you sound sometimes? Or do you just like busting my balls?"

His lips quirked upward. "You've got balls? Where do you keep them hidden?"

"No place you need to know."

He heard her fingers tapping on the table and knew the lighthearted moment was over. "So what else can you show me today," she asked, "or do you just want to reinforce that other stuff. The palm in the nose. The kick in the knee or groin. See, I was paying attention."

"I'm glad you were. Might prevent an attack, but I hope that never happens." He slurped his coffee. "We'll do a refresher and I might show you one or two more steps. Don't want to overload you."

While Natalie cleaned up the dishes, Brent went out back to take Sam around the common grounds. They returned a short time later.

"Guys will be here in less than an hour," Natalie told him. "So, let's go. We have a bet that I can't take you down. What do you say, Sam? You think I can do it?"

Brent took the leash off Sam and sensed that Natalie was standing near. Before he had time to react her foot snaked around his knee and exerted pressure. He buckled and fell on all fours.

"What the hell?" he sputtered.

"Oops. Was that fair?" She laughed. "Remember the element of surprise."

He grabbed her leg and pulled her down on top of him. He found her tummy and tickled her as Sam jumped around them in excitement.

She laughed and kissed him, then pulled him to his feet. "Sorry, Brent. I couldn't help myself."

"Okay, smartass. You proved you're devious, now let's make sure you're effective." He showed her how to get out of a choke hold either in front, or from behind. "Pull his fingers back if you can, then rotate like this, to break his hold." He twirled her around. "Attack by kicking or stomping on his feet. These things sound like common sense maneuvers, and for the most part they are. But doing it correctly is critical to be effective."

He reinforced the pressure points and how to use the forward weight of the body as leverage against the attacker. They ran through the routine time and time again, until Brent was relatively sure that she knew the basic moves sufficiently to disarm an unsuspecting attacker like Carl, who'd think she'd be too frightened to strike back.

There wasn't a cowardly bone in her body, Brent figured, but he hoped that theory would never be put to the test.

They had time to shower and then the service men showed up. Brent and Natalie tried to stay out of their way as they went to work. It wasn't a large apartment but both bedrooms had small windows, and of course the balcony was most vulnerable.

Once they had all the wireless sensors in place, infrared motion detectors, new locks installed on the front door, panic buttons in each room, and a monthly contract for this home security, one of the men said, "We have one more thing we can install if you like. It's a voice monitor warning the intruder that he's been detected. Should scare the pants off a guy."

Natalie answered before Brent could say a word. "I want it."

"You heard the lady. We want it." Brent took Natalie by the hand and they went out to sit on the balcony until the workers were done. Sam sat at their feet, tied to the rail. He'd been a nuisance for the past hour, following the men around, trying to nip at their feet.

"How do you feel about all this? I don't know how else to keep you safe."

"It's good, Brent. Thank you for doing this. You could have just asked me to leave."

"Never." He laced his fingers with her. "You okay about talking to the police? You're not going to back out, are you?"

"No. It's the thing to do. Someone will believe me. Why would I make this up?"

"You wouldn't. Can't understand why he got away with it in Washington either."

"Maybe I didn't pursue it enough. I was too scared, I guess. I figured his partner knew, and a few other guys he hung around with. But that was just his group, not the entire force."

"Well, we'll make sure this goes to the very top. The fact that he came here to threaten you is enough proof of his guilt."

"Unbelievable, isn't it? Like he thinks he's above the law and can get away with anything."

"Well, he's not going to. You'll be free of him at last." Even as he said the words he realized that that meant she'd be free to leave him as well. He felt a pang, a tightness in his chest. She would go. He couldn't stop her and wouldn't if he could. What kind of life would that be for a young woman, trapped with a man who couldn't see beyond today? He couldn't ask Natalie or any woman to share his life, not until he had things figured out, a career in mind, some damn inkling as to what his future held.

CHAPTER TWENTY

Natalie's mind was calm during the short drive to the police station. She had little choice but to report Carl's most recent attack on her, and didn't want to spend one more hour as a prisoner of his making. Besides, the upside was well worth the risk.

Brent didn't have much to say on the ride, and she wondered what he was thinking. Probably asking himself how their worlds had collided. She was supposed to be looking out for him, and instead he'd ended up protecting her. It wasn't fair, but she knew as an honorable man he could do nothing less. By rights he should fire her ass instead of getting mixed up with this, plus he'd laid out thousands of dollars for that new security system, and yet he wouldn't turn his back on her.

"Brent. I'm sorry. This isn't your battle and I never should have brought my problems home to you."

"You didn't," he said shortly. "Seems like Carl wasn't through with you yet. He's the one causing the problems, not you."

"I'm supposed to be helping you, not the other way around."

"You have helped me. In more ways than you know."

Her throat tightened, and she swallowed a lump, feeling very emotional suddenly. She wasn't going to cry. She had to be strong. For him, as well as for herself. Until Carl was caught, every second they were both in danger.

"What am I going to tell the police to make them see how dangerous he is?" She licked her bottom lip. "I have no physical proof. Even the hospital records will state that I took a bad fall. It's his word against mine."

"He came after you. Here in California. Grabbed you and tried to force you to go with him. Waving his shield around, as if he had a right to make an arrest." He spoke with disgust, "Who the hell does he think he is? He's not an officer of the law in this state."

"I did take his car and sold it in Oregon."

"He can't arrest you in California, no matter what you did. He has no authority here. Sooner he knows it, the sooner we can have some peace."

"I agree." She was quiet for a minute, thinking about how much she could tell the cops. What about the fact he'd forced her to have sex after a fight? They'd been living together, was that still rape? And what about the few times he backhanded her when she'd made a comment he didn't like? She had put up with it, so perhaps she'd been a willing accomplice. Why hadn't she simply walked away? At the beginning, she could have told him to stay away from her, but she hadn't known the depth of his cruelty. She'd been lonely and he had played on that.

"What's on your mind?" he asked.

"I'm worried, Brent. Even after he grabbed me yesterday, I have nothing to show for it. No bruises. Just my word. And you couldn't see what was happening."

"I have ears. I could hear well enough."

"I know and I'm sorry I put you through that. I should have told you the truth instead of that ridiculous made-up story, but I've been ashamed for so long." Her stomach knotted. If she had ever lied to Carl he would have exacted his revenge, one kick and one punch at a time. But Brent would never lift a hand to her.

"No need for you to be ashamed with me."

"Thank you." She bit her lip and sucked back tears. Then she reached out a hand and squeezed his knee. "So after the police station, let's get away from here. Far away from your apartment, him, and leave all our troubles behind. It'll be a celebration."

"Not sure what we're celebrating, but I definitely would like to take you to dinner."

"Great. I haven't been to many places since I got here, so you pick the place."

"We can drive up the Pacific Coast Highway and see where we land. Sometimes, it's best not to over plan."

"Good enough." She dreaded the conversation with the police, but she was glad she had Brent at her side. He was strong, honorable, an officer with the United States Army. They'd believe him.

They were nearing the police station when her cell phone rang. "Mind getting that outta my bag? The only person who has my new number is Lori."

He fumbled inside her oversized bag and found the cell. Handed it to her.

"Hey, Lori. Did you call?"

"It's John. I'm at the hospital. Lori's been beaten up and the police are on their way. She wanted me to call you." He released a long shuddering breath. "Shit, man. What the fuck is going on? She said it was your old boyfriend, but he's in Washington. Right?"

Natalie swerved, straightened the wheel, and pulled over to a stop. Her heart leaped into her throat, and her stomach churned as fear and anger raged inside. "What happened to her?"

"She hasn't said much. Just wanted me to call you."

"I'm on my way. Emergency?" she asked.

"Yeah. She's in one of the treatment rooms."

She hung up. Brent turned in his seat to face her. "Carl?"

"I think so." She closed her eyes, thinking of her friend, lying there in the hospital, beaten up. Oh, she wanted to kill Carl. If only she'd kept Brent's gun. "We have to go to the hospital." She felt sick inside and hoped she wouldn't lose her breakfast. She sucked in a couple of quick breaths and wiped the beads of sweat from her forehead.

"Right." Brent spoke calmly, but his jaw was rigid, and there was a tic in his cheek. He looked ready to explode but was holding it in for her sake. "Hopefully, you both can give a report to the police at the same time."

Twenty minutes later they pulled up in front of the ER at Long Beach Memorial. She parked in the lot and they both walked in. Security took their photos and handed them a visitor's card before they were given a room number and directions.

When they found her room, John jumped out of his chair. "I'm glad you came." He grabbed Natalie and held her close. "I'm so sorry. This is all my fault. I should have believed you and not trusted the cops." Tears glittered in his eyes as he pulled away. "Lori was hurt because of me."

She glimpsed her friend on the hospital bed, her head wrapped in bandages, only her eyes and mouth visible. Natalie's knees went weak. Damn Carl—the sick bastard. Why had he hurt her friend? It was her that he wanted. Lori was an innocent victim here—she'd befriended her and allowed her to come and live with them, given her a job.

"John, don't. This is my fault, not yours." She sucked in a breath and tried to steady herself. She couldn't break down now.

She gave him a hug, wanting to erase his guilt. "The police should be trusted. Most of them anyway." She moved past him to take her friend's hand. "Lori, Lori..." Her voice broke. "I'm so sorry, honey. What did he do to you?"

Lori licked her dry lips and struggled to answer.

Brent had been standing in the doorway; now he made his presence known. "John, I'm Brent Harrington. Natalie's been staying with me." He groped his way forward and stopped when he bumped into the bed. "Did Carl attack you, Lori?"

John opened his mouth, staring at Brent in confusion. Then he glanced away. "You're blind," he said, shaking his head.

"Blind, but not disabled." His head whipped around in John's direction. "I don't intend to let this maniac get away with this." He turned back to the women. "Was it Carl, Lori? He grabbed Natalie at the park and we were lucky to get away."

Lori whispered, "Yes."

"He'll be punished for this." His voice was hard, with an edge to it that Natalie had never heard before. She realized she wouldn't want to cross this man, but he was a good person to have in your corner.

John glanced at Natalie. "Why would he show up here and come after my wife? How did he know where we live?"

Lori answered. "He's a detective, so I guess he can get information. He wanted to know Natalie's whereabouts." She sobbed. "I would have told, but I didn't know."

Natalie carefully hugged her friend, afraid of hurting her further. "It's okay. I'm so sorry. I should never have come here. I should have kept running, and kept running, until I had no place left to go."

Lori had been her best friend in college. They'd studied together, partied together, comforted each other over heartaches, bad grades, and celebrated every success along the way. She was closer to her than her own sister. The only person she had trusted with her deep dark secrets, and who had loved her enough to open her home, her heart, and invite her in.

She linked fingers with her. Tears welled in her eyes. Lori was lying in the bed broken and wounded. She'd taken Carl's punches for her. It was so unfair. "Lori, Lori, can you ever forgive me?"

She sniffed, but couldn't hold back any longer, and a sob ripped out of her. Brent put his arm around her and she turned into him. "What can we do?"

His hands ran up and down her back, as if to soothe her. "You both are going to make a statement to the police, and he'll be picked up for questioning. He has to be made accountable for what he's done. It's the only way you're ever going to have any peace." Brent kissed her lightly on the brow, then pulled away. "With your permission, John, we'd like to stay while the police question Lori."

He nodded. "Yes. It'll be a big help. With both of you testifying, he won't get away with this." His voice shook with fury. "Asshole thinks because he's a detective, he's above the law. But not in California. No fucking way."

"How long ago did you call the police? They're taking their sweet time," Brent muttered, clearly agitated.

"Why don't you have a seat?" Natalie said gently and guided Brent toward a chair. The tension is the room was palpable, and both men were losing their cool. Hoping to keep things calm while they waited, Natalie told Lori and John about Brent.

"Brent's a former helicopter pilot. Used to work for CAL FIRE before he went to Afghanistan." She squeezed his hand. "I've been staying with him, helping out since he's only recently out of rehab."

John spoke. "You lost your sight over there? What happened?"

"My helicopter crashed into a mountain. Head injury which resulted in damage to my visual cortex lobe," Brent answered shortly.

Natalie piped in, "He's hoping to regain his sight. Right, Brent? You're able to see shapes and shadows, instead of just darkness."

"Sometimes. It comes and goes."

"I'm glad you two met," Lori said and tried to smile, but the effort ended in a grimace.

"Just rest," Natalie said to her. "Do you have anything broken?"

"My jaw. Nose too."

"Oh, my God. I'm so sorry. Do you want to break mine, so we'll be even?"

Lori's eyes lit up as if she smiled. "Come over here. Let's see if I can."

Just then two police officers entered the room.

"I'm Officer Martin," the tall gray-haired one said, "and this is my partner, Officer Sheldon." He walked over to the bed. "Can you tell us what happened to you, ma'am? We'll need to take down a complaint."

Lori told the officers how she'd come home to find Carl waiting for her in the garage. He'd demanded to know where Natalie was hiding, and when she hadn't told him anything, he'd proceeded to punch her repeatedly in the face.

"He was waiting for you in the garage? How did he get in?"

"We have a keypad outside and our code is pretty simple," John said sheepishly. "It's 3333. Guess it didn't take him too long to figure it out."

"You may want to change that," the officer answered. "And you know for a fact it was Detective Carl Warner, although you say you've never met him?" He looked skeptical. "How can you be sure?"

"Yes, I'm sure," Lori said, "because he asked about Natalie."

"I'm just trying to get things clear. You say he's here for Natalie but he came after you? It couldn't have been a disgruntled employee, or anyone who might have a reason to harm you?"

"Of course not!" John snapped. "My wife told you who did it. Why aren't you out looking for him?"

Brent stood up. "He tried to get to Natalie yesterday in the park."

"Who are you?"

"Brent Harrington—former Warrant Officer in the U.S. Army."

Natalie spoke up. "I'm his aide. And yes, it's Carl, and I'm the one he's after," Natalie said. Then she proceeded to tell her story.

"Thank you, ma'am. We have enough information for now, but please don't leave town. We might have more questions for you. Meanwhile, we'll put out a warrant for his arrest." Officer Sheldon closed his notebook and took a few steps toward the door.

He stopped and turned. "This is quite a story you told us." He pulled at his ear. "You were hospitalized with a broken leg and jaw and the authorities didn't believe you?" he asked Natalie. "And now, someone from that department told this detective that you're here in southern California, so he came after you." He shook his head. "Basically, you're saying that the whole department's crooked. Is that right?"

"I didn't say the whole department. But he's got friends covering for him. How many, I don't know." Natalie took a step in the officer's direction and looked him dead in the eye. "I hope we won't have the same problem here."

Brent put an arm around her, showing his support. "I can attest to the fact he's here, and that he's a real threat."

The two police officers glanced at the four angry faces and retreated. "We'll be in touch."

CHAPTER TWENTY-ONE

After the police departed, Brent and John spoke quietly in a corner, running possible scenarios past each other, while the women chatted. During a lull in their conversation, Brent overheard Lori tell Natalie that she'd been at the consulate's office checking on her work permit.

His chest tightened and he felt like someone had kicked a hole in it. She was going to leave. He knew she would, but not yet. Brent waited for an appropriate moment to speak up. "Natalie, we should probably go and let Lori get some rest."

"Of course," she agreed, getting out of her chair. "I'll check in on you later," she told Lori, and kissed her gently on the forehead.

John walked them to the door and promised to call the moment he heard anything.

As they made their way toward the parking lot, Brent stopped Natalie. "What's going on with that work permit? Has it come through yet?"

"Not yet, but soon."

"You still want to go to France? Why? You could stay here."

"Please try to understand. You've had plenty of adventures in your life, while I haven't had any. I need to learn to stand on my own two feet. If I stay here..." She brushed past him, but he grabbed her arm.

"'If I stay here,' what?"

"I will depend on you. I don't want to do that."

"So you want adventures. Why can't we have them together?" He knew he shouldn't badger her, not now, when her friend was in the hospital and Carl was still running loose. But he couldn't bear the thought of letting her go.

She grabbed his shoulders. Her voice shook. "I told you we couldn't get involved. We never should have slept together. It was a mistake. I knew it would be."

"That was not a mistake. We are good together." He tried to take her into his arms, but she wasn't having it. "If Carl is arrested, you don't need to go. You can stay."

"Don't you understand?" She swallowed hard. "My life was put on hold after my mom got sick. I never got to fulfill my dreams." Her voice cracked. "I wanted to do something really great. Something important, besides teaching school."

He shuffled his feet. He knew he should shut the hell up, but something deep inside of him clung to the hope that he could change her mind. "Well, I'm sure you still can. Doesn't mean you have to go to France, does it?"

"Look. You lived the life you chose. I haven't lived mine." She sighed deeply. "Thing is, I don't want to leave you either, but we both have some growing to do. We have to figure out our own lives before we can ever think of a future." She added, "I'm going to be a tutor for a very nice family with three young children, and live in a country estate an hour or so from Paris. Doesn't that sound perfect?"

"Not to me." He frowned, still unable to let go. "Are you sure you're still not running away from something? Afraid to commit?"

"I want this and it's something I need. I hope it'll be an adventure of a lifetime, and... and... if you can't understand that then..." Her voice hitched. He heard her footsteps running off. She'd left him standing there.

Afraid to take a step, he stood and waited for her return. If he followed her onto the road he might be run over. Likely by her. Deservedly too. What an ass, he'd been. The long and short of it was—he liked her and didn't want her to go.

But he couldn't clip her wings and keep her with him, any more than Carl could.

A few minutes later, he felt a hand tugging on his sleeve. "Come on. I'm sorry I left you, but you pissed me off."

He smiled. "Yeah. I know I did. Sorry about that. I acted like a real jerk. But you know how I feel about you, or if you don't, you should."

"I know and I feel the same, but that doesn't change anything. I still have to leave."

"Well, not tonight. Look, let's put this behind us and enjoy the time we have. Maybe you'll forgive me over a nice dinner. Let's go out."

"Not tonight. I'm not in the mood. Let's grab some takeout. What about Chinese or Thai? Know any good places nearby?"

"Sure do. Just around the corner from our place."

They made a quick stop for the food, and a half hour later they parked in the underground lot, and took the elevator to the sixth floor. They entered and turned off the new security system they'd had installed earlier today. Sam greeted them by dancing around, sniffing at the bag of food.

"Hey boy." Brent bent down to give him some scratches behind his ears, and some loving. "You take care of the house when we were gone?"

"Woof woof." Sam lapped at his face, and then raced around the living room.

Natalie laughed. "He's so smart. I'm sure he knows everything we say."

She took the food containers out of the bag, and grabbed some plastic plates from the cupboard. "You want to take Sam out for a quick walk, or wait until after we eat?"

Sam made the decision for him. He raced to the door and barked.

Brent grabbed his leash. "Back in ten minutes. Lock the door behind me."

"Will do, boss." She followed him to the door and he waited to hear her lock it.

God, he was going to miss her when she was gone. He liked her lippy attitude, her spunk and spirit. Thank God, Carl hadn't been able to beat that out of her.

Soon as they got outside, Sam pulled at the leash, stopping to take a leak in every bush. Once again, they were in the common area between the apartment buildings and near the pool.

"That's a nice dog you've got there."

He turned in the direction of the voice. "Yup. A service dog. Smart as a whip."

"I'm sure he is," the man said. "You had him long?"

"No. Just got out of rehab a few months ago."

"What happened to you?"

Brent didn't like talking to strangers about his blindness or his time at war. Personal questions were just that—personal. Besides he had some spicy Thai and a spicy woman waiting upstairs.

"Nothing to tell. My sight's returning slowly."

"Yeah? How does that happen? Now you see things, and now you don't?"

The man stepped toward him, and Brent's internal antennae sprang to action. He let the leash out, giving Sam more leeway. "Have a nice night," he said, ending the conversation, and headed toward the back door.

"See you around," the guy answered back.

Brent had a bad feeling in his gut. It might not be Carl, but his intuition told him it was. The familiarity of the voice nagged at him. He'd only heard Carl's for a few adrenalin-ridden seconds, but he was pretty sure it was the same. Wouldn't take a lie detector on it, but still.

He knocked softly on the door of his apartment. "It's me," he called out.

"Brent?" She opened up. "Good. I don't know why I was worried. Just had a funny feeling."

He locked the door again, then wrapped his arms around her and pulled her in close. "I had a strange encounter downstairs." He told her about it, adding, "It might not have been him, but as a precaution we need to stay inside and keep safe until he is apprehended."

"God, Brent. How would he have gotten into the common grounds? The gates are all locked and don't they have security cameras everywhere?"

"Not in this building complex. It was built in the eighties, and they've improved security some, but not in the common areas." He let out a breath. "Still, he'd know how to work his way around that."

"I see. And you're right, a little thing like a camera wouldn't stop him."

He gave her a kiss. "Nothing we can do about it now, unless you want me to call the police."

"No. We don't know for sure, and even if we did, I'm just not up to another police encounter today. I've had about all the drama I can take."

"Figured that's what you'd say. Well, we're safe inside." He slipped an arm around her, and gave her a reassuring hug. "I'm just going to wash up, and then let's eat. We've got some work to do tonight."

After they chowed down and cleaned up, Brent took out his gun and showed Natalie how to load a weapon and how to fire. "We can go to a shooting range tomorrow if you like." He couldn't help but tease, "That'll get you out of the house."

"I'll like that."

Brent ran his hand over her hair. "A woman should fill her day with hair appointments and manicures. Not with target practice."

She laughed. "Good God. Did you actually say that? Where were you raised? Hillbilly land?"

"No, but my mother never worked. Dad's new wife doesn't either." He cleared his throat. "Not that I have anything against a woman working. Matter of fact, my lead pilot was a woman. Linda James. Bright, tough, and quick as a whip."

"Wow, glad to hear it. You had me scared for a while."

He chuckled. "I feel protective about you. That's why I seem to say a lot of dumb things."

She kissed him, and he didn't mind the fact that she turned him into an idiot.

"Okay. Now for some more defense work. I'm gonna make you as tough as Captain James."

"Was she your girlfriend over there?" Natalie grabbed his hand and twisted it around his back in one of the moves he'd shown her. She breathed down his neck. "Did you play rough games like this?"

"No, she never gave me the chance. Or any of the men. Don't think we were her type. But I do remember a certain nurse that I knew."

His arm was locked behind his back, and she was right close behind him, so he got a leg around hers and she buckled, breaking the hold. He spun her into his arms. "This is what I did to her." He lifted her chin and took her mouth, plunging his tongue deep, tasting her, wanting her.

Her hands grabbed his ass, and she pulled him close. "What else did you do to that nurse?"

He lifted her shirt and felt her warm flesh beneath. His hand reached higher until he found the curve of her breast. One hand snaked around back and undid her bra, giving him better access. He filled his hands and teased the nipple then bent to suckle one in his warm mouth.

"You did that?" she asked in a husky voice.

"I did worse."

"Show me then. Don't just tell me."

He unzipped her jeans and stuck a hand inside. She sucked in her tummy, and his hand was able to slip into her panties. "I touched her down here."

"What did she do?" Her voice was choked. "Did she unzip you too?" Her fingers deftly had his button undone and his fly down. She ran the back of her fingers against his erection.

"Did you get hard for her?"

"I'm sure I did." He was about busting out of his pants, and thankfully, she pushed them down. "Yeah. I remember she did that to me. Then my shorts too."

Natalie giggled. She put her hands into his shorts and stroked his shaft. "But first, I bet she did this."

"Oh, maybe a time or two." His voice sounded strangled. "I think she put her mouth on me."

"I'm sure she did." She continued her upward stroking then ran a damp finger over his tip. "Does that feel good? As good as the nurse?"

"What nurse?" He grabbed her, and because his pants were down around his ankles, toppled on the floor. She came down with him.

He managed to kick his pants aside and get on top. "This is exactly what I did to that sweet nurse. Are you ready to find out?"

"Oh, yeah. I'm ready. But I'm warning you. I'm sure I'm not as easy."

He dipped a finger into her, and it came out wet. "You wanna make a bet? I'm going to have you screaming in about three secs." He lowered his mouth and found her sweet spot in under one. He licked and tasted, his tongue hot and greedy, flickering over that sweet little nub. His hands were under her buttocks, lifting her for better leverage.

The more she moaned and groaned, the more he gave her.

She had her hands on his shoulders, hanging on for dear life. Her fingers dug into him as she began to peak.

Then suddenly, she buckled under him and cried out his name.

He kissed between her thighs, then lifted his head.

"Like taking candy from a baby." He smiled with pride.

"Not fair." She smacked him lightly on the top of his head. "You cheated."

"Cheated? No." He kissed her softly on the lips. "That was just the way the nurse liked it."

CHAPTER TWENTY-TWO

"Was there really a nurse?" Natalie asked, flipping over so she could rest her head on his chest.

"Do you really want to know?" He ran a lazy finger down her back and she tingled with pleasure.

"No. I don't think so." Her hand began to stroke him. "I prefer that we make our own memories. You don't mind, do you?"

He nipped on an earlobe and put a hand on her ass. "I'm good with that."

"You're good with everything." She kissed him softly and continued stroking. His cock pulsed in her hand. Her tongue slid into his mouth and deepened the kiss. He had his hands in her hair, and his tongue down her throat. His erection prodded her tummy, begging for attention.

He was hot. He was ready and she owned it.

She broke the kiss and straddled him, planting herself on top. He slid in and filled her deeply. His hands cupped her breasts as she rocked against him, at first slowly, then gaining momentum. She controlled the movement, taking him deep, backing off, then giving him her all.

He groaned, and grabbed her by the hips and held her firm, pushing himself into her in one frenzied movement that she met with equal fervor. The momentum built to a crescendo and she couldn't hang on for a second longer, and cried out his name. He shuddered inside her, and she collapsed on top.

They lay on the floor wrapped in each other's arms for what seemed an eternity. Natalie was sure she'd dozed off, and woke when she felt a warm rough tongue on her foot. Sam.

She pushed herself off Brent and stood up. "Whatcha doing, old boy? You want some attention too?"

Brent sat up. "Did I fall asleep?"

She grinned and ran a hand over his head. His hair had grown out a smidgen, and was a little more than a buzz cut. She wished she could stay long enough to run her fingers through it, but it was not meant to be. Well, she'd just have to make as many memories with him as she could in the short time they had.

"We both did," she told him. "Sam woke me up. Didn't you, boy?"

He ruffled Sam's sleek coat, and got a lick on the face in return. "I need a shower. Want to take one together?"

"A quick shower. But we should go over your Braille again tonight."

"No way. We've got too much on our minds to worry about that."

"I know, but time is not on our side. We need to do this." She pulled him to his feet and put an arm around his back as they headed for his shower. "No monkey business, okay? We had our fun, and now we have to hit the books."

"Yeah, yeah, yeah. I like you playing nurse better."

She laughed. "I'm sure you do."

He turned the shower on, waited for it to heat up, then stepped under the hot spray. "You coming?"

She slid in next to him, grabbed a bar of soap and generously lathered them both. His body was wet and slick and it was so tempting to be taken away by the sensuality of the moment and give in to more pleasure. Her fingers ached to touch him, to caress his hard muscles, his still admirable erection, but she needed to stay focused. All this sex was great, but every time he kissed her she felt she loved him a little more. It was a scary thought. The love was growing even as she tried in vain to stop it. It had a life of its own—sprouting like a seed that didn't need nurturing, just a warm bed in which to grow. Her heart thundered at this new revelation. If she gave in to all her carnal desires, she might not have the will power to walk away at all.

"What are you thinking?" he asked, turning off the shower and grabbing them each a towel.

"My mind is in so many directions, I'm not sure how to answer." She sighed, not wanting him to have an inkling of what she'd discovered. If he knew her true feelings, he'd never understand her need to go. "I'm worried about Lori, and wondering why we haven't heard anything from John or the police."

She rubbed herself down and wrapped the towel around herself.

"I could give them a call, if you like. Maybe mention the guy downstairs, suggest they have a look."

"Good idea. I'll get dressed and then we'll see if there's any news."

She put on her Victoria's Secret sweats and pulled her damp hair back in a ponytail. It was only eight o'clock but she was exhausted from all that had happened during the day. The good, the bad, and the ugly.

Brent was on the phone when she returned to the living room. She put a hand on his shoulder, and he shook his head, indicating nothing. "I'm sorry, John. Give our best to Lori, and we hope she has a good night's rest."

After he hung up, he said to her, "John didn't have anything to report, but I called the police a few minutes ago, and they are going to check downstairs and keep a cruiser watching the place."

"That's good. I'm sure we'll sleep better knowing they're taking the threat seriously."

"Better believe it." He yawned. "I'm beat. You wore me out."

"It was an active day. I'm exhausted too. Maybe we could skip the Braille tonight and get on it first thing in the morning. Before our shooting session."

He stood up and stretched. "You want to come to bed, or watch TV?"

"You go on. I might unwind in front of the TV. I'm a little too wound up to sleep."

"Crawl in with me, anytime." He kissed the top of her head. "I don't mind if you wake me."

"Sure, but don't wait up. I've just got a lot on my mind."

"I'm sure you do." She watched him walk away, and wondered why her life had to be so complicated. Here was a man that she was beginning to love, but she couldn't give him her heart, not wholeheartedly. It had to heal first, and so did she.

Carl had stolen so much from her. Her past and now her future too. They needed to subdue their desire and keep the eye on the prize. Getting Brent self-sufficient and capable of living alone was the end goal. That was her job, and all this romance and sex was sidetracking them both. Besides, it was much too easy to confuse passion with love.

~

Brent went to bed alone, wishing she had wanted to come with him. Although they had great sex, she was still keeping a part of herself tucked away, and that was the part he desired more than anything. Still, he knew he couldn't ask her or any woman to share a life with him. Not the way he was. Whether he regained his sight or not, he needed to figure out his plans for the future and learn some new skills. Until he became even a shadow of the man he used to be, he couldn't expect the love and respect from a woman like Natalie.

She was intelligent, educated, kind, and loving in nature, but life had thrown nothing but rotten lemons her way.

She wanted to keep things status quo so she could leave without regrets. It was probably a smart decision on her part. He sure as hell didn't want to be the one who held her back. She needed to go out in the world and carve a life for herself, not play caregiver to a zero like him.

He'd make sure he armed her properly before she left for France. She needed to be someplace safe, and live in the light, not the darkness he knew.

As he closed his eyes, he could hear the voice of Linda James echoing inside his head. "You pathetic wimp! I thought you'd have pulled your shit together by now. What are you waiting for? You want a life—go get it. You want a woman to love—then do something besides feeling sorry for yourself. The Harrington I knew was tough and wouldn't lie down and give up. Get up and fight, dammit, or I'll come back and do it for you."

Brent put the pillow over his head. "Leave me alone, and bug someone else. I'm going to make sure she's okay, then let her go. And why are you hanging around bothering me, James? Don't you have anything better to do?"

Her eyes turned fierce. "Not till you man up, Harrington. Fight, fight, fight."

With those words ringing in his ears, Brent tossed and turned and eventually fell into a fitful sleep.

He woke up to the smell of coffee and the sound of Natalie singing. What the hell did she have to be happy about? Her friend was in the hospital, her crazy ex was stalking her and would kill her if he got a chance, and she was stuck here with him.

Didn't seem like anything to sing about.

He wandered into the kitchen in need of caffeine.

"Good morning, sleepyhead. Or should I say good afternoon?"

"What time is it?" he grumbled and found a cup out for him next to the pot. He poured and sipped.

"It's past eight. I already took Sam out for a quick walk."

"You did what?" He moved so abruptly, he splashed coffee down his bare chest. Fury swept over him, and he tried to control it before he did something he'd later regret. She didn't need anyone screaming or bullying her, but damn he wanted to give her a good shake. "What the hell were you thinking? You have a death wish?"

"No, I don't have a death wish. Did you just burn yourself?" She got up and wiped his chest. "Need ice?"

"No, I don't need ice." He gritted his teeth. "Now will you please explain what possessed you to go outside?"

"I called the hospital and spoke to John. He said Lori had a good night. They've set her jaw and her nose, and the pain meds are keeping her comfortable. She should be released either later today or by tomorrow morning."

"Still doesn't answer my question. What about Carl? Lori might be better off staying put until he's apprehended."

"The police officers came back first thing this morning. Told John that Carl's wanted for questioning, not only in California but back in Washington."

"That's interesting. Tell me more." He slugged some coffee back and managed not to spill on himself.

"Seems as if Carl was married before. His wife died in a boating incident and her body was never found. It was considered a suspicious death since he'd taken a hundred thousand dollar insurance policy on her the year before." She took a sip from her coffee.

"He got away with it?" Brent asked.

"Apparently he claimed they were deep-sea fishing in the Puget Sound and ran into some bad weather. Said he went downstairs to radio for help and when he came back on deck, she'd disappeared. But according to the reports her brother said she hated boats, and would never have gone fishing. She got seasick on their honeymoon, a Carnival cruise, and never had anything to do with boats since."

"So they think…"

"There's more. He had a girlfriend before me who died in their bathtub. Looked like drugs were involved, and it was called a suicide. So you see, women die around this man." She shivered. "He's ten times worse than I thought."

"And yet you went outside?"

"Yes, because I knew I was safe. I spoke to Officer Martin right after talking to John. They have a patrol outside our place, and one at Lori's too. He's going to pay for his crimes."

"But until he's caught, he's even more dangerous. Especially if he knows they are onto him."

"Dangerous, yes, but this is good in a really bad way."

"Two women are dead—what can possibly be good about that?"

"That's the bad part, and I'm really, really sorry for those two women. But..." She took a sip from her coffee, and seemed hesitant to say more.

"But what? I don't get you."

"People believe me now!" she cried. "He will get caught and be punished. I feel as though an enormous weight's been lifted from my shoulders."

She put an arm around his waist. "It's horrible for me to admit this, but it means I'll be free. I can't help those poor women, but knowing about them strengthens my case."

"The police should have been onto him sooner." He was still angry that she'd gone outside, and was torn between shaking her and wrapping her in a protective hug.

"I know, but now I'm really hopeful that he will be caught. And soon."

"So why did you step out of the apartment this morning? Alone?" He released a long breath. "Instead of tempting him, you have to be more careful than ever."

"They have a patrol car cruising our neighborhood and another parked in front of Lori's. They're going to get him. Then he'll know what it's like to run."

"Until we know he's in custody we can't go outside. Could be hiding anywhere, and we could easily be followed."

"I'm not staying locked up. I refuse to be his victim again." Her voice had that stubborn tone he knew so well.

"It could be a matter of hours or a few days. Stay safe with me and let the police do their job. At least you know they're going to investigate this time."

"If he comes near me, I'll stomp on his foot and break his effing nose. Like you showed me."

He chuckled. "I'd like to see that, I would." He kissed the top of her head. "You're one brave soldier."

She sighed and hugged him tight. "Like you. Maybe I'll get a medal too."

"I don't have a medal, sweetheart. Just a discharge." He was silent for a second, figuring out their next move. If he had his sight back he might be more game, but now he preferred to exercise caution. "Okay. I'm going to teach you a few more tricks. These are lethal, and you probably shouldn't use them unless your life is in the balance."

"Trust me, if Carl somehow gets past the police my life is at risk."

CHAPTER TWENTY-THREE

"Okay, big guy. What are you going to teach me now?" They had moved back into the living room and Natalie was amped. The word "lethal" not only got her blood pumping, but her spirits as well. She almost relished the idea of getting her hands on Carl, and taking it to him. For Lori, and for all the times he'd abused her.

She made two small fists and punched Brent lightly on the arm.

Sam jumped around her, snarling and nipping on her heels. "Sam, go sit. We're just playing." The dog lowered his head, and lay on the carpet nearby. He looked docile, but she noticed that he kept one eye on her at all times.

Brent cuffed her hands and put them down. "First of all I want you to watch some videos and get an idea of what might be expected of you. It won't be pretty, but trust me, when it comes to a street fight, you don't want to play by the rules. This is survival defense, military style."

"Yes," she said, triumphantly. "I like it already."

"This isn't a game, Natalie. It's brutal and it's ugly. But I want you to see it, and to practice the moves just in case.

I wouldn't ask you this if I thought I could protect you, but we both know I can't."

"Don't say that. I trust you with my life."

"You shouldn't. As much as I'd like to be your hero, I'm not."

"You are so wrong." She heaved a sigh. "Okay. Where's the video?"

"On the computer. I don't own the tapes but I should. Go to Street Fighter training website. This guy, Robert LeRuyet, is a master instructor of military grade BJJ. That's short for Brazilian jiu-jitsu. The Russian military in the old Soviet Union used a similar combat method."

"Holy crap! I'm going to be a secret weapon."

"I hope so. Let's say he won't be expecting it, anyway."

Natalie found the website and downloaded the five self-defense videos and sat through most of them. Her stomach churned and she wasn't as titillated by the idea of crushing Carl's skull as she had been before.

"So, you want to try to act anything out?" Brent said quietly, sitting in a computer chair directly behind her.

"No. I don't have the appetite. Maybe later."

"I'm sorry, Nat. I know it's brutal, but I want you prepared in case Carl somehow gets to you before the police get to him."

"Right. I get it. Don't like it, but I get it." She stretched her arms over her head and arched her back. "I'm stiff from sitting. Maybe we should take two coffees down to the patrol car on the street. That would get us out for a second and we'd still be safe."

At the mention of going out, Sam raced to the door and started barking.

"See, even Sam wants to."

"What about danger don't you understand?" Brent didn't sound amused. "You're an infuriating woman, with a very thick head."

"My head's not thick, and you don't have to get mad. I'm not going anywhere, unless you think we should go to the shooting range?" Her mood brightened at the thought. "Can we? That will get us out for a little while, and we can take Sam. Could stop for fast food burgers and fries," she added as an incentive.

"Why don't we just stay put until we hear from the police? He's sure to be found soon, and it would be a shame if we were at the range when the call came through." Brent slipped an arm around her. "In fact, you might want to stay away from the windows."

"But we're on the sixth floor."

"There's an apartment building on the left that has a direct view of this place. I'm not saying it would be easy, but he's a detective, and I'm sure he's learned a few tricks in his day."

"That's truly scary." She rubbed her arms. "Why haven't the police caught him?"

"That's the million dollar question." Brent stood close to her and instinctively she moved into his arms. "You all right?" he asked, his voice taut with worry.

"Yeah. Just need to be held for a moment. Then I'll be fine."

"Glad to be of service." He dropped his chin onto her head, held her tight, and she could feel his heart beating next to hers.

She soaked in all his strength, his compassion, his warmth, and let it settle in deep. She breathed him in, feeling a comfort that hadn't been there before. "Thanks, Brent. I needed that." After a quick kiss she disengaged herself. "Okay, what do you want to do if we can't go outside?"

"I have some ideas to entertain ourselves and they don't require getting out of bed."

She laughed, sorely tempted. "That was a leading question, wasn't it? I have a better idea. We did say we were going to spend the morning learning Braille. Why don't you do that while I study my killer defense moves on your iPad."

"Could do, but I still vote for suggestion one."

"You're insatiable," she told him.

"You'd be too if you hadn't had any in a year and a half."

"I wish I hadn't," she murmured. "It was awful." Carl had not made love to her in a long, long time. It was all about his exercising control and power over her, and toward the end, when he knew that she no longer loved him, he'd made damn sure that she hadn't enjoyed a minute of it.

"I'm sorry, that was an insensitive remark."

"It's all right. You didn't know what my life was like."

Sam whined and stood next to the plate glass windows. Natalie opened the door and let him out. They had a doggie pad in one corner which would have to do until they were free to leave.

Out of the corner of her eye, she saw a bright light flash from the building on their left. The apartment complex had three separate buildings that were in a semicircle facing the pool and the common grounds, and offered a glimpse of the ocean two blocks away.

She squinted, trying to make out what she had seen. Then she froze, as a terrible thought entered her head. Was she in his crossfire? Could it be a rifle, or had Brent's warnings simply made her paranoid?

Not wanting to find out, she stepped back and hid behind the drapes.

"What's the matter?" Brent spoke quietly, sensing her fear.

"Nothing. I just let the dog out, and thought I saw something across the way. I'm just spooked, that's all."

"Better spooked then a target," he said gently. "Go back into the bedroom and stay safe. I'll let Sam back in, and then I'll check to see if the police have any news."

"Maybe I will. Let me know if you hear anything."

She returned to her room, sat down at the computer desk and ran through the videotapes once again, trying to retain as much information as possible. Of course, if she were under attack her adrenalin would be running high, and who knew what she'd be able to remember. But she would only get one chance at it, so she'd better pay attention and know instinctively what to do.

"Natalie?" Brent tapped on the door. "Can I come in?"

"Of course." Her heart pounded. "Has he been caught?"

"They took someone into custody who met his description."

"Is it him?" she asked, jumping out of her chair.

"They haven't confirmed it yet. They would like you to come down to the station and ID him."

"Would I have to be in the same room with him, or can I just look through that one-way glass?" She scratched her arms, feeling as though she had a bad case of lice. Her skin crawled from inside out. "Just the thought of being physically close to him again makes me ill. Guess I'm not as tough as I thought." She put a hand to her stomach, feeling like she had a bad case of indigestion. Acid bile rose in her throat. "I might throw up."

"Come on." He put a hand at her elbow. "Breathe slowly, you'll be fine. I have an idea that will make you feel better. We'll go to the station, you can ID him, then we can get those juicy hamburgers you were talking about." He kissed her cheek. "Going down to the beach, it'll be a celebration of sorts."

"What if it's not him?"

"Then at least it'll get us out. Clear our heads for a while."

"Where will we go? Someplace far away from here?"

"Down to Seal Beach—it's about twenty minutes away."

"Really?" She smiled. "Oh, that's a wonderful idea. Lead on." Brent was so good to her, always there for support, and thinking up ways to make her happy.

They grabbed Sam and headed down to the underground parking lot. Sam took his usual seat in the back and Brent gave her directions to the police precinct.

They were ushered into a room right away, and Officer Martin and Officer Sheldon explained that the man in custody couldn't see her, and all she had to do was ID him or not, then leave.

"He's not talking and has asked for his lawyer. While we're waiting we thought it would be helpful if you came down."

"No problem. Happy to do so." She clung to Brent's arm, her palms wet.

The man entered the room. He was the same size and build. When he turned and showed his profile, she knew instantly it wasn't him. Her shoulders dropped. "It's not him. I'm sorry. That's not Carl."

"You're sure? We found him only a block away from your residence. Sitting in a car. Wouldn't tell us what he was up to."

The man turned around to face them and show both angles, but there was no mistake. It wasn't Carl.

"I'm sure. Which means he's still out there." Her hands shook and she felt comforted by Brent's arm around her waist, holding her steady. She leaned into him. "Please find him soon. I can't take this much longer."

"Yes, ma'am. Thanks for taking the time out to come here today." Officer Martin added, "We'll call you the moment we find him. You're right. He's a dangerous man. Stay safe."

Brent kept his arm around her back as they walked out of the station and headed back to the car. He helped her inside, and she couldn't hold the tears back. "Oh, Brent, I so wanted it to be him. What are we going to do now? Head back home? Be his prisoner again?" She thumped the steering wheel over and over. "I hate this. Why won't he leave me alone?"

"I don't know, my darling, but I do know you need a break from all this. Come on, let's go get those hamburgers, and let Carl be damned."

She wiped her eyes, and sniffed back her tears. "Yes. Let's."

Natalie put the windows down, letting the fresh air and the smell of the Pacific calm her nerves. It was a warm day, mid-eighties, but with a good breeze and no humidity. Billowing clouds dotted the sky, and seagulls flew overhead. If her stalker ex-boyfriend wasn't hell bent on killing her, it would be a lovely day.

They found a parking spot near Main Street and a short walk from the pier. Sam jumped out of the car, yipping with excitement. Natalie felt like yipping too. Damn Carl and the horse he rode in on. Hopefully he'd rot in prison, and she could walk in the sunshine and live without fear. She deserved that, and he had no power over her anymore. With a stunning revelation she realized he never had, it was her who had given it to him. Well, now she was taking it back.

She handed Sam's harness to Brent and linked her arm through his. "Lead on, my dear man, and let's sniff out a good burger."

"Mmm-hmm, I can practically taste it already."

Sam pulled at his leash, obviously forgetting his training manners. "Heel," she said, reminding him of his duties. Instantly he obeyed, and she almost felt sorry for him. He couldn't play or be ordinary like other dogs, and maybe in his own way, he was imprisoned too.

She bit back her guilty feelings toward the guide dog, determined not to let anything ruin this unexpected pleasure. They walked down the tree-lined street, and Natalie glanced in a few of the shops. She bought a chime for the patio, and a nice pottery bowl that she would use for fresh flowers.

"This is a little like Belmont's main street, with all the restaurants and tourist shops, but they both have their own charm." Natalie asked, "Is this what all southern California is like? Miles and miles of quaint little beaches and towns?"

"Yeah. Pretty much. Why, you like it here?" He turned his head in her direction, his unseeing eyes on her face. "Maybe you'll want to stay after all."

She smiled. "You never know. I may return."

They were like a couple of kids for an hour or so. No responsibilities, no worries. Just enjoying each other's company and a sense of freedom. They found an outside table and ate their hamburgers and fries, and sipped on a light beer.

Natalie fed Sam the second half of her burger before they resumed their walk. The pier was quiet, only a few fishermen out at this sunset hour. They strolled to the end, then turned around, heading back to the car.

"So glad we came here." Natalie threaded her fingers through his. They were only a few feet from the car, and she dreaded the thought of returning home. "This was a great way to unwind. Can't we stay a little longer?"

"It was good, but we should get back before dark." He squeezed her hand. "Maybe we can do this again soon."

"Don't count on it." The voice came from behind.

Natalie froze. She knew that voice only too well. Her heart stopped, and everything around them seemed to stand still. Carl had followed them. How had they not known?

She turned her head slowly. She could feel the color drain from her face, her joy and brief happiness flee, and her warrior spirit wither and die. "Carl. How did you find me?"

EPISODE SEVEN

CHAPTER TWENTY-FOUR

Something pointed and sharp was jammed into her back. A gun?

"Isn't this nice?" Carl sneered. "The three of us out for a little walk." He lowered his voice and dropped the friendly act. "Don't do anything stupid, Natalie, or your friend will be dead before he hits the ground."

Brent swirled around. "Leave her alone. You want somebody, come after me." He swung his arms around searching for his foe. "Come on. Fight me, dammit. Or do you only hit women?"

"You're too easy." Carl laughed and jabbed at him. "What's the matter? You can't see me?" Jabbed again. "You like that, big guy? You're a pretty tough guy, right?" Carl's voice turned ugly. "You fucking my girl?"

Natalie swung the pottery bowl at his head and missed. Terror filled her lungs, suffocating her. She couldn't scream. Only a whimper came out. Sam snarled and balked at his leash. She tried to remember some of her self-defense moves, but nothing came to mind. Her brain, as well as her body, was paralyzed by fear.

Carl grabbed the leash out of Brent's hand and shot the dog in his foot. No sound was made. He'd used a silencer.

That act of violence freed her, and she launched herself at him, beating him with her small fists. Carl grabbed her hands and gave them an evil twist.

"Sam! He shot Sam," Natalie cried, finding her voice at last.

"He'll live," Carl said quietly, "which is more than I can say for you."

Brent swiftly turned and kicked, and Natalie prayed he'd make good contact with Carl's knee. Unfortunately, his kick missed the intended target. "You sick bastard," Brent snarled. "Come on. Hit me, not the dog."

"I'll deal with you later," Carl said, and grabbed Sam, tossing him in the back of the car. "You go next," he said to Brent, giving him a shove.

Brent swung around and grabbed him by the throat. "Run Natalie," he shouted. His brave move gave her a brief moment of hope. Maybe they could overpower him. Two people were stronger than just one. Except that one had a gun which was now pointed at Brent's head.

Her heart sank. "I'm not leaving you," she whispered, terrified that Carl would pull the trigger. Brent had put his own life in danger, offering her a chance to flee, and that alone would be enough to love this man. She looked at him and blinked back tears.

"You heard that? She's not leaving you." Carl shoved the gun against Brent's temple. "Now get in the car before I put a bullet in your brain."

Brent released the hold he had on Carl's throat, but used an elbow aimed at his nose. All he got for his efforts was a left hook on his chin that sent him reeling, stumbling into the side of the car.

"In the backseat with the mutt," Carl told him, prodding him in the back with the gun.

Brent lunged forward, attempting to head butt his opponent, but Carl was much too quick. He ended up smacking his forehead against Carl's forearm. He righted himself and swung again. "Fight me, dammit," Brent cried, fists ready to pummel his opponent.

Carl grabbed his wrist, and snapped his arm behind his back. In response, Brent stomped on Carl's foot and tried to elbow him again, but Carl didn't loosen his grip. He shoved Brent into the backseat, as Natalie shouted out for help. No one was in hearing distance, and if they had been, she was sure they'd be too frightened to interfere.

Natalie thought about all the videos she'd watched. What had she learned? Not a damn thing, it seemed. Carl still had control, and if they didn't get it and soon, they'd be dead. Aim for his weak spots, eyes, nose, crotch. Yes, but what if she failed? He'd shoot them both for sure.

The gun was no longer at her back, and once they got into the car with him, they wouldn't stand a chance. Better to make a move now. One way or the other.

Taking a deep breath she swung around and aimed for his knee, kicking hard, using as much strength as she could muster. She made contact with his knee cap, and he stumbled, then righted himself.

"Why, you bitch." He back-slapped her and then forced her into the driver's seat. "If you don't want to die right here, you'll keep your cool and drive us nicely back to your little love nest."

"What do you want with me? Why don't you leave me alone?" she cried.

"I tell you when you can leave. Not the other way around." He hopped into the passenger seat. "I gave you everything, and this is how you treated me?"

Natalie wondered what Brent was doing. Could he reach around the headrest and get his hands around Carl's neck? What the hell was going on? All that bullshit about disarming a man when he least expected it, well, it didn't seem to be working out. Self-defense—right! The man holding the gun was the one with the power.

Natalie swallowed the bile rising in her throat and attempted to hold the wheel steady with shaky hands. She pulled out into the street, driving slowly, praying for time.

"Step on it, sweetheart. I have a big night planned for both of you, and you won't want to miss a minute." Carl jammed the revolver into her side. "Hey, you. Lover boy, in the back. Don't try anything heroic. I've got a gun planted in Natalie's side. Tell him, Nat."

"It's true." Tears glittered in her eyes. The last thing she wanted was to be at his mercy again. She'd rather die first. "Brent, don't listen to him. Do what you have to do."

Brent spoke softly, "That wouldn't be smart, Natalie. He's got the gun." He nudged the back of her seat. "Stay cool, and think things through."

Natalie glanced back in the rear-view mirror, noticing Brent had Sam's head on his lap. His voice had been as calm as if he were discussing the weather, but she could see the tension in his jaw and the glint in his eye.

Wait a minute. Wait one damn minute. His eyes were not staring straight ahead, sightlessly. They were making eye contact. With hers.

Did that mean? Could his sight be coming back? Hell, even if it only lasted only an hour or two, she'd take it.

He winked, and she almost laughed, giddy with relief. He could see. Dear God, he could see. How much, she didn't know, but this amazing turn of events had come in the nick of time too. Maybe somebody upstairs was looking out for them or that misplaced head butt had done him a world of good. Whatever it was, as long as it lasted until Brent could come up with a way to disarm Carl, it was a much-needed miracle.

Her shoulders relaxed, and she could breathe again. Maybe if she distracted Carl long enough, Brent might act.

"So Carl—I heard a little story about you. Seems like you might be questioned about the disappearance of your first wife. Imagine my surprise. You may have forgotten to tell me about that."

"Go to hell."

"Oh, I've already been there," she answered sweetly. In the rear-view mirror, she could see Brent disengaging the dog and shifting his weight. She decided to keep up the chatter.

"What did you do to her? Heard she fell off a boat. Don't suppose you had a hand in that, did you?"

"Shut the hell up." Carl's mouth was an angry slit, and he shoved the gun harder against her side.

She winced. "Okay, okay. You don't want to shoot me here. Not while I'm driving, right?" She laughed, which she knew would infuriate Carl even more. He loved his power over women, the fear he instilled.

Well, hell. She just wasn't going to give it to him.

"You don't frighten me. Not anymore."

"Oh, yeah? We'll see about that. I have plans for you, baby, and trust me, you'll be on your knees begging for mercy."

"That's not likely to happen. You'd have to kill me first."

"That too can be arranged."

"Oh, wait!" Natalie said pleasantly. "Didn't you just hear the sound of a siren?"

Carl's head whipped around. "Pull over. Let the cruiser go past."

"What if they are looking for you? What will you do then, Mr. Bigshot? You can't shoot us all."

"I'll take out the officer, and you'll be next."

Brent spoke up. "Pull over, Natalie. With any luck he's on his way to something else."

She did as they instructed, checking her side mirror, hoping like hell he was right. If the patrol car stopped, Carl would shoot him, she had no doubt. He wasn't bluffing, and he had nothing to lose. He was already a suspect in at least one murder.

She glanced at Brent, who was watching the cruiser too. Their eyes connected. He gave her a brief nod, and she didn't have any idea what he had planned, but knew he was working it out.

The element of surprise might be their best weapon. Their only one.

∼

Brent breathed a sigh of relief as the patrol car flew past. The cops had no reason to stop the BMW they were traveling in, and had no idea that a crazed detective had a gun on them. That lack of knowledge saved some officer's life.

Speaking of saving lives, getting his sight back had been a lucky break. The doctors, after operating on his occipital cortex lobe, said his vision loss could be psychosomatic and could come back anytime. Perhaps the stress had triggered its return, or the fear of losing Natalie. Hell if he knew, he was just damn glad that it had, and hoped to God that it would last long enough to pull them through.

The bright light from the sun was driving bullets through his head. His vision was out of focus, but he had to save Natalie and it better not slip away.

He still didn't have a good idea of how he was going to turn this situation around, but one thing for sure, he'd find a way. It couldn't be done in the car. Too many variables. The gun was too close to Natalie, and he was extremely limited in the backseat. Even when the car came to a stop at the side of the road, he decided to wait.

The opportunity would come. Being reckless could get someone killed. The idea that that someone could be Natalie made the decision for him. He didn't want her death on his conscience, the way he had Linda James and his other crew mates. But of course it was more than that. He cared about Natalie, more than he could ever remember caring about anyone. He wanted to protect her, sure, but more importantly he wanted to see her happy and living the life that she dreamed.

Everyone should have that option.

"Drive," Carl ordered and glanced back to see what he was up to.

Brent put a blank expression on his face. "Where the hell are we?" he muttered. "What happened with the cruiser?"

"Luckily for you and the lady here, it had something more important to do. Didn't stop for losers like you."

Brent rubbed his jaw. "Way I see it, you might be the real loser in this scenario. If you harm either one of us, you think the local police won't put out a manhunt for you? With your history, you'll be pretty high on their list. Just below home terrorist, I'd imagine."

"Why don't you shut the hell up, smartass? You don't think I could blow your brains out right now?"

"Actually speaking, I think you could. But it would be messy and it wouldn't be wise. You're a smart guy. You've gotten away with a few things before. I'm sure that you have something clever planned for Natalie and me." He patted Sam's head, noticing that his paw had stopped bleeding. Sam was injured but not seriously.

He gritted his teeth. That asshole was going to pay for shooting his dog and for his cruelty to Natalie. And he didn't like being threatened and pushed around either.

Carl preened, liking the compliment. "You got that right. I've had lots of time to figure things out."

"Great," Brent said cheerfully. "Mind sharing it?"

Carl wasn't amused. "You've got a smart mouth, haven't you?"

"Not that smart. I just see humor in the situation, don't you? Come on. It's a little bit funny. You've got a woman next to you that you've terrorized for years, and she's not afraid of you. Me, a blind vet, can't see my way out of a paper bag, and hell, I'm not afraid either." He chuckled. "Think about it. What do I have to live for? This is no way to spend the next fifty years. So when you get the urge, go ahead and pull the trigger."

"Don't think I won't," Carl muttered.

"Might mess with your plans a bit. You're a control freak, right? Killing me now would probably screw things up." Brent shifted a little. "Wonder how it's all going down. First you probably want us all to go upstairs, and then maybe you'll shoot us both with that silencer of yours. Make it look like a murder/suicide thing. Your ex-girlfriend could have been a psycho bitch and she decided to take me out. Or, I'm so fucked up from the war that I took the gun and blew her head off, then swallowed the next bullet." He shook his head. "Come on. Am I right? I'm right, aren't I? Figured out your little plan. I'm a fucking genius, I am."

"That wasn't the plan," Carl replied. "But it's a darn good one. I could always adapt."

"Okay," Natalie spoke up. "If you guys are through with your pissing contest, I need some direction. We're nearing the apartment building. Want me to pull up front or use the underground parking?"

"Dumb question," Carl answered. "I'm not letting you guys on the street. Park underground, and start saying your prayers."

CHAPTER TWENTY-FIVE

Natalie dared a quick look back at Brent and he gave her another quick nod. He looked relaxed and calm, which under the circumstances was just ridiculous. Her own stomach was jumping around like a nest of honeybees, her palms were wet, and sweat trickled down her spine.

Relaxed? She didn't think so. In a few minutes, without intervention, they might be dead. Oh, please, Brent, she silently prayed, do have a plan, and make it a mighty good one.

The only saving grace was that he was a military man, born in a family of men who went to war and came home safely. His father was a general, his older brother a marine, and all three men had battled their enemies and conquered other demons as well. What could one man do to them that the Middle Eastern terrorists could not?

And there was always the element of surprise.

She used the remote control to open the garage door and drove to the designated parking spot. She trembled inside, but struggled to control her fear. The last thing she wanted was for Carl to see the power he had over her. She refused to give him the satisfaction.

Natalie glanced around the parking garage hoping to see some sign of action, but it was deserted at this after dinner hour. They wouldn't have a diversion. Would he kill them right here and now, or take them upstairs and have a little fun first? He liked to play mental games, preferring to stretch the torture out. That's the kind of guy she'd almost married. No, not married. She'd learned how evil he was in plenty of time to walk away. Why had she waited so long? Why hadn't she gone to school one day and just disappeared?

Was she that weak? Pathetic? No! No, not anymore. She was a warrior now, and she would fight to her death.

She glanced back at Sam. Poor, poor Sam. He looked half asleep. How much blood had he lost? Would he be of any help at all? Well, there was only one way to find out.

She turned the engine off and opened her door. "Okay, Carl. What's your next move? I'm sick and tired of your games. Played them long enough." She put her hand on the revolver poking at her and pushed it aside. "You going to shoot us right here and now, or want to drag this out for a while?"

"Killing you now would be too easy. And besides, your friend here had a pretty good idea."

Her chin shot up. "Whatever you decide doesn't matter. Your days are numbered too." She laughed. "So tell me, Carl. What would you prefer? A shootout with the police or to be thrown in jail for the next forty years? Sure you'd get plenty of action there, a hunky guy like you."

"Shut up, bitch. Get out, and leave the dog here." He pointed the gun at Brent, forgetting that he couldn't see. "You, step out of the car. Don't try any funny business."

"I can't leave the dog," Brent said, and scooped Sam into his arms. "I'll do whatever you want," Brent said, "just let me bring him upstairs. After all, if you kill us and make it look like a suicide/murder, the dog wouldn't have been left in the car. Think it through, dude."

"Good point. Bring him." He waved his gun. "Let's go, folks. The show's about to begin."

∽

Brent lifted the dog out of the car, and cradled him in his arms. The garage was dark, with only dim overhead lighting, but he could make out the revolver pointed at Natalie's back. Things were not as clear as they had been out in the daylight. A little fuzzy, but he could see enough. He stumbled a few steps, on purpose, hoping to put a plan in action. He didn't want to wait until they got into the apartment because once there, he was pretty sure that Carl would take control. Right here in the parking garage he wouldn't be expecting it. He was glancing around, keeping an eye out for anyone who might drive by as he hurried them along.

With Carl's attention not totally centered on him, Brent knew he had to act and act fast.

"Hey, won't somebody give a blind man a hand? I can't find my way to the elevator without Sam here to lead."

Carl stopped and turned back. "Then leave the fucking dog. Your choice."

"All right." Brent lowered Sam to the ground. Although the dog limped and favored his bleeding paw, Brent was confident that he'd leap into action when given a command. He gave the dog a push forward and shouted, "Attack!" At that exact moment, he kept his body low and launched himself at Carl.

Sam bared his teeth and snagged Carl's leg. Carl swiped at the dog and tried to get away, but Brent had his arms locked around Carl's middle, his head buried in the man's abdomen, and fought to wrestle him to the ground. With Sam's help, Carl collapsed and Brent pummeled him a few times in the gut, and managed a good right hook to his chin, and then both men rolled around with the gun between them.

Natalie screamed, and tried to intervene. Sam shook his head with fury, never letting go of Carl's calf even as the men rolled about.

Brent had Carl under him, and punched him several times in the face. Carl used his legs, wrapping them around him so he couldn't break free. The gun was still wedged between their bodies, but Brent's weight made Carl's hand useless.

Sam let go of Carl's calf and sunk his strong teeth in his arm, drawing a lot of blood. Brent rolled off him, and Natalie kicked the gun out of his hand. She added another kick in the groin for good measure. He crumpled up in a ball, and Brent pulled back and gave him a right hook, then grabbed his wrists and forced them behind his back. He was breathing hard, but his adrenaline was pumping pure oxygen into his veins. He'd had a few fights in his day, but nothing had ever given him as much pleasure as this.

"Natalie, see if I have something in the trunk of the car. A rope, anything that binds." He shoved his knee into the back of Carl's, so Carl's leg would cave in. He intended to keep him at a disadvantage until he was properly tied up.

She looked and came back with a bicycle chain. "Will this do?" She glanced at Carl, and Brent could see the contempt in her face. Her fear was gone and she wasn't gloating, but she had a different air about her. No longer weak, no longer a victim.

Brent grinned. "Nicely." He pulled Carl to his feet, and wrapped the chain around his wrists. "Natalie, before we take this bastard upstairs, you want another go at him?"

Her eyes met Brent's, and he was able to really see her for the first time.

God, she was beautiful, but this was no time to soak her in. He still had to get this jerk upstairs, call the police, and then after he was taken away, he could look at her forever.

Natalie seemed to be aware of this special moment too. She looked deeply into his eyes, as if she didn't want to lose that connection. Then she smiled, and Brent felt his heart expand double the size.

"No. I'm good," she said. "He's not worth my energy." She picked up the gun, and put it to Carl's back. "Why don't you carry Sam, and I'll take great pleasure in using this to prod our guest along?"

She glanced back at Brent and her eyes sparkled. "So when did you get your sight back?"

"Things have been a little less fuzzy the last few days. Kind of like the fog is lifting but I'm still in it. Anyway, not sure if it was that little knock on my head that did it, or the whole thing was psychosomatic like the docs have been saying. All I know is it came in handy." He slipped a hand around Natalie's waist. He had seen her many times in his imagination but she'd never looked this beautiful. "Not sure if I'm seeing you clearly, but wow—you are one gorgeous lady."

"Your sight's not that good," she said with a warm laugh.

Carl made a grunting noise and tried to pull away but she slid the gun up to the back of his head. "Careful there, partner. I'm a little trigger happy." They were at the elevator and she hit the button. She leaned close and whispered in his ear. "In what world did you ever think you could get the best of us? We're the good guys. Don't you watch any TV?"

Carl had his arms shackled behind his back, but he still raised his head and sneered. "You think this is over? I'll get out of this, just like I did the others."

"Not this time," Brent answered. "Your luck has run out." Once again, he slid an arm around Natalie for emotional support.

They exited the elevator and shuffled down the hall to the apartment. Natalie used Brent's key and opened up, then turned the security system off. She gave Carl a not-too-gentle push that made him stumble forward.

Brent put Sam down gently in his doggy bed, then turned to Carl and shoved him in a chair. "I should shoot you in the foot for what you did to Sam. And break every bone in your body for what you did to Natalie. But I'd rather keep you in one piece so the guys in prison can take turns with a nice detective like you." He stood inches away from the man who had made Natalie's life a living hell, and he wanted to rearrange a few of his facial features, but knew there had been enough violence today.

"Go fuck yourself," Carl answered.

He still had the tough, badass sneer on his face, and Brent clenched and unclenched his fist a few times, undecided if he wanted to loosen a few front teeth.

"No, I don't think I will, but, hey, you'll get lots of that where you'll be going." He aimed the gun at Carl's crotch. "Sit tight while I contact the police. They have a nice cell with your name on it."

Natalie gave Sam some water and a few doggie treats, but her eyes kept darting between the two men. "I'll call a vet. He'll need to be looked at, once this jerk is out of here. And out of our lives for good," she added with extra emphasis.

A half hour later the police came and took down their statements and led Carl away. He couldn't resist one more taunt as he left. "You've not seen the last of me," he shouted to Natalie. "I'll be back to finish what I started."

One of the cops told him to shut it. He gave Natalie an apologetic look. "Don't worry about that, ma'am. From what I've seen, there's a long list of things he needs to answer for."

"Thank you. And make sure you lock him up for a long, long time."

The men left, and Natalie turned to Brent. She grinned. "Well, you were quite the hero today, Captain Harrington." She put her arms around his neck and nuzzled up to him. "My God, you were so brilliant and brave."

"Warrant Officer, not captain. That was James. May she rest in peace." He put his hands around her waist and pulled her in close. "Did I ever tell you that you have the prettiest little nose, and the sweetest lips God ever put on this earth?"

"Uh, no. Pretty sure you didn't. But then you couldn't have seen that before."

He bent and kissed her lips. He felt his heart stutter, knowing how much she meant to him, and how close he'd come to losing her for good. What if his sight hadn't come back? Would he still have been able to overpower Carl? Were all those defensive maneuvers just a bunch of hogwash, and completely ineffective against a man with a gun—as Natalie had stated more than once? He was glad he didn't need to know.

"Well, I'm seeing it now. Not as clear as I'd like, but enough. God, it is enough. I could gaze at you forever and never grow tired of it."

He kissed her again, taking it deep this time. He wanted to hold on to her forever, but he knew that he had to let her go.

Finally, he took her arms and pushed her away. "Well, I sure don't feel like going back outside, but I guess we better get Sam to the vet. You up for it?"

"Of course. Sam was a hero today too. Let's get him taken care of."

Brent carried Sam back down to the car, ignoring the blood on the backseat. He'd deal with that another time, but right now all he wanted was to get Sam fixed up then spend a night with Natalie in his arms.

The veterinarian's office was only a few miles down the street and they had emergency hours. The vet put Sam on a table, cleaned up his wound, and told them the bullet had gone right through. Once he cleaned up the gash, he told them in a few days Sam would be good as new.

Brent sat in the back with the dog, telling him what a good boy he was, and Sam licked his hand, seemingly enjoying his few minutes of fame.

They were home within ten minutes, and Brent got Sam settled in his bed, then turned his attention to Natalie. He lifted her shirt over her head. "You've got blood on it," he said softly. "Your shorts too." He unzipped her shorts and pushed them down to her feet. He kissed her neck and undid her bra.

She tried to cover herself, but he pushed her hands down. "Don't, please. Let me look at you. I've wanted to see you for so long."

She shrugged out of the bra. Then closed her eyes. "I hope you won't be disappointed."

He took her breasts in his hands, his eyes devouring her. "God. You're beautiful. No wonder Carl didn't want to let you go."

"Please, don't talk of Carl. I want you, Brent. I want to be in your bed and feel safe in your arms."

He bent his head and kissed each of her breasts, sucking on one nipple, then the other. "I can't wait to love you tonight, but first, we need to shower." He grabbed her hand and led her to the bathroom. "What I want to do with you tonight deserves a clean body."

He stripped his clothes off and tossed them on the floor. Once the water was warm he stepped in under the shower and pulled Natalie into his arms. He kissed her deeply, running his fingers through her thick head of hair. He'd never seen her beautiful face before, her straight shoulders, firm breasts, tiny waist, slender thighs. He intended to spend the entire night drinking in his fill of her. One inch at a time.

He shampooed her hair, then took the soap and lathered her down, taking his time between her legs. Her breath hitched, and she scooped some of the soap from her own body to stroke his shaft. He rubbed up against her, needing a place for his erection.

She moaned his name, and he lifted her leg and slipped inside. She clung to him as he claimed her body, repeatedly driving himself deeper and deeper, butting her body against the shower wall.

Her mouth was open, giving him hot, demanding kisses, and her breathing had quickened. Her fingers dug into his back, holding him fast. Her hips moved frantically, then she bucked and swayed, collapsing into a heap on the wet floor.

He picked her up, wrapped her in a towel and took her to bed.

The night was long, and neither of them slept. He kissed every inch of flesh he could find, getting to know her intimately, committing every single detail of her to memory in case he forgot. He wasn't sure how long he could keep her, but he had her for now, and didn't want to waste one precious minute of it.

CHAPTER TWENTY-SIX

The following morning, Natalie slipped out of bed, not wanting to wake Brent. He had fallen into a deep sleep only a few hours ago, and she watched him for a moment, feeling her emotions rising to the surface, threatening to spill over. With Carl behind bars, she had her freedom back. For the first time in so many years she was safe, able to do anything she wanted without fear. Right now, what she wanted was simply to feast her eyes on Brent.

His face was buried in his pillow, and he had one arm stretched out as though searching for her. The cover was down at his feet and she could admire his body from head to toe. He had filled out some in the past few weeks, but he was still painfully thin, yet beautiful, like a sculpture. Broad shoulders, slim at the hips, shapely legs and ass.

She swallowed a sudden lump. She would miss him when she was gone. But he didn't need her now, and she was free to leave, or would be in a day or so when her work permit came through. The idea of going to France didn't thrill her as it did before, but everything she'd told Brent was true. They both needed to heal, to grow, to become whole again, and she had to do it alone. She'd never been independent or assertive, and although she'd be living in someone's home and tutoring children, she would be in a unique environment, something totally different than she'd ever experienced before.

She couldn't tell Brent about having second thoughts either. Not unless he asked her to stay.

Perhaps he would. He might have fallen in love with her, as she had with him. Of course he'd never used the word love, but he certainly had enjoyed her body, that's for damn sure.

She went into her bedroom, slipped on a robe, then padded down the hall to the kitchen and started the coffee. They had lots to do in the next few days. This morning she wanted to visit Lori and give her the good news in person, if she hadn't been told already. She had the coffee mug in her hand when suddenly it dropped out of her hands. She bent to pick it up, but all she could see was Carl, his ugly face inches from hers, with a gun at her back. A sob ripped from her and tremors ran up and down her spine. She was caught in the nightmare, as the terrifying moments flashed through her mind. She put a hand over her mouth to ward off a scream.

She picked up one piece of the stoneware mug and then another, and another, placing them on the counter. She breathed deeply and, hands shaking, reached for another mug. She forced her mind away from Carl, away from the man who'd made her life so miserable for so long, and remembered that he didn't have any power over her anymore. Not in her thoughts, not in her head, and not in her bed.

She poured her coffee, and closed her eyes, thinking of Brent. He would probably want to see his doctor, and

Shane, and everyone else in the world that he cared about to share his wonderful news. Tears filled her eyes. He could see again. Oh, God, how wonderful was that? She was so grateful, so intensely happy for him, that the tears continued to flow.

She turned when she heard him behind her. "Brent, the coffee is ready."

"I see that." He lifted her face, and wiped away a tear. "Why are you crying?"

"I don't know. Relief, happiness, I'm not sure. I'm just emotional all of a sudden."

He kissed her lips softly. "Of course you are. Carl's no longer a threat, and you're free to live the life you want."

She lifted her eyes to his, able for the first time to see the warmth and emotion that leapt in his. "That's right. Happy tears, of course." She turned away. "You didn't sleep much. You must be busting to tell everyone your great news." She poured two cups and handed him one. "I'm so thrilled for you, Brent."

He took a sip from his coffee, his eyes never leaving her face. "Yeah. It's great. Actually can see better this morning than I did last night."

"That's wonderful," she said. "Everything worked out, didn't it?"

"Guess so. Who knows what would have happened if it hadn't been for that knock on my head." He laughed. "The head butt idea worked out great, even if I missed my intended target."

"You were brave and clever. I was so darn proud of you." She smiled, and said lightly, "Here you were, asking him to fight with you, willing to do battle so I could get free.

No one's ever fought for me before." She wanted to tell him how much she loved him, but she kept quiet. With his sight, everything had changed. He probably didn't want her hanging around anymore. He could go back to work, find himself someone who wanted to get married, stay home and raise kids. Seemed like that was the kind of girl he fancied.

"You too. You didn't run when you got the chance." He swallowed another sip. "And Sam. Can't forget Sam."

At the mention of his name, Sam looked up from his bed, and hopped over to them. Natalie buried her face in his fur. "You took a bullet for us, didn't you boy?"

Brent bent to scratch behind his ears. "Sure did. That makes you a hero dog, and you should get a nice big medal. How about a rawhide treat instead? Will that do it for you?"

He grabbed a treat from the pantry and tossed it to Sam. He caught it midair, and sat down with it between his paws and his jaws.

He watched the dog for a minute, then his expression changed. "Guess this means I'm going to have to give him up. That's gonna be tough, but someone now needs him more than me."

"I'm sure you can keep him if you want to. Shane said he's a retired service dog and that was why he was able to pull strings for you. He was up for adoption, isn't that right?"

"Not sure about that. I'll check." Sam flipped over and Brent rubbed the dog's belly. "And to think I didn't want him." He waited a second, then added in a low voice, "Or you."

Natalie glanced away. The memory brought her a stab of pain. He'd been so angry, so afraid of his future, and had not wanted anyone to witness him in that pitiful state. This strong heroic man had been at his weakest moment when she had walked in. No wonder he hadn't wanted her around.

She felt a floodgate of emotions open up inside of her and knew at any second the storm would burst. She supposed it was natural after all they'd been through to feel this distraught, so emotionally undone. As though she were falling apart at the seams. And she didn't know how to fix it.

The fact she was free to leave should have her dancing around the room in joy, instead of wanting to fling herself into Brent's arms and beg him to let her stay.

Obviously she was overreacting to last night's stress. Once she was on the airplane halfway across the Atlantic, she'd never look back. Her future was ahead of her, it wasn't here. Not with Brent. They would never visit the children in the hospital, bringing music and a smile to light up their lives. She'd have enjoyed that, but it was only a fanciful dream.

"I'm going to shower. Then I want to visit Lori." She left quickly, holding back tears.

She turned on the shower and stepped underneath, allowing the tears to come. Sobs ripped her apart but she didn't stop them. She hadn't meant to care so much for Brent, but he had wormed his way into her heart, and now she didn't know how she'd live without him. And yet she had to leave, she told herself. She had to move on, grow, have her adventures. Without Brent. His world had opened up again and she couldn't hold him back.

When at last her tears stopped coming, she turned off the shower and stepped out. She dried herself, then dressed. One glance in the mirror confirmed her swollen bloodshot eyes, red nose, and blotchy skin. Why couldn't she be one of those women who cry pretty?

She blotted her face, used eye drops, and did her best to repair the damage, but Brent would have to be blind once again not to see the heartbreak seeping out of her.

She needed to buck up. Fast.

He was dressed when she came into the kitchen, and frying up some eggs.

"I'd like to come with you," he said, and slid scrambled eggs on two plates.

"That's not necessary," she told him. "I'm sure you're going to be very busy today. You need to see your doctor, call your family and tell them the great news. And Shane. Everyone." She forced a smile. "You'll have so much to do, and plans to make. Just think. You'll be able to work again."

He buttered two pieces of toast, put one on each plate, and handed one to her. She took it and sat down.

"What's up with you? You're acting strange. Like you don't want me around or something. I know things will be different around here, but my feelings haven't changed toward you, and I'm not in any hurry to see you leave. Stay as long as you want."

She sat down at the table and took a bite out of her toast. Stay as long as you want... Why did those words sting? They were warm, polite, but what did they mean? That she could live with him for another week or two and he'd continue to pay her? Well, she didn't want his money. Besides, now with Carl in jail, she could access her own bank accounts and withdraw the small savings she had after her grandma passed away. She wasn't destitute, and she didn't need his pity.

She swallowed hard, darn near choking on the toast. "Thank you. Lori told me my work permit will be here in a matter of a few days. I can always stay with her—she might need my help."

Brent sat next to her and ate his breakfast. He didn't look at her, and she couldn't read his face. "If that's what you want."

She took a bite of the scrambled egg and tried to get it down. It tasted like sawdust in her dry throat. "It's not what I want. It's the right thing to do."

"What do you want, Natalie?"

"I don't know. I used to be so sure, but now everything's upside down. I'm free to leave but I like it here. I was thinking this morning how we were going to go to the hospital and cheer up the sick children. We won't be able to do that now."

"We could take a few hours and visit the children before you leave."

She blinked rapidly. "I won't be able to wake up to coffee and scrambled eggs. Not with you, anyway."

He reached out and took her hand. "You'll have another family to take care of. Three little children that you can converse with in every language. You won't have time to miss me. On your days off you'll be cavorting all over Paris, taking side trips to Versailles and Nice." He smiled. "I'm jealous. It does sound like fun."

"What will you do?" she asked.

"I'm not sure yet, but when I figure it out I'll let you know." He ran a finger down the side of her cheek. "There's no reason why we can't still be friends, is there? We can Skype and email. Maybe I'll come visit one day."

"One day you'll forget all about me, and marry that girl just like your mother."

"I don't want a woman like my mother. I want a woman like you. But not right now. You have things you need to do, and so do I."

He didn't love her. He didn't want her to stay.

She nodded and stood up, taking her plate into the kitchen. She dumped the breakfast in the bin. "That's right, Brent. After I visit Lori, I have some shopping to do. Can't go to Paris looking like this." She gave him a brave smile. "I'll see you back here tonight."

He stood up and came into the kitchen, putting his hands on her hips. "Something is bothering you, but I'll be damned if I know what it is. Talk to me. Don't shut me out."

"There's not much to say, is there? Your life is here, and mine is in France."

With that he let her go.

CHAPTER TWENTY-SEVEN

Brent stormed out of the apartment, taking his keys with him. He hadn't driven for damn near a year and a half, but it was a good day to start. Hell, it was a good day to start anything. Fresh starts—that's what the day offered. No regrets, and nothing to hold him back. No woman, that's for sure.

Why were women such a mystery to men? Why couldn't they be straight up and say what was on their mind, instead of getting all moody and quiet? What was bothering her, anyway? Dammit, he thought she'd be delighted that Carl was finally locked up and she was free to go, but instead she'd been emotional, irrational, and distant with him too. But what did he expect? That was half the reason he'd stayed clear and hadn't let his heart get involved. Women were so damn unpredictable.

He put the top down hoping the breeze would clear his head. In the two weeks he'd known her, she'd messed with it good. Hell, it wasn't him that wanted to see her go. He was quite content to keep things just the way they were. They lived together, got along fine, had great sex, and were perfectly comfortable. She was the one who wanted adventures, but he'd had enough for one lifetime. Right now, he longed for peace, a quiet existence, and some solitude to put everything back in perspective.

He needed to heal from the inside out.

Having a restless nature, he'd soon look for a day job, but right now he wanted to look around at the world he'd been missing and simply enjoy the simple pleasures.

He drove slowly down the Pacific Coast Highway, getting used to the feel of driving again. It was almost surreal and he felt like a fish out of water. Keeping the car under twenty miles an hour gave him time to get used to the simple mechanics and allowed him to glimpse the ocean, and watch pretty young women strolling or skating down the sidewalk. He'd missed both views. Pretty women abounded in California and if Natalie left, he would be sure to find someone else to spend his nights with. Not if, when. When Natalie left. He'd find a new flavor of the week, and make damn sure she didn't smell like some kind of fruit.

He rubbed a spot between his eyes. He had a pounding headache. Of course he was glad for her, she was finally going to be able to do all the things she'd never had the chance to do. Great. Fucking great. He could find himself a blonde bimbo and have great sex too.

The pounding grew worse. Maybe a drive across town would cure him of whatever she'd afflicted him with. Damn well hoped so. He had no inclination to spend a moment of his time wishing for things that couldn't come true. If she wanted to go, fine. Let her. He'd find appeasement elsewhere.

He had his sight back, and no way in hell was he going to waste time feeling bad because she intended to leave. Matter of fact, after he drove across town he'd be over her.

Like that! Love 'em and leave 'em, wasn't that his motto? He'd been rather proud of the fact that he could care deeply for someone, but if things didn't pan out, he never hurt for long. Well, that wasn't quite true. There had been one special girl, but she hadn't waited for him to commit and moved on. Now she was a mother and had two little toddlers, so he'd been told.

He'd carried her picture in his wallet for a long time. Would look at it once in a while to remind himself of what he'd let go. Well, he didn't have any pictures of Natalie, and didn't want one either.

Pulling out his cell, he decided to call Shane. His buddy would cheer him up. He always did.

"Hey, what's up?" Shane said in way of answer.

"So much has happened, I'm not sure where to start. Want to meet me for coffee?"

"Meet for coffee? Well now, that's really something." Shane cleared his throat. "I'm working, but, for you, I can make time."

"Good. Tell me where and I'll be there."

Brent had an hour to kill and decided he'd swing by his ophthalmologist's office and deliver the good news. Dr. Green couldn't see him immediately, but Brent set up an appointment to come in at the end of the week for a thorough exam. That killed some time before he was to meet Shane near the hospital at a small coffee house.

Arriving first, Brent ordered a cappuccino and sat at a table window. He turned and waved when Shane walked through the door.

Shane lifted his hand in greeting, then stopped, dead still. His eyes opened wide and his mouth gaped. He moved his hand again and watched Brent's eyes follow the movement. "No fucking shit!"

He strode over and slapped his buddy on the back. "When did this happen? How come I wasn't the first to know?"

"You're the second, and my vision cleared up last night. Grab a coffee, and I'll tell you the full story. It's a humdinger." He laughed at the expression on Shane's face. Just being able to see it was priceless.

Shane got his iced mocha frappuccino, a couple of donuts, then grabbed a seat next to him. "Okay, shoot. What happened?"

A half hour later they were still sitting there. "Holy shit. I can't believe that Natalie was in danger all that time and none of us knew." Shane wiped chocolate icing off his mouth. "Do you mind if I share this with Lauren? She'll probably want to help her out in any way she can."

"Yeah, you can tell Lauren. I'm sure that Natalie will want to see both of you before she says good-bye." He bit into the glazed donut that Shane had bought, then pushed it aside.

"What do you mean good-bye? Where's she going?"

"France. She's got a job tutoring some children in a country villa outside Paris. She's never been anywhere or done anything, and this is a big deal for her." Brent shrugged. "She can't wait to go. It'll be an experience of a lifetime."

He knew it was true, but still, he wished it didn't hurt quite so much. He wanted to be happy for her and in some ways he was, but... She made him laugh. She made him feel.

"What about you?" Shane gave him a skeptical look. "How do you feel about that?"

Brent took a sip from his cup, and thought about his answer. "I'm staying put. I've had enough excitement and now I'm looking forward to some peace. Figuring things out, one day at a time."

"But you love her, right?" Shane stirred his frappuccino, a frown on his face.

"Sure, but what's that got to do with it?"

"You can't let her go. You don't find a good woman every day of the week, and when you meet someone special you hold on tight." Shane shifted in his seat to look at him better. "Come on, Brent. You're not a kid anymore. Isn't it time you got married, had a family of your own?"

"Not yet. One day, for sure, but I still have some healing to do."

"Well, I certainly understand that. Took me a good long time to get my act together."

"You had a lot of issues to deal with, but now I have my sight back, so I've got no excuse."

"Sure you do. Stress disorder takes a long time to go away. Don't beat yourself up about it, just accept the fact that you're still going to have bad dreams and anxiety for some time to come."

"Sucks, doesn't it?"

"Yeah, but it gets better over time."

"So, it's just as well that Natalie's going to leave. Sure I'll miss her, but I'm not going to be like that psycho ex of hers and cling to her. No way. I'm happy to let her go. Don't want a woman in my life until I'm a hundred percent whole."

"So you say." He took a sip from his drink. "But I don't believe you for a second."

"Well, as long as she does, we're good."

"Where is she now?" Shane avoided looking at Brent as he asked.

"Not sure, but she was going to visit Lori in the hospital today. Unless Lori's been released. Then she'd visit her at her home, I suppose." Brent shrugged. "Soon as she gets that permit, she's out of here." He stretched and yawned, as if it didn't matter one bit. "Once I get things figured out, who knows? I might take a trip over the pond. See how she's doing."

Shane grinned. "Now you're talking. Don't make it too long."

The two friends talked a little longer, then left the coffee shop, going their separate ways. Brent was eager to get home to see Natalie. Not to plead or beg, just to see her and talk to her again. He missed her already and she wasn't even gone.

Brent returned home and found the place empty. Sam was in his doggy bed and lifted one eye in greeting. He looked as dejected as Brent felt.

"Where did she go, boy?" He rubbed Sam's belly. "Is she coming back?"

He walked down the hallway and entered her room. Her bag was gone and the closet was empty. Natalie had left.

∽

"How good did it feel to kick him in the nuts?" Lori asked Natalie. "Darn, I wish I'd been there."

Lori was sitting up in a makeshift bed on the couch. She'd only left the hospital this morning and with Carl captured, John had wanted her home. Natalie had picked up some food to share and now sat opposite her, eating and talking.

She'd just given Lori the intimate details about Carl showing up at Seal Beach and how they'd managed to escape.

"I'm glad you weren't there, because it was scarier than shit, but yes, that part was extremely satisfying. It might not have been necessary, but he had it coming. And then some."

"Wow, were you guys lucky that his sight came back in the nick of time."

"I know. He said it's been coming and going, so perhaps he could actually see more than he let on. Told me it may have been psychosomatic. Who knows? But we were lucky."

"He might have pretended not to see, to keep you with him longer. He loves you, you know."

Natalie's stomach clenched, and she felt a wave of yearning inside. "Why do you say that? You only met him once, and you were certainly in no shape to judge."

"Damn, Natalie, surely you could see it. It was clear as day—the way he was so protective of you, the way he looked when you talked about him. Even John noticed." She reached out a hand and touched Natalie's knee. "Brent's a good guy. A keeper, and I'd have said that sighted or not."

"I know he is." She bit her lip. "But, Lori, I don't think he wants me. He had an opportunity to ask me to stay. But he didn't. Told me I'm free to go." Natalie sipped her iced tea and pretended indifference. "So here I am. Thanks for saying I could stay with you. Being with Brent right now would be too painful."

She glanced out the window, not wanting to see pity in her friend's eyes. It was her own fault that Brent was letting her go. She'd told him repeatedly that she would be leaving as soon as the permit came through and that they both had healing to do. She'd given him no choice. But still, it hurt that he didn't intend to fight for her.

"It might very well come today or tomorrow. But if I were you, I wouldn't be in such a hurry to leave. Stay awhile and see how things fly with you and Brent."

"No. He's made it clear that I'm free to go, and he has big decisions to make that don't include me. Now that he's sighted, he'll have more job opportunities. Who knows what he'll decide to do."

"Well, anyway. I wish you'd stick around a little longer. I know the couple in France want you for the summer, but it's only June." She sat up straighter. "You could push it off until after the Fourth of July weekend. That'll give you one more week."

"It'll probably take me that long to get everything sorted out. I need to close my bank accounts in Washington, and have plenty to do to get ready for this trip." She thought about all her clothes that she'd left back home, but no. She didn't want anything from her life with Carl. She wanted to start fresh. "I have to shop. Get my hair done, and look like my old self again. I left with only the clothes on my back and what little cash I could get from ditching his car."

"Oh, he must be furious about that," Lori said with a laugh. She straightened the blanket around herself, and then put her fingers to her face. "I can't wait to look like myself again either. Or get these darn bandages off. They itch."

"I'm sorry. That was kind of insensitive of me." Natalie got up and kissed her friend's forehead. "How long will it be?"

"Not sure. A few weeks, maybe." Lori held her hand. "Taking a few hits from him was worth it, now that he's been arrested. I wonder exactly how many others he tormented over the years?"

John walked into the room. "What are you girls talking about?"

"Talking about Carl's past," Lori said. "I wonder if there are more women out there eager to testify."

"Like Tiger's girlfriends."

"Yeah. Something like that. But much worse."

He kissed Lori on the head. "How you feeling, love?"

"The pain meds help. I'm fine. Look like hell though."

"You're always beautiful to me."

Natalie smiled at the two of them, and thought about Brent. They did have something between them. It was more than just physical. She was sure of it. The way he touched and kissed her—with both tenderness and passion—it went soul deep. She knew the love was there, but their time wasn't now. They both had work to do. He had scar tissue from his time at war, and the rest of his life to figure out, and she had to become strong emotionally and not use Brent as a safety net.

John handed Lori an envelope. "Something from the French consulate. Could be that work permit you've been waiting for."

Lori shot Natalie a look. "Here we go." She ripped open the envelope and there it was.

Natalie's ticket to freedom.

EPISODE SEVEN

CHAPTER TWENTY-EIGHT

Brent went for a long walk on the beach and played with Sam—tossed him a tennis ball and watched as he chased it into the surf. During this peaceful pastime he figured out some stuff too. For some unknown reason, the powers that be were giving him a get-out-of-jail-free card and a second chance. He didn't intend to waste it either. Eventually he'd do something meaningful—once he figured that part out.

Meanwhile, he could get the old surf board out—hit some waves, maybe go carousing down Santa Monica Pier and check out hot chicks in tiny bikinis. That would be a sight worth seeing. It sounded good. Real good.

Then again, he could take a drive to Sacramento and speak to Human Resources about getting his old job back at CAL FIRE. The idea of flying again made his heart feel years lighter. He could still be useful and help people in trouble.

He liked that idea a lot.

Grabbing a pizza to go, he led Sam back to the apartment and they sat out on the patio to have dinner together. Brent had an ice cold beer, and Sam lapped up his ice water. They couldn't be happier. Didn't need a female around to make them complete. A man and his dog were perfect companions.

But he couldn't help but wonder where Natalie was tonight. What scent would she be wearing? He chug-a-lugged the beer and went into the fridge for another.

Damn woman. How could she leave without saying goodbye? What had he done wrong? He'd said all the right things. Told her that she was welcome to stay as long as she wanted—that they'd remain friends, and email and Skype. It had seemed to piss her off. What had she wanted from him? Had he missed something?

"What do you say, buddy? What the hell was Natalie pissed about? We caught her asshole boyfriend. She can be safe now and do damn near anything she wants. Just like me. We are both free and able to forge on with our lives and have adventures or not. It's up to us if we become happy."

He tossed a pizza slice to the dog. "Funny thing is, I was happy even when things got rough around here. Taking care of Natalie made me feel good inside. Ya know?"

The dog licked his foot and looked at him with his big, clear eyes. Clever dog could probably understand more than he did.

"So what do you think? Should I just let her go? Or find out where Lori lives and tell her to come back here where she belongs?" He put the cold bottle on his forehead and rubbed it back and forth. Head hurt thinking about her. Felt a sharp pain around his heart too. "She didn't say good-bye. That's just not right. She has some explaining to do. I think I should demand an explanation. Don't you?"

The dog blinked. "Woof woof."

"You do? You think that's a good idea!" He took a big bite out of his pizza and munched away. "Maybe I will. Got nothing better to do tomorrow. Just might have a little talk with her. See if she might change her mind."

Once the pizza was finished, he took Sam downstairs for a final walk, then watched a little sports on TV. The day had worn him out, and he fell asleep on the couch and didn't wake up until dawn.

Sam was licking his foot, and, startled, he glanced around, realizing he was still on the couch. He got up, stretched and yawned, and decided to go for a long swim. He hadn't done that since Natalie had arrived. She'd distracted him by making coffee, having breakfast, and her damn scent. Tantalizing woman. She made it hard to forget.

He grabbed a towel and a thermal cup of coffee, put on his flip flops and headed downstairs. He enjoyed doing laps, not so much as a physical activity but because it cleared the head. He placed his coffee cup on the edge of the pool and dived in.

He had the pool to himself in this early morning hour, and he worked hard, pushing himself lap after lap until his arms could barely rise one more time, and his legs were weak with exhaustion. He pulled himself up and out of the water, and sat on the edge sipping his tepid coffee.

He'd warred with himself for the past half hour, and not even the physical activity had cleared his mind. He knew he should leave Natalie alone, but he couldn't. He had to see her once more. She couldn't walk away and start a new life without knowing how he felt. If she didn't feel the same, okay. He'd let her go and wish her well, but not without a proper good-bye. He deserved that much, didn't he?

Once upstairs, he called the hospital and was told that Lori had checked out. He called John's cell to ask if Natalie was staying with them, and after some hesitation, John had confirmed it.

"Yeah, she's here." He added as an after thought, "She's a nice girl, but I think she's confused. Going to France was supposed to be a way to escape Carl, but now he's no longer a threat. Not sure if she's that keen anymore."

"Thanks, John. I'm going to see if I can change her mind."

He wrote down the address, then went into the bathroom to shower and shave. Dressed in a clean black tee and worn jeans. Flip flops and a squirt of cologne and he was ready. Brent put the top down and whistled as he drove across town to find Natalie and hopefully bring her home.

∽

Since Lori was laid up, Natalie answered the door.

"Brent! What are you doing here?" She backed up with her hand at her throat. Her heart did a double bounce and raced like an Olympic skier. She lowered her hand to her chest to try and steady the beat. "How did you know I was here?"

"I figured it out and John confirmed it when I called this morning."

"He gave you this address?" Why would he do that? Hadn't he already messed up once by not minding his own business? Yet she knew that both times he'd only been trying to help. She wasn't angry with him, only frustrated. It was so hard to face Brent and know that she might never see him again.

"I looked it up. Why did you leave without telling me?"

Lori called out, "Brent, is that you? Come on in."

Brent glanced at Natalie and walked past her. She followed, unsure what to answer him. What words could she use to explain that her heart had leapt with joy when she saw him standing on the porch? To tell him that he looked so handsome, so healthy, and so dear to her, that she'd wanted nothing more than to run into his arms. She wanted to stay more than she wanted to leave, but leave she must. Staying would be safe, it would not allow her to grow emotionally, become the strong person she needed to be. She'd stayed with Carl out of fear, and she didn't want to live with Brent for another wrong reason. If they were to be together, she wanted to make sure the decision was based on strength and love, a choice they'd mutually make.

Brent bent and kissed Lori on the forehead. "How're you feeling?"

"Feel like crap, but I'm on the mend. It was worth a few bruises to make the police realize how dangerous that man was."

"You're a good friend," Brent told Lori and glanced at Natalie.

She moved forward, tongue-tied, heart thundering, stomach doing backflips. To avoid looking at Brent, she focused her attention on Lori, taking her hand.

"You're sweet, but you shouldn't have to deal with all this."

"You wouldn't be lying here," Lori answered gently. "You'd be in the morgue."

"That's true," Natalie spoke softly and tried to smile. "But now none of us need to worry."

Lori looked at Brent and back at Natalie. "I'm sure you two have things to discuss that don't include me. Why don't you both go out into the back garden, since I'm not getting around too well?"

"Can I get you anything first?" Natalie inquired. She was anxious to hear what Brent had to say; she needed to know for her own peace of mind. Had she been the only one who'd fallen in love? Did he share those feelings too?

"I'm fine. Don't hurry back because of me."

Brent rested a hand on Lori's shoulder. "Thanks," he said quietly, then followed Natalie through the patio glass doors.

Lori and John lived in a large home in a beautiful residential area of Long Beach in a Spanish-style home built in the early nineteen hundreds. It had a red tiled roof, white stucco walls, and corniced gates. The private backyard had a large rectangular pool with flowered shrubbery and palms, blocking off the view from their neighbors.

Brent and Natalie sat at a wrought iron table that sat six, with plush red and yellow cushioned chairs, and a Mexican pot in the center with fresh flowers.

Natalie reached out a hand and touched his arm. "Brent, I'm sorry I left the way I did. It wasn't very kind of me. I was going to call you and apologize." She licked her lips and fidgeted with her hands. "You know how emotional I was that morning. So much had happened so quickly, and I needed to get away and clear my mind."

He jumped out of his seat, clearly agitated. He walked over to the pool and back. When he returned, his jaw was set, his eyes on fire. "And is your mind clear?" He leaned closer to her. "Do you know what you want?"

She glanced away, breathing deeply. "I'm going to France. You know that." She ran a nervous hand through her hair. "It was decided before I met you. The family in France made the arrangements." Her eyes pleaded with him to understand. Leaving him was not easy—it was something she had to do. For her and for him. To become a better person. Someone that she could admire. Not the frightened little mouse she had been for so long. "They had to initiate the process, and justify hiring me. Because of my language and teaching skills, I was screened and accepted for the job."

"Right. I get that." He leaned over her seat, and she could feel his breath on her neck. "So did you get your permit?"

She nodded and squirmed. "It came yesterday. My long-stay visa and work permit. It came UPS from the French consular services." She swallowed and looked away. Why was she defending her actions? That was ridiculous. He'd given her no reason to stay. "So I'm going. The decision's been made."

Brent cleared his throat. "You could change your mind. You always have a choice. What you do is up to you. Like when I went to war. Couldn't cry over losing my sight—it was a price I willingly paid for doing what I thought was right."

"It was a heavy price just the same."

"Yes it was. Just like staying with Carl when he beat you was a decision that you made, and paid dearly for."

"How dare you!" She jumped out of her seat. Pain shot through her. It was worse than a slap in the face, more cruel than Carl's fists. "You have no idea what it was like. How he controlled me by fear." She backed away, fists knotted at her side. "How could you say that to me?" Her eyes filled with tears.

"Sit down. Please, Natalie." He put a hand out in apology. "I am sorry. It was a terrible thing to say. Please sit and hear me out."

She took her seat, but stuck her chin out and glared at him.

"I was trying to make a point—not a very good one, but my intention was clear." He put a finger under her chin and looked into her eyes. "We all have choices. You could stay with me for a little longer. See how things work out."

She opened her mouth to tell him what she thought of that, but he touched her lips, silencing her. "Look at me, Natalie. Do you want to go to France?"

"Why? Why are you asking me this? You know I have to go."

"What if I asked you to stay?"

Her mouth trembled, and she felt a swell of tears forming behind her eyes. It wouldn't be long before that storm broke, and she didn't want him to see her cry. She wanted him to remember her as she looked today. Confident and pretty, her hair recently cut and highlighted, manicured toes peeking out of her flip flops, wearing a flowered sundress, sitting out in the California sunshine with a warm smile just for him.

That's how she wanted to be remembered.

She stood up and put a hand on Brent's cheek. She bent and kissed him, then gave him a loving smile. "I would say our timing sucks. If things were different... Well, who knows? But they aren't, and you have things to do and so do I." She took a small step back. "Brent, you know I care for you. Very much. But I don't like who I am, and I have to go away to find myself."

She sniffed back her tears and straightened her shoulders, determined to be strong. Strong enough to walk away. "I'm so thrilled that your sight came back and that you can go back to flying, or whatever it is you decide to do. And yes, you can write me if you like. I'd love to keep in touch. And maybe one day I'll come back here to visit or you'll find yourself in France. This doesn't mean good-bye forever. It just means farewell for now."

He got to his feet. "Is there nothing I can say that'll make you stay?" he asked quietly.

Yes, she wanted to answer. You could tell me how much you love me, and will miss me when I'm gone. Yet she knew he wouldn't. Even during their most passionate moments, words of love had never been spoken. And if she told him? It wouldn't change anything. She needed to go to grow. Living here with Brent was too easy, too safe, something the weak, the frightened Natalie would do. If she came back to Brent, she wanted to come back, full of confidence, strong, courageous, a woman they both could admire.

She shook her head sadly. "I'm afraid not."

He nodded. "When are you leaving?"

"I have a flight booked on July fifth. I need a week to get my affairs in order."

"Right." She noticed a tic in the side of his face. His jaw was set, and his eyes had lost hope.

"I'll walk you to the door." She led the way back inside, and he stopped in front of Lori.

"Will you stay and have lunch with us?" she asked, looking from one unhappy face to the other.

"No, I'm sorry. I won't be back again, so I wanted to wish you a quick recovery and thank you again for helping out Natalie. You're a wonderful friend."

"You too, Brent. You saved Natalie's life."

"Naw. That was Sam. He got Carl on the ground and then we all took turns doing the rest."

She smiled. "Well, don't be a stranger. You're welcome here, anytime."

He nodded. "Tell John thanks."

Natalie walked him to the door. Their eyes met for one last time. "Au revoire," she told him, and before she lost all control, she turned and closed the door.

Lori looked up as she ran past. "Are you all right?"

"Yes, yes, I can't talk about it." Natalie flew up the stairs and ran into the guest bedroom. She threw herself on the bed and a huge sob ripped out of her. She hadn't had the courage to say good-bye back at his house, and had cowardly snuck away. She had wanted to avoid this heartache altogether. Seeing him today had not only brought the pain back, but had intensified the ache.

Tears flowed down her cheeks, and she hugged the pillow and cried.

What was she to do? She loved Brent and yet she had to send him away. Why couldn't she accept his invitation to stay with him, instead of running off to prove herself? Other people lived safe lives. They didn't have to have adventures and force themselves to be more than they were. Brent liked her fine just as she was—or did he? Would he grow bored with her too? Well, one thing was for certain, she didn't like the woman she was, and that was the only thing that mattered. Self-respect was everything, and until she could look in a mirror and like the woman she'd become, she was not worthy of love.

Staying was not an option. Besides, she had more serious problems on her hands. Her period was never late and it was now three days overdue. She was sure it was stress, it had to be stress, but what if... no, no...

Stupid! She was so stupid, how could she have had sex without protection? Of course they both knew better and yet common sense had flown out the window whenever Brent touched her. His kisses and his passion had made her mindless with need. Why hadn't either of them stopped for one damn minute and thought about using a condom? She had used birth control for the two years she'd been with Carl, but her prescription had run out and she hadn't had time to see a new doctor.

She stopped sobbing and went into the bathroom. If her period didn't arrive soon, she'd go to the pharmacy and buy a pregnancy kit. Pregnant or not, one thing for sure, Brent must never find out. The last thing he needed was to be trapped by a woman he didn't love.

CHAPTER TWENTY-NINE

Brent didn't feel like going home so he drove to Sacramento to speak to someone there about getting his old job back.

A young guy sat behind the desk with a pen between his teeth. "Look, when you called I pulled up your work history with CAL FIRE and I see you had an impressive record. Seven years without fault. I wish we could welcome you back into the captain's seat, but I'm afraid with your medical discharge and recent loss of vision, that will be impossible."

"But if I can pass the medical exam there's no reason I can't fly." Brent said stubbornly, resenting the attitude of this young, preppy kid. Looked fresh out of high school, yet he sat in his leather chair, twirling around, a pen stuck in his mouth. He was in Human Resources, a desk jockey; how would he know the skill set required to fly choppers during the thick of fire or dodging missiles in mountainous terrain? It took a helluva lot more than 20/20 vision. Things like guts, instinct, dexterity, and luck.

Kid in those situations would probably be scared shitless, like most normal people.

"Even with your stellar career record," Gary Marshall said, "I'm sure you won't be cleared for flight duty." He took the pen out of his mouth. "Next month we have an opening for an Air Operations Officer position. It's level one, which is a ground entry job. Basically you'd be a lead pilot, meaning you'd provide technical instruction to new recruits. You'd be responsible to develop and administer the training and monitor their flight assignments." He twirled his seat around and stood up. "What do you think? Would you be up for that?"

He shifted his feet. "Would I get to fly?"

"Your position as lead pilot is to train and guide the other pilots, but one of the requirements is that you have your commercial airman certification, which you have. This could be a good career opportunity. A nice fit."

"I'll think on it. How soon do you need a decision?" Brent asked. This was a decent job offer, he knew that, but being around the action and not being able to fly—well, he just wasn't sure that he could do that.

"We won't be interviewing until the end of next week. If you want the job it's yours."

"Thanks." He stretched out his hand and they shook. "I'll get back to you."

The young man put a hand on his arm. "We'd love to have you here. You know the territory, and you have good leadership skills. You'd be an asset, sir."

Asset, my ass. Training a bunch of snotty nose kids, that's what he'd be doing. But hell, he had been one of those once, and everyone had to start somewhere. On a positive note, he'd be back with some of the old comrades he'd shared good and not so good times with. He'd be in the swing of things, contributing to his 401(k), and he had a future here. Even though he wouldn't be sitting in the captain's seat where he liked to be, he'd still be involved, doing a worthwhile job.

But the adventurous, kick-ass part of him told him he'd be bored silly.

Unless something better came alone, he'd ignore that part of himself, and for once in his life accept and appreciate a non-life-threatening existence. Hadn't he had enough dangerous missions for one lifetime? If it was peace he was after, he wouldn't find it fighting fires. A nice desk job might do the trick.

He drove back home, thinking about his possibilities. Perhaps he could do this for a while, and maybe after a year or two he might be cleared for flight duty. Being in the right place at the right time had a way of opening doors that would normally be shut tight.

Once he was back in Belmont Shores he picked up some Chinese food and took it home piping hot. Sam was at the door to greet him. Brent wasn't sure if Sam's excitement was due to his return or the smell of the Chinese food, but in either case the dog deserved a good reward and a good home. He planned on keeping him and making sure the dog could enjoy the rest of his days as a dog should. Chasing balls, lazing around when he felt like it. His working days were over.

Brent dumped a good portion into Sam's dish, and put the rest on the kitchen table and dug in with his fork.

He had enjoyed Natalie's healthy, delicious home cooked meals, but now that he was a bachelor again, Sam and he could get used to fast food.

She was leaving on July fifth, which meant she'd be around for the Fourth of July celebrations. He was sure that Lauren and Shane and Josh would want to see her and maybe they could all go out on a boat and watch the fireworks.

Maybe Lauren could call and invite her. And what if she said yes? Could he take a hit one more time? Her rejection had cut him to the core but he understood her decision, and in some small part of his soul could agree with it too. But seeing her, being with her would only increase the pain, and yet not seeing was unthinkable too. What a mess he was. Just knowing that she was only a few miles away made him weak with need. He had to see her one last time. The decision was made. He'd see her, say his goodbye, and then in his heart he'd let her go.

~

The following day Natalie ran around, buying luggage, new clothes and lingerie, suitable shoes for running after three children, and two pairs of high heels for the adventures she was going to have. She'd wear them on the side trips that Brent had mentioned, and to prance down the Champs-Élysées. The expensive designer heels were for dreaming big and, hopefully, she'd have plenty of opportunities to wear them.

Her bank transfer had come through, and although she was far from wealthy, she was no longer penniless, and it felt so good to dress well and feel pretty again.

She had donated her old Toyota Corolla to a women's shelter, and used the earnings from Brent to buy her new belongings, keeping her savings intact.

Shopped out, tired from running around all day, she only wanted to go home, but the taxis were either on strike or "off duty" or just not around. She'd stood at a corner with all her bags at her feet for at least ten minutes when Lauren rushed by. She didn't see Natalie right away, and would have kept going except her large shopping bag knocked into Natalie's and spilled the contents into the street. She stopped to apologize and her eyes widened with surprise.

"Natalie. My gosh! I'm so sorry I didn't see you. Here, let me help you gather your things up." They quickly shoveled the clothes back in the bag and placed it safely back on the corner, away from the oncoming traffic.

"What are you doing here, Lauren? Not working today?"

"No. Just rushing around as usual. I had an hour free so I decided to run out and buy some maternity clothes. Everything is getting too tight on me," she said patting her stomach.

"You look great," Natalie told her and meant it. "You've got that glow."

Lauren rolled her eyes. "Probably more flushed from the heat and running around." She glanced at Natalie's four shopping bags. "Looks like you had a busy morning too. I hear you're going to France. You must be excited."

"I am. I leave after the weekend. I wanted to tell you that night when we were all at your house, but I couldn't. I didn't want anyone to know where I was going in case my ex found out." She bit her lip. "I'm sorry. I didn't mean to hide the truth."

"Look, this is silly talking in the middle of the street. My car is just around the corner. Can I give you a ride somewhere?"

"I'm staying at my friend's near Huntington, but I don't want to put you out if you're in a hurry." She could really use the ride, but seeing Lauren made her uncomfortable. She would want to know every little detail, and Natalie was so tired of talking about it. Heartsick too. Yes, this job and opportunity was a dream come true, but she didn't have the enthusiasm for it right now. And explaining it meant digging deeper into herself, and she wasn't ready to do that.

"No trouble. I'll just call Shane and let him know to pick up Josh from his friend's. Then I don't need to rush."

"That's not necessary. I'm waiting for a cab."

"Oh, they're never around when you need them. Come on. It'll give us a chance to catch up."

That's what she was afraid of. But she needed the ride, and it would be rude to refuse. "If you're sure…"

"Of course I am. I want to hear all about your new job."

She picked up a couple of Natalie's bags and marched toward her car. Natalie had no choice but to follow. She stopped in front of a white Mercedes sedan and popped the trunk, then dropped the shopping bags in back.

It was a beautiful car, understated, classy, just like Lauren herself.

"Thank you for doing this. I really appreciate it." She blew her bangs out of her eyes. "I didn't want to go back to Washington for my old clothes, too many unpleasant memories. I also heard that clothes are very expensive overseas."

"Definitely better bargains here, but you'll enjoy the new fashions too." Lauren gave her a quick look. "I'm so sorry you're leaving. I'm sure that Brent will be disappointed to lose you."

Once they were on the road, they resumed the conversation.

"You know that I spent years studying languages," Natalie said quietly, "waiting for the opportunity to use them. And now that day has come. I tried to explain how much this meant to me, and I think Brent understands. He's done so much with his life, while I've done so little."

"I do understand. It's just that I'd hoped you might be able to do them together."

Natalie clenched her hands together. "Brent's an amazing guy and he'll have his pick of girls in no time."

"I don't think he wants his pick of girls, Natalie. A man never does when they find that special one."

"Yes, well, I'm sure that your Shane felt that way, but not Brent. He asked me to stay, but not once has he ever mentioned the word love."

"Ahhhh." Lauren took her eyes off the road to glance at her. "I see. That explains things better."

"What do you mean?"

"I mean it's clear to me that you love Brent and that he loves you. Have you told him?"

"No. My reasons are strong for leaving. Trust me on that." She crossed her arms, almost defiantly. "Besides, I want to go to France. Imagine, living in a chateau a short distance from Paris. Doesn't it sound like a dream come true?"

"It does. And I wish you all good things, but if for some reason you're not happy, won't you please let Brent or someone know? Email me, and I'll make sure you get home."

"That's very kind of you." Natalie gave Lauren a fond smile. "You're a wonderful person and you care about your friends." She was silent for a few minutes, then figured she needed to emphasize one more thing. "I'm sure that Brent will get over me. We grew close because we both needed the other. He'll be fine. I'm sure of it."

"Yes. Shane and I will take good care of him. Don't you worry." She spoke almost absently, looking deep in thought. "We're heading toward Huntington now. Let me know where we're going."

"Right. Carry on past Sunset Beach, and then you're going to turn left, but I can't remember the name of the street. It'll take you to their development. It's Oak View."

"Got it."

Natalie navigated the remainder of the ride, which was a relief so she wouldn't have to carry on this conversation. It was bad enough having them running nonstop in her brain, let alone having to clarify her reasons for others.

They parked in front of Lori's pretty Spanish-style hacienda, and Lauren helped her out with her bags.

"Would you allow us to take you for dinner before you leave? If you're not too busy, of course."

"I can't say for sure since I'm a guest here in their house. I'll give you my cell phone number and then we can talk." She wrote it down and handed it to Lauren. "Thanks for the ride and for the friendship. Take care of Brent for me, won't you?"

The two women looked into each other's eyes. "Men can be fools sometimes. They know what they want. They just don't know how to ask for it."

"I wish it were that simple. I haven't told him everything either." Natalie leaned forward and gave her a hug. "Take care of junior here. I hope to meet him or her one day."

"I hope you will too."

Natalie turned away, thinking how wonderful if must be to bring a child into the world with that much love. If she were having a baby, would her love be enough? It seemed so unfair, but if she told Brent he'd want to do what was honorable, and she'd never know for sure. Did he love her, or would he be acting out of compassion and honor? She didn't want anything from him unless it came from his heart.

CHAPTER THIRTY

Time flew by, and the weekend was upon them. Because Lori was still recuperating they were sticking close to home, and Natalie was free to make her own arrangements. It was too painful for her to see Brent, so she made excuses when Lauren called to make plans.

She had said her good-byes, and it was time to go. The future was before her, whatever it held—and no matter what, she had to close the door on the past. Regardless of how painful. Alone in bed it was impossible for her not to remember resting her head on Brent's broad chest while his arms held her safe. She had loved his inner strength and compassion, the goodness and purity in his heart. Not to mention the passion in his kisses, the way they made love.

So many tender moments, in and out of bed. She missed their morning coffee together, the silly little banter, the laughter and camaraderie they shared. Mostly, she missed the feeling of being safe and cared for, a sense of belonging, of being loved for who she was, not what she could be. She couldn't remember that kind of acceptance, not since her father left home.

The memories of her short time with Brent brought tears to her eyes, and a ripping pain in her chest. It hurt to know that she might never see him again. It made her heart ache and left a big empty hole inside of her that she was afraid would never be filled. How many Brents were there in this world? And even if there were an abundance of kind, generous, good men, she didn't want them. She wanted him.

But what could she do? He wanted her to stay, but he hadn't told her he loved her, hadn't promised her any kind of future. And if he did? What then? Would she stay and never have this chance to grow? No, it was better that their love was left unspoken. It was better for her to go away quietly, and for the two of them to keep in touch.

She had another matter to worry about, as her period still had not come. Maybe she was a coward in refusing to take a pregnancy test. But one way or another she'd have to deal with it—for her an abortion was not an option. Hopefully it was stress; surely she had had enough of that lately to cause her hormones to be more than slightly off kilter.

If she was having a baby, the family in France might decide to let her go. Or they might still insist that she work for the year her contract stated. But it was all guesswork, and until she knew for sure, there was no sense in worrying. She'd just have to take one day at a time.

On a positive note, the local police had told her and Lori that Carl was now being questioned on the disappearance of his first wife and the death of his former girlfriend, so he had a lot more problems to focus on besides her. Whether convicted or not of previous allegations, he'd be tied up in a legal battle for some time to come. He would always have a cloud of doubt over him, and his days as a detective were numbered.

The next morning she went downstairs early and called for a taxi to the airport. John and Lori had made coffee and toast, and she sat down to an early morning breakfast. It was only five, the sky was still dark, but her flight left in a few hours.

John carried her bags downstairs and put them near the door. "You know, I could take you. It's not necessary for you to get a cab."

"We talked about that last night," she answered softly. "Going to LAX this time in the morning will be a nightmare. The traffic is always horrendous, but coming home it would be worse. I don't want you to do that. You two have already been so kind to me." She kissed his cheek. "Thanks for the offer just the same."

Lori refilled her coffee. "After college we swore we'd stay friends, and yet so many years went by without us seeing each other. I don't want that to happen again. Maybe next spring, John and I will come over for a visit. Wouldn't that be wonderful, John? We haven't gotten away for years."

"It's not easy when we run our own business, but we could certainly try. Or you two could have a girl's weekend together."

"Now that would be fun," Natalie answered with a smile.

"We'll do that for sure. Remember to call us when you get there, and let us know that you arrived safely." Lori grasped her friend's hands. "I think you might be very happy working for his family. I can't wait to hear all about it."

"Of course, I'll call and give you updated reports."

"Excellent. If you don't call, at least email. If for any reason it's not a good fit, we'll handle things from this end and see if we can get a different position for you elsewhere."

"Don't worry," Natalie said. "I'm sure it'll be fine. They look very nice, don't they?" They had all Skyped last night, and she'd had a glimpse of the children and their parents. From what she'd seen, the place and family were very impressive.

"They do," Lori agreed. "But just in case. The husband is younger than I expected and handsome too. Let's hope he's not too French," she said with a meaningful smile.

Just then the taxi tooted his horn. "Well, that's it then." Natalie hugged Lori and then John. "Thanks for everything. Love you guys. And Lori, get well quick, you hear?"

"Good-bye, Natalie," she answered, hugging her again. "Meet your prince over there, okay? I want to see you with a dashing, darling Frenchman, and babies of your own."

Natalie swallowed a sudden lump in her throat. She hadn't mentioned the fact her period was late, not wanting her friends to have that worry as well.

"One day, perhaps."

John carried her bags to the taxi, and Lori stood at the doorway and blew her kisses. She waved, and John opened the rear door.

Natalie slipped in. "Los Angeles airport," she told the driver.

The traffic at this early hour wasn't too heavy and they pulled up at the Air France terminal in plenty of time for her flight. She had her boarding pass, but had to drag her two heavy bags into the terminal since it was an international flight.

She dragged one through the door and was about to return for the second, when a man behind her spoke. "I've got your bag."

Natalie turned at the sound of his voice. "Brent." Her heart raced. "What are you doing here?" She felt breathless and had to physically restrain herself from flinging herself into his arms.

"John told me your flight number. I've been waiting an hour." His eyes caressed her face. "Didn't want to miss you."

"An hour?" She licked her lips, and blinked rapidly, forcing back tears. "Why? We don't have anything left to say to each other. Do we?"

"You wouldn't let me see you. Why?"

"You know why. I have to go. I have no choice. It hurts me to see you." A tear dribbled out and she turned her head, hoping he wouldn't see. Her heart cracked a little more, not just for her, but for the two of them. "You shouldn't have come. It doesn't help, it only hurts. I do love you, you know." There. She had said it. She couldn't leave without letting him know. She lifted her chin. "It's true. I should have told you before."

He turned her face to his, and used a thumb and wiped away her tear. "You love me? Oh, Natalie, that's why I'm here. To tell you that I love you too." He kissed her forehead. "Why didn't I say it sooner?"

Her breath hitched, and her heart beat wildly in her chest. "Hearing it now is enough."

He kissed her again, softly this time on the lips. "I love you so much. I didn't know it before, but once you were gone I realized that I missed you. More than I've ever missed anyone before. I even took a drive across town and that didn't help." He tried to laugh, but Natalie could see it didn't come easy.

She touched his face, and put a finger on his lips. "Don't." Her pulse raced, and her heart ached with a pain that might never go away. "Don't say any more, because it only makes it harder to bear."

"You don't have to go. Stay with me, Natalie. Please." His eyes searched hers, and she could see the pain in his. She knew that look as it mirrored her own.

"I want to stay. More than anything," her voice broke, "but I can't." She sucked in a breath and released it slowly, fighting for control. "I have an obligation to fulfill and I would never feel right if I backed out now. I also have an obligation to myself. I don't like the person I was, and I need to prove that I can be strong. Do you understand? If we're to be together, I want us both to be able to stand on our own two feet."

"It's that important to you? More important than us?"

She nodded and gulped down some air. "Yes. I do have to go. If you still feel this way about me a year from now, then we can always meet again. But Brent, you don't know yourself yet, how can you ask me to stay?"

"I know enough. I know that I want you."

His words made her weak with longing, but now more than ever she had to stay firm and not surrender to the seductive temptation. "And I want you." She stepped up and kissed his cheek. "If our love is strong enough, it'll survive a year apart. I don't want us to stay together out of need, but to come together on our own free will when we're strong."

"Sometimes life doesn't offer second chances." He put his arms around her back and drew her close. "I'm afraid that I'll lose you."

"If you lose me, then I'm not worth keeping." She didn't want to think about the possibility that she might be pregnant, and what this would do to him if he knew.

If they really loved each other, their love would find a way. It would survive. And meantime they both could find themselves again and become whole. They were two damaged people who had a chance to grow and be strong on their own, and if they came together then, their love would be greater for it.

She gave him a final kiss and felt her heart split in two. One for him and one for herself. Tears blinded her, and she swiped them away, wanting to see him clearly one last time. "I do love you. Write me, and often. One year, Brent. Wait for me."

He nodded, unable to speak.

He carried her bags to the counter, then turned and walked away. Natalie watched his back, wondering, not for the first time, if she was making a terrible mistake. What if their love didn't survive? What if she lost him for good? How would she feel then?

EPILOGUE

Four months later.
It was a beautiful autumn day, a slight chill in the air, but the sun was shining, and the children were playing hide and seek in the maze. Natalie, of course, had to be the one to count to twenty while her three charges hid and laughed at her when she got lost.

Mirabelle, or Belle for short, was nine, and she was the ringleader. Her younger sister, Carisse, or Cary, was six, and Felix was four. They were delightful children, surrounded by adoring parents, a live-in nanny, house staff, and a menagerie of pets, including a sheep dog, a bird dog for hunting, and two ponies.

Chateau Le Fleur was in the Loire Valley, and Natalie had not been prepared for its impressive size, the grandeur and elegance. It had separate staff quarters, but the main house had eight bedrooms and nine baths. The eighteenth-century manor was completely remodeled, with granite counters in the bathrooms and kitchen, beautiful wood paneling, and limestone floors. The main hall and dining room had several magnificent fireplaces, chandeliers, and French doors that opened to the enormous pool, the rose gardens, the maze where the children now played, and a serene lake with a fountain and swans.

Sweeping lawns led down to the lake, and as you walked there were numerous benches to sit and admire the flowered gardens. The outdoors was lit up in the evenings and was the most amazing sight Natalie had ever seen.

She'd pinched herself several times since her arrival, wondering if she were dreaming or had she actually found this little piece of heaven?

Madam and Monsieur Montfil, the children's parents and her employees, were as delightful as everyone else she encountered. She'd been welcomed and made to feel as though she were an important part of this family. Even though she missed Brent with all her heart, and not a day went by without her thinking about him, she knew she'd done the right thing. Growing in confidence, she had begun the long journey of laying her fears and insecurities to rest. She could laugh and smile more easily now, and little things filled her with joy. It was a rebirth, a time of revelation and healing.

The only thing marring her happiness was the fact that her baby would not have a father. Brent had not been in contact with her, and so it seemed he had moved on. Well, she had no one to blame but herself. And she didn't blame him. Not at all. He had told her he loved her. He had given her a choice. She had chosen her future without him, and if she regretted it, what more was there to say?

When she realized that her period was not late—in fact it was not coming—she had told her employees at once, and offered them a chance to get out of their contract.

They'd said she was welcome to stay and rejoiced with her, telling her another baby was always a blessing.

Life was close to perfect.

"Mademoiselle Natalie. What are you doing?" Bella asked, with a pout. "We've been hiding and you forgot to come and look for us."

"I'm sorry." Natalie hugged her. "I must have been daydreaming. This is like a fairytale place, and you and Cary are princesses, while little Felix makes a fine young prince."

Felix tugged on her skirt. "Why won't you play? I want you to chase me. I don't like hiding. I get scared and Bella won't hide with me."

She took his hand. "It's almost time for lunch and then your lessons. Why don't we go back?"

The children reluctantly agreed and they were making their way around the pool when the housekeeper came out of the house, beckoning to Natalie.

"Miss Natalie, you have a caller. A right handsome man too."

Natalie's heart skipped a beat, and a rush of heat swept through her, warming her blood, bringing fresh color to her face. Could it be? It had to be. Who else would come to see her? Why had he never written or called? A week ago, she'd sent a letter, but would he have received it by now?

She wanted to run, to fly, but managed to keep both feet on the ground. "Did he give you a name?" she asked, trying to act casual although her pulse raced with excitement.

"He did, miss." She grinned and clapped her hands. "Brent Harrington. He's in the library waiting for you."

Natalie put a hand to her chest, as her heart leapt with joy. She squirmed with excitement. "Oh my. Do I look all right? Did he say anything?"

"You look beautiful, and I'm sure that he will tell you why he's come." She whispered so the children couldn't hear, "Is he the father?"

She nodded. "Do you mind taking the children in?"

"Not at all. You go ahead. I've got the little ones."

Natalie tried to walk, but her feet wouldn't let her. She ran toward the house, flung the door wide, and reached the library, slightly out of breath.

He was standing there, and what breath she had left.

His hair had grown in, thick and lush, and her fingers itched to reach out and touch. Her eyes grew moist as she drank him in. His body had filled out and he wore his clothes well. He was more handsome than she'd imagined, and as he faced her she could see the strong, confident man he used to be.

"Brent," she breathed, and moved to his side. "What are you doing here?"

"You know why I've come." He smiled slowly, his eyes never leaving hers. "I couldn't stay away any longer."

"But, but..." She licked her lips. "Why didn't you write?"

"I tried several times, but the things I had to say to you couldn't be put on paper. And email was too impersonal. Besides, you were right. I had a lot of things to figure out and I wanted to give you space."

"I see." Her heart fluttered. Her pulse beat like a butterfly's wing. She swallowed the lump in her throat. "And now?"

"Now I'm here. To stay, whether you want me or not." He stepped away and walked around the room. "I'm not going to pressure you, Natalie. I know that you have a job to do, and I must admit that you've done well." He came back and took her hand in his. "You sure know how to find an adventure." He glanced around the room and smiled. "This tops the list. And you're glowing with happiness. I've never seen you so beautiful, and so content."

"Yes, I do love it here, and they have been so kind to me."

He pulled her into his arms, and she could feel his heart pounding next to hers. "I'm not here to take you away, although you're welcome to come." He kissed her lightly on the lips. "I'm going to be in Germany for the next few years. I took a job as a Warrior Outreach coordinator in Landstuhl."

"You did?" Her eyes found his and held on for dear life.

"Yes. I'll be setting up the Wounded Warrior Project in the major military facilities here in Europe. I'll be working closely with the warriors and their families, making sure they get the support and medical treatment they need."

"That is wonderful, Brent. I'm so, so proud of you."

He swallowed hard, looking suddenly less sure of himself. "The job will require a lot of travel, but I would like to see you on weekends or anytime you can get away." He put his hands behind her back, drawing her near. "Would that be okay with you?"

"Yes, it would be more than okay. It would be wonderful. Oh, Brent." She sighed. "I'm so happy. You have no idea." She wanted to squeal with excitement and run and tell everyone, but she was a proper tutor now, and how would that look to the children? She grinned, and tried not to jump up and down. "Brent, I'm so happy that you got a job close by."

"Me too." He kissed her eyes and her cheeks. "I love you, Natalie, and I know that you're not ready to make a commitment to me, but I came here so I could be close to you. I don't want to let you go, but I don't want to force myself on you either."

"You're not. I've missed you so much. I was so worried when you didn't write. Thought you'd gotten over me."

"Never. I could never get over you. I love you."

"And I love you too." She cocked her head, and gave him a long look. "I have something important to tell you."

"What is it?" He smiled, waiting.

"I'm not sure how you'll take this news. It does affect you. And me."

"Tell me. Why are you being so secretive? Whatever it is, I'm sure it'll be fine."

"I hope that it'll be better than fine." She took his hand and put it on her small baby bump. Butterflies leapt around inside of her, as nervously she wondered what he would say. Did he want to be a father? She licked her lips then gave him a weak smile. "We're having a baby, Brent."

He pushed her away so he could see her better. Shock registered on his face. "You're pregnant?"

She nodded. "I didn't know for sure when I left."

"Why didn't you write or tell me?"

"When you didn't write, I wasn't sure if you still wanted me. Or a baby. But I sent a letter informing you last week."

"I can't believe it!" A huge grin spread across his handsome face. "I'm having a baby?"

"Yes." She laughed. "Yes. Isn't it wonderful?"

"Well, in that case, we'll have to get married now, instead of waiting, won't we?" He took her face between his hands and kissed her deeply. "You have made me the luckiest man in the world. Marry me, Natalie. Say you'll marry me."

She blinked back tears. "I will. You know I will." She grabbed his hands and held on tight. "I'll have to give notice, of course."

"You can do whatever makes you happiest. I'm going to be busy for probably the first several months, spreading the mission of WWP, coordinating projects throughout Europe, organizing activities. I want you with me, but if you want to work another month or two, that's fine by me."

"I want to be with you too. More than you know." She thought about it for all of two seconds. "Why don't I give them two weeks? That's long enough. I can't wait to start our life together. But we should probably marry soon."

He laughed. "I'll marry you today, tomorrow, just say when." He kissed her again, softly, tenderly. "And if you want adventures, my darling bride, I promise you that you will have plenty every day for the rest of your life."

"I want you. But yes, your job and our life together will be extraordinary." She grinned. "And I'm so darn glad that I studied languages. Now I can use them. Isn't that great! Aren't you happy, darling?"

"I'm happy, delighted, and glad for many things. And that's only one of them." He took her hand. "Shall we tell the family that we're going to a chapel and going to get married?"

She laughed. "Let's!" Then she sighed with pleasure. "When I took that job as your live-in aide, I never expected it to be a permanent position. But I wouldn't have it any other way."

They looked into each other's eyes, knowing how lucky they had been. Adversity had brought them together, and strength had pulled them through. Not only were they bringing a baby into the world, but had found a love for a lifetime.

She stood on tiptoe and wrapped her arms around his neck. "Isn't it proper to kiss the bride?"

"Not only proper, but mandatory." His mouth claimed hers and Natalie knew that her heart had found a place to call home.

ABOUT THE AUTHOR

Patrice Wilton was born in Vancouver, Canada, and knew from the age of twelve that she wanted to be a writer. She also knew that she had to grow up first and see the world that she wanted to write about, so she became a flight attendant and for seventeen years traveled the world. At the age of forty, she sat down to write her first novel—in longhand!

She is the proud mother of two, with four lovely granddaughters and a wonderful, supportive man at her side. They live in West Palm Beach, Florida, where he teaches her golf, and she teaches him patience.

Kindle Serials

This book was originally released in Episodes as a Kindle Serial. Kindle Serials launched in 2012 as a new way to experience serialized books. Kindle Serials allow readers to enjoy the story as the author creates it, purchasing once and receiving all existing Episodes immediately, followed by future Episodes as they are published. To find out more about Kindle Serials and to see the current selection of Serials titles, visit www.amazon.com/kindleserials.

Made in the USA
Charleston, SC
22 December 2013